# The Swift Seasons

# THE SWIFT
# SEASONS

—

*Mollee Kruger*

Kruger, Mollee
The Swift Seasons


1.Aging_2.Retirement communities_3.Humor_4.Oliver Wendell Holmes_5.Jews_

ISBN: 0991228901
ISBN 13: 9780991228904
Library of Congress Control Number: 2016904962
LCCN Imprint Name: Rockville, MD

**Printed in the United States of America**

# DEDICATION

---

To the children, grandchildren, and dear friends of the
elderly everywhere and to the devoted professionals,
caregivers, and volunteers who touch their lives

# ACKNOWLEDGMENTS

———◆———

THE FOLLOWING POEMS: "Brotherly Breach," *Admiral of the Mosquitoes*, Maryben Books; "A Woman Ignored," *A Purse of Humorous Verse for the Jewish Woman*, Biblio Press, N.Y.; thanks to the University of Maryland Libraries and Professor Emerita Ruth Alvarez for the extended loan of books by and about Dr. Holmes, to Anne Turkos, Sunil Freeman and The Writer's Center, to David, Ray, and Ginny; also deepest gratitude for the past three years of loving, time-consuming assistance from Len, Joe, Dina, Cynthia, Isaac, and Mira; and a special thank-you to those feisty neighbors who continue to inspire me each day with their strength, courage, and humor. And I'm forever indebted to the immortal Oliver Wendell Holmes.

**Other Books by Mollee Kruger**
Unholy Writ
More Unholy Writ
Yankee Shoes
Daughters of Chutzpah
Admiral of the Mosquitoes
Ladies First
A Purse of Humorous Verse for the Jewish Woman
The Cobbler's Last

# PART ONE

---

*"Here I have related, at length, a string of trivialities. You must have the imagination of a poet to transfigure them."*

OLIVER WENDELL HOLMES
(1809–1894)

# FRITZI'S PRELUDE

————◆————

WHEN I WAS YOUNG, IF anyone ever told me, "Fritzi Schnell, some day you'll eat breakfast every morning with a bunch of old crab apples, " I'd have split my sides laughing.

You think nothing much ever happens in a place like this, but believe me, the things I see, the things I hear. Take the bunch at mealtime. For starters, there's Jake the Jaded Journalist, who has always been mean to me; why, I can't figure out. I even reported him to the front desk for not being friendly. Next to him sits Lydia, who used to be a librarian, big deal. Plus Diana, Goddess of the Hunt. Jake came up with all these dopey names, including his. God only knows what he calls me. It's hard to remember who's who, but you'll get used to it, like the rest of us when we come here. In fact, some residents never bother to learn what to call anybody and others are happy if they even remember first names. But I keep up to the minute on things. Not much gets by me.

A few ladies here are single, never married. Most are widows. We have a newcomer at our breakfast table, Willa, who's not exactly new. They used to sit across the dining room, she and her husband Aaron, who was not in good shape. Although he passed away months ago, she keeps the same apartment. I guess she prefers living here in a kosher place that serves potato latkes and matzo balls for dinner instead of pork chops and ham. She's quiet, tall, and skinny, sort of creepy, with big gray eyes that water a lot. Jake named her Willa the Wordless because she doesn't speak much.

People say Jake led a dog's life. I hate animals in general. My ex-husband once bought a pet shop, and we lost our shirts.

Busy day. There's a talk this morning in the Leviathan Lecture Lounge on how to think like a young Jewish person, and then I have to rush to the lobby or lose my spot next to the aspidistra plant, where I can see who comes through the front door and who goes out. Jake says I don't miss a trick. Did I tell you he can be very mean to me? Why, I don't know. I'm a nice person. Or I can be if people behave themselves. So anyway, welcome to SVM: A Retirement Community. And don't ask me what SVM stands for. Nobody knows. See you around.

# CHAPTER 1

———

"I HAVE MANY MEMORIES, BUT I don't remember them," Diana said to Jake the Journalist, a wild-eyed man who gobbled down oatmeal with her at the breakfast table each morning. He had long ago taken stock of his fellow tenants at the retirement home and felt he knew them as well as the arthritic fingers on his left hand. "Joint tenants with pains in their joints," he said in his guttural voice.

Now, in spite of glittering chandeliers overhead, carnations jammed into stem vases on each table, and pastel-green-uniformed waiters who spoke with tropical accents, the dining room reminded Jake of his less-than-euphoric high-school days. All their lives, no matter what their age, Jake thought, people could be divided into two groups: the "ins" and the "outs," the conformers and the troublemakers.

Nearby, a band of wrinkled, white-haired rebels occupied what they called the Ha-Ha Table. Receiving envious looks in their direction, the Ha-Ha consortium, an ingathering of three widows and three widowers, entertained themselves at breakfast with sarcastic asides and frequent laughter. They appeared to be having all the fun and received envious looks from the other residents.

Jake didn't sit with them, didn't want to. In the cavernous space of the Esther Essenvarg Dining Den, he occupied a seat at what he had labeled the Ho-Hum Table.

"Why do people here watch so much TV, the same Turner Classic Movies, over and over again?" he asked to keep the conversation going.

"My first wife used to force me to go to the movies with her to see all those tear-jerkers. They were rotten then, and they're still no good. Right?"

He addressed the skin-and-bones woman on his left, a reserved eighty-ish lady. Jake, with his knack for bestowing descriptive names, referred to her as Willa the Wordless—but never to her face.

Willa pretended not to hear him or bosomy Diana, sometimes known as Goddess of the Hunt. A tad under eighty, suspiciously brunette, Diana longed to join the Ha-Ha Table, where no vacancies ever existed. She spent her time seeking out quality people, preferably quasihealthy men, whom she pursued from their first day of arrival. Less desirable but better than nothing were old-timers like Jake. Permanently bent but still resilient, Jake claimed to be "somewhat over eighty-five" on his last birthday.

"What was the name of that book you were reading the other day, Jake?" Diana asked.

"*The Joy of Art?*"

"Anything like *The Joy of Sex?*" She used a fake coy voice. "Who wrote that one anyway?"

"You did," Jake said. The eavesdropping Ha-Ha Table chuckled in appreciation. "*The Joy of Sexual Art* is even better," he added, now at the top of his game. Everyone who could hear him laughed except Willa the Wordless, who unsuccessfully stabbed hard at her fresh-fruit cocktail with a slightly bent fork.

Diana, Goddess of the Hunt, changed the subject. She watched her tablemate attack a bowl of cornflakes as if they were in danger of disappearing before his spoon could reach them. "Did you just get a haircut, Jake?"

"Too much off the top?" Jake asked.

"It's OK," Diana said. "Not wonderful, but OK."

Jake looked hurt. "My Korean barber doesn't use scissors. He uses…"

"A sword?" Diana asked. Eavesdroppers at the Ha-Ha Table found that hilarious and gave the remark the reception it deserved.

An aide from an African country, the name of whom had been changed to something residents couldn't remember or pronounce, approached, pushing a wheelchair. "Ready to go?" she asked her employer, Lydia, the former librarian.

"Lydia the Encyclopiddia is leaving us," Jake announced. He could be gruff but never to Lydia, a calm little woman with a constant smile on her face. She had a kind word for everyone, including the woman who bathed and dressed her each day.

Most residents still managed by themselves, but their number decreased week by week as formerly independent people changed status and joined the frail elderly. At that point home-health aides took over. It was an unlikely stew, a smattering of Sephardic Hebrews blended with Ashkenazi Jews who were Russian, Polish, German, Romanian, and Hungarian in origin. They were tended by Mexicans and Central and South American exiles, or Caribbean nationals with faint French or British accents, ambitious Filipinas as well as Ethiopians and Eritreans with their finely chiseled features, dark East Indians, Pakistanis, and other miscellaneous Asians. The majority were native African women, some in towering wraparound head gear and tribal smocks, the colors inspired by rain forests and exotic birds. Paid by the hour, these tireless helpers assisted the Judaic elderly suffering from every known ailment, including neglectful offspring who never visited.

Grasping the aide's plump arm, Lydia transferred to her wheelchair and announced, "Nine o'clock doctor's appointment." She gave them a broad smile, as if old age were one great joke played on all of them.

"An honor having you with us," Jake boomed in his most gallant manner, in case she wouldn't be returning the next morning, and maybe she wouldn't.

With Lydia gone, Fritzi Schnell stepped into the spotlight. "See that aide who just took Lydia away?" she said. "When I was walking down the hall yesterday morning, I saw her knock hard on the door of, you know, that woman with the pinkish hair, the one who sits at the table opposite us and pretends she doesn't know me? Anyway, she comes to the door and"—Fritzi lowered her voice—"Guess what?"

"What?" Diana asked in a wary voice.

Hesitating, Fritzi glanced at Jake. She decided the story was not for a man's ears. "Tell you later," she said and slipped away to find an all-female audience. The eaters around the table continued dipping spoons into their oatmeal. No great loss.

As if on cue, The Centenarian, having finished breakfast elsewhere, plodded to a point behind Jake's chair. "I'm a hundred and one," he began, as he did morning after morning.

"We know," said Jake, not bothering to look up. "Tell us something we don't know." Each evening he ate dinner with this ancient man. Every evening they sat together at a distant table in the spacious SVM dining room with its mahogany sideboards and sturdy carpeting that refused to show stains of frequently spilled food.

"One hundred and one and I believe in nothing," The Centenarian said. "How d'you like that? Know what else I don't believe in? Doctors. Biggest con game in the world."

"Sometimes you con," Jake said, "and sometimes you con't." The Ha-Has snickered.

"Medicine. The curse of mankind." The Centenarian always spoke in the positive manner of a latter-day prophet. "I don't take pills. Don't waste time going to doctors. Never did. Never will. Just got back from vacation with my grandkids in St. Thomas. Must be doing something right."

"You told me women were the curse of mankind," Jake said. He winked at Willa, who had no appetite for funny remarks. She took a quick look at the Centenarian's skeletal face and concentrated on stirring her oatmeal.

The Centenarian talked but never bothered to listen. The others often agreed that although they didn't know him back then, they were certain The Centenarian's personality hadn't changed since his younger days. "Obnoxious in," Jake observed, "obnoxious out."

Jake prided himself on being the only person at the table to know what to call this man, especially after Diana made an error by insisting, "Somebody who lives a whole century is a centarian."

"Not a real word," the Jake said, with the assurance of a seasoned news-paperman, and people respected him for that. "Call him a centenarian.

And you can call me Ishmael." Although Willa the Wordless caught the literary reference, she stayed expressionless. It was important to keep a distance.

"Actually, the right word is 'centaur,'" Diana said.

Jake corrected her. "The old geezer may be many things, but he's not mythological, and he doesn't have the head, trunk, and arms of a human attached to the body and legs of a horse."

Impressed, the others nodded, everyone except Willa the Wordless, aiming for a quick getaway. She wasn't in the mood.

The Centenarian stood speechless in one spot for thirty seconds. Still at center stage, he concentrated on making his essential points before departure. "Kill the income tax. It corrupts the whole system. Put all doctors in jail. Do away with vitamin pills. That's the biggest fraud of all time."

"Vitamin C is nice," Diana said. "I haven't had a cold in two years."

The Centenarian muttered to himself as he plodded toward the French doors. "Trouble is, billionaires run the show and idiots believe them."

Jake leaned toward Diana. "Did you see him last night at dinner? He tripped and fell over a parked walker jutting out too far from the wall. When 911 came with the gurney, they lifted him up to his feet and he hollered, 'Get the hell out. I don't need your goddam help.'"

"He wouldn't let them take him to the hospital?" Diana asked.

"Nope. Put up a fight and won."

"We can learn from him," Diana said. "He's a role model."

In the SVM community, eighty-year-olds marveled at the endurance of nonagenarians, who kept an eye on the handful of centenarians. The freshmen aped the sophomores who studied the juniors who admired the seniors. Few looked forward to graduation.

The table watched as the very old man hobbled away. "This place," Jake said, shaking his wild head of hair. "I ought to write a novel about it except there are too many characters to keep up with."

And while the Ha-Ha Table chuckled at Jake's latest remark, Willa the Wordless stood, gathered up her lightweight canvas handbag from the floor and left her companions in the glorious sunshine of the Esther

Essenvarg Dining Den. She headed toward the elevator, which carried her to a quiet, book-fortified apartment on the eighth floor. There she would retire to her journal and a more sedate world ruled by a certain Boston physician, dead for one hundred twenty years.

———————

*June 12, 2013.* Now is the Summer of My Disconnect. I treasure this paisley-covered journal Aaron bought me in his final healthy year, even though the pages are too tightly bound and I have to fight every inch of the way to keep the covers open as I write. My daily repository of un-lovely thoughts lacks a title. Cynical Jake at breakfast could supply one. He strikes me as a dogmatic tyrant with a touch of hysteria thrown into the mix. That annoying Fritzi took me aside the other day and told me "behind your back," as she put it, he calls me Willa the Wordless, which Fritzi thought was "mean of him." Mustn't get involved.

Aaron has been dead four months, and I still haven't gotten rid of all his socks. They turn up like fuzzy dark phantoms whenever I open a dresser drawer. Someday my energy will recharge long enough for me to decide what to do with the thermal underwear left over from those years when he cleared the snow from our driveway. And his tennis racket. And his baseball cap.

Eating with strangers at breakfast and listening to what passes for conversation drains 50 percent of my strength. Dinner with a hearing-impaired couple consumes another 20 percent, and that leaves 20 percent for hours alone in the company of Oliver Wendell Holmes, my only pas-sion these days. Maybe he'll prescribe a miraculous nineteenth-century potion to blot out the dreary nights. Fat chance.

Unbearable household clutter lies around me...bank statements to shred, Aaron's suits to inventory for tax deductions and then banish from my sight forever, his leftover hospice medications to dump, hundreds of his paperbacks. Lydia, the retired librarian, suggested I donate any throwaways to her pet charity, the Biblio Boosters, a group that sells used books to help inner-city school libraries.

It's hard to imagine how a ninety-year-old woman in a wheelchair can serve as president of any group, but Lydia does get results. If not for her, I wouldn't have rifled through our stack of Agatha Christie discards and unearthed *The Poet at the Breakfast Table*. Once on a summer vacation to Otter Pond, Aaron paid a dollar for the book at a barn/bookstore. The amber flyleaf bears a date, 1891, handwritten in flowery Victorian style. Whoever owned this book must have bought it when Oliver Wendell Holmes was still living. That gives me goose bumps. The final ten pages are missing; it's worthless as a collector's item, but it sat on our bookshelf for years and somehow got packed when we moved to SVM.

"Those three desiccated initials, SVM, tell no tales," Aaron once commented. True. Not much institutional memory here, and who knows what the letters mean? Other retirement homes these days have fancier names like Tranquility Towers or Kindly Korners, and there's a Verdant Valley nursing facility nearby. The phone book even lists one flowery residence as Petunia Palace.

Aaron could do better than that. A wordsmith supreme, he gave birth to the most outrageous ideas in the business. I remember the night when his slogan "Advertising Never Sleeps" won a *Tide* magazine award for its originality. The next morning a newspaper article called him Mr. Advertising. Other agencies in town envied his chutzpah. He told me once that if SVM were his client back then, he would have loaded each room with free boxes of Kleenex and renamed the place GezundtHouse! Me, I'd rather stick with the truth and go with Aging Acres.

Rambling again. This journal eats up too much of my time today, keeping me from my daily clandestine tryst with Dr. Holmes. Long ago when I first discovered him in that awful American Lit course at college, he seemed dry as stale challah. Now seventy years later, starved for decent conversation, I'd love nothing better than passing the Sweet'N Low to Oliver Wendell Holmes each morning. Of course if he ever popped up, it would scare me witless.

Holmes referred to his Breakfast-Table books as *slight dramatic backgrounds* that *show off a few talkers and writers, aided by certain silent supernumeraries.* Perhaps like his boardinghouse tenants, the residents here are also supernumeraries, actors without lines, hired for the occasion, especially the mob scenes at mealtime. If so, they deserve Oscars. I keep hoping they're white-wigged young actors heavily made up to look old, performers trained in slow motion, low-paid extras shuffling in and out of the Esther Essenvarg Dining Den each morning and evening. Jake, that gloomiest of the lot, calls them "the walking wounded."

Oliver Wendell Holmes would appreciate that. Lately, I've become sort of addicted to reading his stuff, except that he irks me when male characters at his breakfast table are identified by their noble professions: The Divinity Student, The Young Astronomer, The Register of Deeds. In contrast, women rate generic names like The Lady and The Young Girl, with exceptions for The School Mistress and The Landlady, a humorous presence sharing meals with her boarders. Of her, the autocrat of the breakfast table writes patronizingly: "Our Landlady is a most respectable person, who has seen better days, of course,—all landladies have,—but also, I feel sure, seen a good deal worse ones."

My residence hasn't any landlady spouting humorous remarks in a nasal Yankee dialect, only our long-suffering, harried administrative staff, who endure stress magnified beyond belief. No matter what they sow, they reap a harvest of dissatisfied comments from malcontents. As a silent listener at the breakfast table, I'm aware of impressionable newcomers who complain less frequently when they first arrive until they realize that in order to be accepted, they have to learn to complain often and bitterly or risk being considered an outsider by the others. That wise old librarian, Lydia, remarked the other day, "Idle hands are rarely accompanied by idle tongues."

# CHAPTER 2

———

IT WAS THE WORST SCENE the residents could ever imagine at 8:15 a.m. Those absent that day had to be satisfied with the embellished version later provided by Fritzi Schnell, proud to announce she witnessed it from beginning to end. Even Jake was shaken by the vitriol of the moment. "Madam Frankenstein meets Madam Dracula," he called it.

The contest: in one corner, challenger Diana, Goddess of the Hunt, a squatter floating from table to table, against the defender, Renee Richmond, a feisty eighty-seven-year-old, who arrived fifteen minutes later than usual for her bagel and lox because she had hired a new person to help her get dressed. "They always slow me down," she said.

Earlier, Diana, having noticed Renee's vacant seat, leaned her fuchsia snakehead cane against the wall and lowered her brand-new hip onto the unoccupied chair. It happened to be next to a man known as Howie the Unwholesome Wholesaler, called by that name because three irate women had recently accused him of putting his hand on their thighs.

By the time Renee arrived, she found her place taken. "Get your freak-ing *tush* off my chair," she told Diana. Renee did not say "freaking."

"Such language," Howie remarked in a pious tone to Lydia. He poured himself a glass of orange juice from the decanter on the table. "No need for a woman to talk like that."

Diana refused to look at Renee. "It's open seating," she added with cool edge to her voice and an overwhelming interest in a smudged spoon. "At breakfast we can sit anywhere we like."

Renee, whose four husbands had left her "well fixed," wasn't one to be pushed around. "You know I sit in that freaking seat every day." The Esther Essenvarg Dining Room had grown silent. Smothered laughter engulfed the Ha-Ha Table.

Howie continued his quest to impress both Diana and Lydia with his gentlemanly University of Virginia routine. "You're being very rude to this lovely lady."

"Just keep your gums shut," Renee said.

"Plenty of empty chairs at this table," Diana said. "I'm sure you can eat breakfast three feet away from where you usually sit."

"I'm going to stuff your words down your throat," Renee said.

Diana confided in the person on her right who happened to be Willa the Wordless. "Did you hear that?" she asked. Willa shook her head and buttered a Kaiser roll.

A flustered breakfast supervisor in impossibly high-heeled wedges and a gray business suit passed by, pushing a heavy cart loaded with juice, coffee, and milk. Two pregnant employees had gone into labor, according to Fritzi, and the kitchen was understaffed.

Diana raised a gnarled hand to stop the supervisor. "I think," Diana said under her breath, "this woman has personality issues." The younger woman smiled brilliantly and continued across the room with the cart. When Diana finally left for an acupuncture appointment, residents applauded, glad the unpleasantness was over. From time to time, the elderly may enjoy a no-holds-barred verbal confrontation among their peers but never during meals.

Jake twisted his shaggy head from side to side as if he were trying to shake away a cloud of massive unhappiness. "Where's the kid with the coffee?" He pounded on the table with a cereal spoon. "Over here! Over here!" The women, including Willa, flinched. Why did this man remain angry day after day, week after week? Even on rare occasions when he joked, he begrudged the moment.

A beautiful young Nigerian woman with an intricate orange hairdo pushed her cart in his direction. "I'm coming. You're not the only one in this place."

"We thought you ran away and got married," Jake said.

The waitress narrowed her eyes at the table of old white people. She opened her mouth as if she had a sharper answer planned, but merely said, "I can't think straight this morning. My braids are too tight."

Jake almost laughed. "First time for that excuse. And I've heard them all. Used to be an editor." He turned to Willa. "Did I ever tell you my newspaper won awards from the Jewish Press Association?" Willa shook her head but didn't speak.

"The oatmeal here is always good," Diana said to no one in particular.

Willa excused herself from the throng. At an earlier time in her life, a younger, less-passive Willa would have moved away to a sleek high-rise apartment in the nearby city. Now the slightest change of routine swallowed up energy she couldn't quite muster, and yet, never having been an old lady before, she didn't know how to be one.

She glanced at the Timex strapped to her wrist. Time to seek comfort in Oliver Wendell Holmes, but first an errand. Lately, she had been waking up with a chronic dry-eye condition for which her ophthalmologist prescribed artificial tears five times a day. For Willa, not yet out of mourning, it was like carrying coals to Newcastle.

Outside, an early-morning drizzle had ended, and the weather turned sunny enough for a walk to the neighborhood pharmacy for a bottle of Systane. At the drugstore checkout counter, a handsome Sikh cashier in a white turban handed Willa change for a twenty-dollar bill. She stuffed the eye medication and sales slip into her handbag and directed her lace-up black Nikes toward home. Viewed from a distance, the solidly built SVM building acquired a maternal kind of dignity, its red-brick annexes reaching out in all directions like open arms. She crossed the crescent-moon driveway and passed white hydrangeas circled by a green fringe of juniper bushes. On nearby streets of this busy inner suburb, split-level houses had long ago replaced what had been acres of cornfields. Retirement facilities had cropped up with roomier apartments, airier balconies, and more inspired landscaping, but only SVM served glasses of Kedem concord-grape wine at Friday night Sabbath dinners, where assorted gentlemen in skullcaps stood at their tables to recite Kiddush over the wine. No other place offered apples and honey for a sweet New Year, Passover meals complete with *matzo brie* or a daily minyan for the pious or High Holy Day services for every brand of Judaism on the books. That's why Willa and Aaron had chosen this homey place, although he often said, "Actually, I got hooked on the chocolate Hanukkah coins."

Remembering him, Willa managed a pensive smile as she approached the magical front doors that opened without ever being touched. Later when she would check to see if any Holmes characters ever clashed fiercely like Renee and Diana over seating arrangements, she would find only meaningful conversations tempered by Bostonian civility.

———◆———

*Wednesday, June 19.* Question: Why are old books and old buildings more lovable than aging people? Although I never become emotional remembering our crowded apartment above my parent's bakery, Oliver Wendell Holmes goes into raptures over his childhood home:

> *…dear old house…I want to gather up my recollections and wind a string of narrative round them, typing them up like a nosegay for the last tribute…We Americans are all cuckoos…we make our homes in the nests of others…*

He might have enjoyed SVM, this dear old house, but would he be impressed by our brand of odd birds and their ruffled feathers? Ah, Holmes would say, "Every person's feelings have a front-door and a side-door…… This front-door leads into a passage…opens into an ante-room, and this into the inferior apartments. The side-door opens at once into the sacred chambers."

Dr. Holmes, if you ever tried to peer into our sacred chambers, you'd find a mah- jongg game in progress. People here don't speak much about former occupations or careers, and that's the greatest difference between us and the characters in your books. Real life people keep too much frozen inside themselves. Your boarders never shut up. The Scarabee rattles on and on about the insect world. The elderly gentleman known as The Master introduces such items from his library as "An Essay on the Great Effects of Even Languid and Unheeded Local Motion." The Poet confesses that although he loves to speak, he doesn't know what he's thinking until he says it. My tablemates talk at breakfast too, but not like yours. On sleepless nights, I still hear the aimless chitchat at my table and excuse myself for not feeling more attached to fellow elders who choose self-preservation as their only goal in life. (OK, Madam Superiority, what tops *your* list these days?)

Back to Dr. Holmes for salvation. Stamped inside the front cover of my favorite Breakfast Table book are the words "Tigers Athletic Club, Freeland, Pa., 1891." What muscular athlete in long johns once owned this book? I envision a boxer of the John L. Sullivan school lifting weights, the wordy volume of Holmes in one hand and the Marquis of Queensbury rules in the other.

Aaron interpreted it differently. "What if Casey at the bat belonged to the Freeland, PA, Athletic Club?" he asked. "What if, after the mighty Casey struck out, he dashed to the club to find comfort in *The Poet at the Breakfast Table*. Willa, do you think the guys down at the nineteenth-century version of Gold's gym actually read this stuff?"

I thumbed through the faded chapters. "Of course," I said to him, "they became addicted to sentences like this: 'Our epizoic literature is becoming so extensive that nobody is safe from its ad infinitum progeny.'" We laughed so hard I dropped the book on the floor and seven more pages fell out.

Last night during a fractured dream, none other than Oliver Wendell Holmes himself materialized. I read somewhere that he was a wisp of a fellow, "the little doctor," they called him. Anyway, before this pint-sized creature disappeared, he promised that one day soon he would open his black leather bag and produce "an effective nostrum" concocted just for me.

"Is it kosher?" I asked, and woke up before he could answer.

# CHAPTER 3

———•———

"A WOMAN IN A NIGHTGOWN wandered into my freaking apartment last night," Renee Richmond announced at breakfast.

Renee liked to shock persons who had just arrived at SVM. Two of them now occupied places at the table. Like many of the elderly inhabitants, they hailed from out of state but felt the need to move closer to their middle-aged children, who worked at the nearby community college. Only a minority of the boarders were local.

"We're supposed to keep our doors locked at all times," Bertha the Bingo Baby said.

"I don't lock my door, "Renee said, with a pout that was hard to manage because she had undergone cosmetic surgery in recent months. "I have claustrophobia."

"Who was it?" Fritzi asked.

Renee gave her a freezing look. "I don't remember names of people here. Everyone seems to be Florence or Mary or Sylvia."

Lydia the Encyclopiddia sipped her coffee and felt it her duty to explain one basic fact to new arrivals at the table. "You can identify our generation by the names...Frieda, Hattie, Bessie, all born in the 1920s or before, but it's perfectly fine if you don't bother with names. Some people do, but as time wears on, they forget."

Bertha liked the philosophical turn the conversation had taken. "Like me. The longer you live here, the less you care. Unfamiliar faces keep coming, older ones disappear."

"It's difficult to stay current," Lydia said.

Renee Richmond asserted herself once more, determined to continue her story. "So this strange person wandered into my place last night, and all the time her husband was in their apartment sound asleep…snoring so loud I could hear him through the wall."

"And what did a resourceful woman like you do?" Lydia asked in her gentle way.

Renee's face produced the equivalent of a frown. "I was jealous and asked myself why he deserved to be sleeping. So I woke up the freaking son of a bitch."

The recent arrivals gasped, but old-timers were used to spicy talk from Renee. Most Jewish women of her generation, the Rachels, Sonias, Belles, and Sarahs at SVM, did not express themselves that way. They may have known Yiddish equivalents of rough language, but the curses of their immigrant parents sounded more homey and less coarse than English versions of the same words. World War II or Korean War veterans took creative swearing in their stride. When old women weren't in hearing distance, the men used their own favorite obscenities, but sparingly in a kosher place like SVM, which also housed several retired rabbis within earshot.

"Lots of Barbaras, Bettys, and Ruths," Bertha said, getting back to the original subject. "Ever notice that around here every other woman is named Barbara, Betty, or Ruth?"

"Or Selmas. And a good supply of Sarahs, Rebeccas, Leahs, Rachels, and Deborahs," Lydia said.

The two newcomers, who had come to breakfast early, deserted the table at this point and were replaced by Jake's friend, Sidney the Savvy Salesman, arriving unusually late but happy to reclaim his rightful place from people he saw as interlopers.

"Sidney, we were discussing how difficult it is to remember the names of our neighbors," Lydia said.

Sidney always scorned such frivolous female chitchat. "They come and go," he said. "Who can keep up?"

"They were the names of the girls we knew in school," Lydia said with a wistful note to her voice. "I wonder what happened to all of those sweet young things?"

Sidney released a plaintive, "They're here!" and dug into his omelet.

"We forgot to mention the Tillies and Fannies," Bertha said.

Sidney couldn't hide his boredom. "Change the channel, Bertha," he said. "Ah, here's the new guy. He's a musician. Over here, Eric, this chair. From now on, nobody sits there except Eric Revelle."

Diana, Goddess of the Hunt, evaluated the newcomer as another prospect. She surveyed his head of gleaming white hair and neatly trimmed Van Dyke beard. She took a detailed inventory of his physical infirmities, probably caused by Parkinson's and then, to underscore her position as leading soprano in the SVM Chorus, belted out the opening line of a Broadway musical.

"Consider yourself at 'ome," she sang, in what she considered a Cockney accent.

Sidney used his handkerchief to brush away pieces of scrambled Eggbeaters from an empty chair. "This seat will be easier for Eric to get to. My friend Jake often sits over there, but he has an appointment this morning with the ophthalmologist. Has to get shots in his eyes or he'll go completely blind. How he can still drive at night with one good eye is beyond me."

Eric hesitated, but Sidney wouldn't give up. "Sit. We need another guy to even things out. The girls have a tendency to take over." He lowered his voice. "With four sisters and five daughters, all my life I had too much of all that female stuff at home."

It was impolite for Willa to stare, but she had already noted Eric's stiff gait and dependence on a walker. His head was lowered, and at first she couldn't see what his eyes were like. His hand trembled as he sought the arm of a nearby chair for support. When he looked up, his lively blue eyes startled her. He nodded in her direction, and she acknowledged his silent greeting. Then she wiped her lips with a paper breakfast napkin, excused herself from the table, and escaped to her morning ritual: journal notations, followed by a search for wisdom in the sensible paragraphs of the illustrious little doctor from Boston.

———◆———

*Friday, June 26.* Keeping quiet is no sin. Oliver Wendell Holmes captures my sentiments perfectly when he writes: "...if I had my life to live over again, I think I should go in for silence...This language is such a paltry tool! The handle of it cuts and the blade doesn't...It always seems to me that talk is a ripple and thought is a groundswell."

Yet in a sequel, *The Professor at the Breakfast Table*, he contradicts himself, referring to untalkative "fellow boarders" like this: "The rest being conversational noncombatants, mostly still, sad feeders, who take in their food as locomotives take in wood and water, and then wither away from the table like blossoms that never came to fruit."

Silence begets silence. Although most women here are widows and we ought to have something in common, they rarely mention their late husbands, at least not to me. Month by month at SVM, new patches of widows grow like Queen Anne's Lace in all corners of the lobby, and I'm not about to join them, even if they invite me, which they haven't. The whiteness of the widows' coiffures is blinding, blizzards of curls. How do they get and stay that way when my hair remains a pewter color with no future prospects? Do the ladies own stock in the beauty parlor? Is everyone wearing wigs? Well, maybe the handful of Orthodox ladies. Or Diana, Goddess of the Hunt, and others like her. They're not fooling anybody. Jake made a penetrating remark this morning after Diana left the table: "An old lady wearing too much eye makeup may think she looks young and glamorous, but she only looks like an old lady wearing too much eye makeup."

When Lydia commented, "You're a cynic," Jake answered, "I'm a realist." And Bertha said, "I'm Jewish."

Even at this age, widowers, the divorced, and the never-marrieds seek their own kind. So do the religious and nonreligious. Friends we once knew at dinner and breakfast have vanished. Too bad. When we first arrived at SVM, Aaron used his electric scooter to get himself to the dining room. I always arrived at the table beforehand to create a parking space for him by removing a chair. Fruma, a pleasant widowed member of what Aaron called the Army of the Snow Whites, would join us with a smile and whisper. "Keep doing this. You'll have no regrets later on."

Aaron grew worse; I missed countless breakfasts, and in the meantime Fruma disappeared. Perhaps she never even existed or was one of those biblical angels who appear to the right person at the right time and afterward don't bother to write or call. I wish we had exchanged reminiscences about our marriages. I wanted to hear about hers and tell her about mine, a sweet union that expired with no leftover resentments, no unresolved conflicts, no dangling participles. Toward the end Aaron even insisted that I not remain alone for the rest of my days, but he's an impossible act to follow. Always funny, always enthusiastic, he seemed young even in those years when he wasn't.

In time, I may seek out my contemporaries. Some appear kind, smart, worth knowing—others not. Old age is a time to make do with what you have, Jake says. You take what you can get. Maybe he'd even advise me to settle for less, a latter-day Prince Charming in an unstained polyester shirt who will thunder to my rescue in a mechanized wheelchair, scoop me up, and carry me off to meet his newest physical therapist. At this very moment the man of my dreams, albeit pudgy, gassy, or wheezing, could be hovering nearby, worshipping me from afar, but I can't even see him without putting on my glasses. Caution and decorum, old girl. God forbid that Fritzi should ever manufacture libelous stories that cast me in the same light as Diana, Goddess of the Hunt.

Meanwhile, as the World War II song goes, I walk alone. Yesterday the SVM bus took us to a live butterfly exhibit called "The Wing-Dingers." I counted twelve walkers and one wheelchair loaded onto the bus, a lot of heavy lifting for the driver. By the time everyone managed to stumble aboard, navigate the aisle, and choose a seat next to a reasonably alert traveling companion, it took a couple of eons.

Fritzi entered the bus with her usual demands. "I'm looking for a warm seat," she said. I liked the way Sidney wrinkled his nose and said, "A warm seat? Winter or summer, no one is ever satisfied with the temperature of this bus." That new man, Eric, didn't show up. Our field trips must be difficult for him to maneuver.

At the nature center, we filed into a plant-filled room featuring tables with ripened cantaloupe slices on paper plates set out for the butterflies to nosh on. Overhead hundreds of wings circled, freestyle. Fritzi kept ducking and batting the insects away with a rolled up magazine. "I don't want those bugs in my hair," she said.

Jake overheard her. "Maybe," he said, "the winged creatures take one look at all our white heads and mistake them for dandelions gone to seed, like the ones we used to see in Central Park." Jake, the grouch, can be poetic when he wants to be. Fritzi's complaining reminded me of an old ad for bug killer. Jake must have read my mind because he whispered in my ear, as a swarming mass of Lepidoptera came at us from all sides, "Quick, Henry, the Flit!"

"Ethel, what are those camouflaged ones?" Bertha asked. "The printing on the sign is too small for me to read."

Ethel consulted her brochure. "Morpho. Wait, I'm wrong," she said. "Common Anglewing. Aren't they lovely? At first when you see them drooping on a stalk, they look like dead leaves, all colorless and dull, but when they open their wings, they become gorgeous shades of fuchsia, gold, and purple."

I twisted around to look at this newcomer. Placid, barely lined face, matronly figure, a thick salt-and-pepper braid hanging down her back. Ethel wore what we used to call a housedress, buttoned up the front, printed with tiny flowers, a dusty brown cardigan over her shoulders.

"I think," she said to me in a pleasant voice, "we old folks may be drab on the outside like those butterflies, but if we get the chance, we can still open up and show our beautiful colors."

"Yeah, when fish wear pantyhose," Fritzi said.

I quickly moved away from both of them. Although Ethel shows promise, starting a new friendship is not top priority for me right now.

# CHAPTER 4

———

"Would you like a drink?" asked the young woman balancing a tray of plastic glasses filled with what looked like thick tomato soup. Blond, slim, fortyish Doreen, the assistant dining-room manager, labored hard to bring variety to the breakfast table. A devout Catholic new on the job, she hadn't grasped that this first generation of Jewish American women had little experience with alcohol except for sweet concord-grape wine preceded by prayer, Kiddush, on the Sabbath and religious holidays. Second generation ladies like Willa, Flo, and Renee, further removed from Eastern European immigrant experience, were more flexible.

"Care for a Bloody Mary this morning?" Doreen asked again. Jake and Sidney would have accepted immediately, but they had signed up for a Jewish War Veterans bagel and lox brunch at a nearby synagogue.

Bertha screwed up her face. "What did she say?"

"A Bloody Mary," the young woman repeated, "they're very good."

"*What* is it? *What*?" Harriet the Happy Homemaker asked.

"Mostly tomato juice," Doreen said.

"Oh, that's nice. I'll have some," Bertha said.

"With a touch of vodka in it," the assistant manager added, handing out a glass to the nearest outstretched hand.

"Vodka?" Bertha said. "Who drinks vodka at eight o'clock in the morning?" Her thin lips tightened. "Never mind."

Yetta the Yiddishist also declined with a wave of her hand. "Do I look like a *shikkor*?"

"God forbid," Bertha said.

Yetta continued in distain. "Only a shikkor, a drunkard, has vodka so early in the morning."

"The Cossacks in Russia drank vodka, and look what they did to the Jews," an unidentified newcomer said in a mournful voice. Most of the breakfast-table ladies refused the abomination.

"*You* drink it," Yetta said to Doreen, and added, "Feh!"

Eric, the new man, arrived in the middle of this dramatic confrontation. After he lowered himself into a chair with difficulty, he accepted a glass and raised it in a silent toast to the company at large. He nodded to Willa, who was sorry she had downed her Bloody Mary so fast. Tilting her head, she lifted her empty cup in his direction.

Eric tackled the drink with the savoir faire of someone accustomed to after-concert champagne soirees with wealthy patrons and beer-cozy hours with fellow musicians in raucous German rathskellers. As he sipped his drink, he said to Willa in a soft voice, "Shall we ask for seconds?" She laughed. They shared a bond at that moment, Willa thought, and she was heartbroken when he finished a single cup of coffee and apologized for having to leave early. "I can't keep my neurologist waiting," he said, and then looking into her eyes, decided to stay a bit longer.

While the others tackled their pancakes, already tepid under the onslaught of cloying maple syrup, Harriet the Happy Homemaker took the floor. "My grandson is perfect," she announced in her husky voice. The other women glanced at each other. "Phi Beta Kappa, top of his class. They don't accept mediocre students at Yale, only the perfect ones, which he certainly is."

Bertha couldn't stand it another minute. "So is mine. My grandson always makes the dean's list."

A chant rose from the table. "Mine too, mine too, mine too." Eric seemed amused but said, "Excuse me," reached for his walker, and left before Willa could engage him in more worthwhile conversation.

"Mine three," Yetta the Yiddishist said. "If you asked me to list all the prizes my granddaughter has won for her artwork, I'd be exhausted, *oysgemahtert.*" She often threw Yiddish words into her conversation, whether the others understood it or not.

Willa regretted the lost opportunity with Eric but kept her thoughts to herself. A bespectacled woman occupying Jake's available seat rose to make a quick getaway. "Forgot to water my plants this morning," she said. "Have a good day."

Harriet the Happy Homemaker checked to make sure the woman passed out of earshot and said, "She told me she talks to those plants."

"In English or in Yiddish?" Yetta asked. The child of Workman's Circle socialists, she had attended a Yiddish-speaking school while growing up in the Bronx.

Harriet gave a good-natured laugh. "What does she know from Yiddish? She says her grandparents came to America in 1895. Not her parents, her grandparents."

Yetta shook her head. "You'd think in a Jewish place like this, more people would know *mamaloshen.*"

Harriet took advantage of the opening. "My grandson speaks five languages." Before Harriet could continue, Fritzi Schnell hurried in to claim a vacant chair across from Willa and said, "See that lady at the table next to the window? I don't know her name, but what goes on here, you wouldn't believe."

The others stayed quiet and listened hard. "The woman has a very sick husband in the hospital," Fritzi said. "She thinks he's going to die, so she took up with another man. See that guy next to her, the one with the crutch? She's always climbing into his car and driving away with him, who knows where. It's not right."

"Who? Gladys?" Harriet couldn't hide her indignation. "She was the membership chair of our Hadassah group in Florida."

"Oh, it's not her fault. She's very nice. *He's* the one to blame."

"Benny? He's my cousin," Harriet said. "Gladys doesn't drive anymore. My Cousin Benny gives her a ride to the hospital every day out of the goodness of his heart."

Fritzi grabbed two slices of seedless rye bread from a wicker basket in the center of the table and retreated to an adjacent table. "See that woman over there?" she said, gesturing toward Harriet. "She was mean to me. I'm not going to sit with her anymore. She's not friendly."

Willa the Wordless groped under the table for her handbag. It always went missing among the tangle of chair legs, the Velcro-tabbed shoes, the battered cane tips, and napkins that slid off laps more convex than concave.

"You didn't finish your french toast," Harriet said to Willa.

"Not hungry." With Eric gone, there was no reason to remain. She murmured a few apologetic words that others couldn't quite hear and headed for the elevator, where she pushed the Up button. Waiting there, she felt a tap on her shoulder. She turned around fast, hoping it would be Eric, and discovered Ethel, the woman who, weeks before, had spoken to her at the butterfly display.

"Excuse me," she said. "This fell from your bag." In her hand she held something that Willa had removed from her mailbox before breakfast. "I've never seen this magazine before. *Our Voice*? Is it new?"

"No. It's been around awhile."

Ethel squinted and read aloud. "Published by the National Spasmodic Dysphonia Association." Ethel gave her a sympathetic smile. "You have a problem speaking?"

"Yes."

"The cantor at my friend's synagogue had the same thing. He had to quit. We never know what's coming next, do we?"

She handed the newsletter to Willa, who raised her hand in what she hoped was a grateful gesture and said, "Thanks for your trouble."

Ethel gave a healing sort of laugh. "Just the right thing to do." She put her hand on Willa's arm. "What floor are you on?"

Willa squirmed and pushed the elevator button again. "Eighth."

"I'm in an efficiency on the lower level, but the front desk told me there's a bigger apartment they're renovating on the eighth floor, and I'm thinking of switching when they finish."

Willa felt uncomfortable in her presence. "That's nice," she said, ducking into the elevator, empty except for a purple-turbaned African aide speaking a tribal language into her cell phone. Before the door closed, Ethel waved good-bye.

"Going up?" Willa asked. The aide nodded, continued her animated conversation, and left at the seventh floor. Ethel, Willa thought, seemed like someone to avoid. It was more gratifying to concentrate on the musician. Eric, with his curly white hair and those magnificent cheekbones, must have been a handsome devil when young. Even now his eyes retained a certain hidden excitement. At upcoming breakfasts, she wanted to hear more about him and less about Harriet's perfect grandson.

———

*Friday, July 4.* Happy Independence Day from SVM, the Pantheon of Independent Living! Lots of little American flags here but no fireworks, unless Renee and Diana sit at our table. I envy Dr. Holmes. If he didn't invent them, where in real life could he ever have found people chatting casually about entomology, philosophy, and theology over their porridge so early in the morning? Even his rarefied circle must have had its limits. Although he rubbed elbows each week at the Saturday Club with the likes of Ralph Waldo Emerson, James Russell Lowell, and Henry Wadsworth Longfellow, who would want to face that exhausting bunch at breakfast every single day?

Mine is a different breed, not proper Boston Brahmins but Jews, for God's sake—an ingathering of performers, storytellers, upbeat, downbeat, pious, secular, agnostic, idealistic, worldly, naïve, saints, and schlemiels. They grew up in a hostile world, and now as they dip into the reality of old age, they don't like it one bit; Jews don't suffer fate lightly. Fate, a word that pops up at our table when you least expect it.

No question about it, there is a multitude of ambitious retired people at SVM, hard workers and topnotch achievers who fought great odds to succeed in their fields. And I'm equally certain the apartments are filled with upstanding citizens, paragons who never miss a chance to vote, who knit for the military overseas, attend religious services, enjoy opera and ballet, join book clubs, love Israeli music, take art lessons, and attend community lectures and string quartets. But their little planets must spin without me. I feel no urge to bridge the space. Not yet anyway.

All my life I've listened to a running dialogue in my head. Reality whispers to Romance, "Do you come here often?" And Romance answers, "Not so much as I'd like." Reality asks her, "Why not?" and she answers in a sad voice, "Because you don't let me."

Reality jostles us wherever we go. Today Fritzi informed the table that a woman on the fourth floor has just depleted all her savings to care for a husband who didn't have long-term health insurance. "Now she has nothing left," Fritzi said in a fake sympathetic voice, "and she has to find a cheaper place to live."

Renee Richmond raised a brown-penciled eyebrow. "No excuse for that. She should have planned ahead." The others looked at each other and didn't speak.

Reality barges in unannounced. It not only strikes the elderly; it also leaves its graffiti on the faces of their boomer offspring, those infants who brought them such joy at war's end. Harriet remarked the other day, "My daughter's hair is as white as mine, and my son's hairline has receded as much as his father's did." At the SVM entrance, the once-beautiful young brides and handsome grooms, now stoop-shouldered and overweight, load their parents' walkers and wheelchairs into cars. Hail Reality! Reality rules the waves of grown children shlepping grocery bags filled with Ensure and adult diapers. It's payback time.

In spite of its obstacles, I do believe with a perfect faith that Romance will outlive us all. In a recent meditation session to which Lydia dragged me, I abandoned all that mindful relaxation abracadabra long enough to post an imaginary classified ad in the rarified air. Wanted: an old-fashioned Romantic hero, a dashing Errol Flynn, to fend off the villain Reality, who is up to no good.

Jake reported more this morning on the newcomer and named him Eric the Maestersinger. We were surprised to learn that Eric sang with the

Metropolitan Opera, a bass/baritone, imagine that! I had him pegged as a starving violinist. Not much chance for private communication between the two of us. I wonder, does Oliver Wendell Holmes ever introduce any musicians into his breakfast clique? So far no trace, but while turning pages, I uncovered this passage that struck home: "Oh these boarding-houses! What forlorn people one sees...coming down day after day...to sit...with strangers; their hearts full of sad memories which have no language but a sigh, no record but the lines of sorrow on their features;...how sad...when the solitary, whose hearts are shrivelling, are not set in families!"

You're not always a lot of laughs, Dr. Holmes.

# CHAPTER 5

———❖———

ONE MORNING WHEN HARRIET THE Happy Homemaker left the break-fast table for an exclusive, early-morning tour of the strictly kosher SVM kitchen, her seat was taken by a puffy-faced man whom Jake called Moshe the Mambo Maven. A former dance teacher at Arthur Murray's, Moshe considered himself an integral part of show business and immediately informed them, "I'm a natural-born comedian. People say I can be very humorous."

Jake rolled his eyes as Moshe continued. "I was at the podiatrist's yesterday and asked her, 'When do you want me to start giving you dance lessons?' And she says to me, 'I don't need them, but my husband does. He has ten left feet.' And I'm quick on the trigger and say, 'That's because you're a foot doctor.'" He paused for audience response.

"I saw in the paper that Rabbi Zabba died yesterday," Bertha said.

Jake shrugged. "Rabbis die too, you know. Why should the rest of us have all the fun?"

With two bandages on her left cheek from a visit to the dermatologist the day before, Fritzi arrived late to describe in graphic detail two growths she had removed from her face. "If you think this is bad," she said, pointing to the bandage, "last night a woman on the fifth floor had a real bad fall."

The simple word "fall" sent a chill into the sunlit morning. One mere slide off a mattress could result in a 911 call and a hospital stay, a month in rehab, and then what? Did the resident return to SVM and struggle down the arduous path of hiring aides to help with dressing, bathing, and feeding? Did a harried son or daughter arrange to move the parent into the child's home or decide on a full-time assisted living place like Verdant Valley, costing thousands and thousands?

"Tripped over her bedroom slippers," Fritzi said. "I told her to wear regular shoes in her apartment and throw away those floppy blue mules, but she never listens."

Yetta the Yiddishist noticed that Willa showed less sympathy than the others. "Aren't you afraid of falling?" she asked.

"No."

Yetta looked as if she were seeing Willa for the first time. "You don't say much, do you?"

"No."

"Ever read the Yiddish story by I. L. Peretz? *Bontsha Schweig*, meaning *Bontsha the Silent*?

Willa shook her head and tried to concentrate on her omelet while everyone at the table stared at her.

Yetta beamed. "It's about a poor man who lived in silence. After he quietly died, he was tried in a celestial court by the angels of paradise. The defending angel testified that no matter what had ever happened to him, Bontsha never raised his voice, never protested, never complained."

"He didn't live here," Jake said.

"When they decided that he had suffered in silence long enough, the judge offered him a reward, anything in paradise he wanted, just name it. This humble man had never expected anything in life or in death."

The other residents wanted to know what he asked for.

"All he craved was a hot roll with butter for breakfast each morning."

"I wouldn't mind that myself," Bertha said.

Yetta's story didn't brighten Willa's day. She would have deserted the group except for the appearance of a hearing-impaired couple with whom she ate dinner each evening. Ordinarily at breakfast, they sat at a secluded table for two, but that day they moved, according to Fritzi, because somebody she knew, another resident, had invited his son to drop by on the way to work, and the father needed that smaller private table where they could eat alone and discuss business.

"The son is a terrible gambler. He wants power of attorney," Fritzi said. "I warned the father not to give it to him."

Renee Richmond had no patience with the hard-of-hearing newcomers. "Who needs them?" she whispered to Willa.

The tall man in question carried himself with military precision, forward march, his skinny arms swinging through the air with robotic precision. He let the others know immediately that he had been a colonel in the US Army.

Trailing behind, his tiny companion in her pink lace blouse, a matching silk rose tucked into her white ponytail, could barely move, even with the help of a walker.

"This girl can't hear worth a damn," announced the colonel in an ear-splitting voice. "I'm Goldberg, Chip."

Lydia the Encyclopiddia/Librarian smiled. "And your wife's name?"

"I don't sleep with her, so I don't know," Goldberg, Chip said for all the world to hear. "She's just a nice lady I met here."

Lydia became rattled by that. "But what do you call her?"

"Don't call her much of anything. I think her name is Gertie. Not Dirty Gertie from Bizerte. Not one of those. She doesn't say much, but we understand each other." He bent toward her and roared, "You want pancakes, honey?"

Gertie gave him a loving smile. He speared two from his plate. "Here, take mine. I'll order myself some more." Then he turned to Jake. "They were cold anyway. You could use a shave. Are you the rabbi guy?"

Jake frowned. "No, but if you need one, that's Rabbi Lottman standing near the window." He pointed to a bearded man in a dark brown suit and embroidered green and orange yarmulke. "He's the *machgiach* here."

"The *what*?" Goldberg said. "Forgot the goddamn hearing aid again. So did Gertie."

"The machgiach, the person who makes sure the kitchen stays kosher," Bertha said.

Goldberg nodded, gave her a devilish grin, and making sure everyone could hear him, yelled to the Haitian waiter close by, "Could we have some ham and eggs over here? This morning I'm in the mood for *ham and eggs*!"

The appalled women at the table looked at each other. "That's no way to talk in a kosher place," Bertha said. Willa paid little attention except to note that Eric the Maestersinger didn't make an appearance on stage that morning.

------

*Tuesday, July 9.* Score one for romance after eighty! Lately, instead of signing up for bus trips to local concerts and ballets, I prefer in-house events, especially after dinner, when my energy gives out. Our residents volunteer family members, sometimes visibly reluctant, to provide free entertainment for us. Last night when Bertha's musical granddaughter was scheduled to perform at an early evening piano recital, I slipped into the auditorium and found a seat on the back row for quick and easy escape.

Earlier in the day, Dr. Holmes had regaled me with an outrageous critique of a pianist, and it stayed with me as we waited for the show to begin. Holmes showed no mercy:

> The old Master was talking about a concert..."I don't like your chopped music...the music you POUR out is good for sick folks, and the music you POUND out isn't. I have been to hear... a young woman with as many white flounces around her as the planet Saturn has rings...She gave the music stool a twirl or two... Then she pushed up her cuffs as if she was going to fight for the champion's belt...Then those two hands of hers made a jump at the keys as if they were a couple of tigers coming down on a flock of black sheep......Dead stop, so still you could hear your hair growing......Then another jump...and a grand clatter and scramble and string of jumps up and down, back and forward, one hand over the other, like a stampede of rats and mice more than like anything I call music.

A Harvard-educated gentleman who loved classical music, Holmes must have written this tongue-in-cheek review for pure shock value. Seated alone and smiling to myself at Holmes's deliberate attempt to rile pretentious Bostonians, I jumped when someone tapped me on the shoulder.

"May I join you?" Eric Revelle said in a hushed voice.

Startled, I fell into a brief, unexpected spasm of coughing but kept the presence of mind to move over, give him my aisle seat, and offer to push his walker to the back of the room so that the army of latecomers wouldn't trip over it in the dim light. He seemed grateful. After that, the two of us sat lost in the music, breathing it in and exhaling it, not even speaking to each other. I liked it all: Chopin's "Polonaise," courtesy of that old Cornell Wilde movie, *A Song to Remember*; Tchaikovsky's melody borrowed for a once-popular song, "I'm Always Chasing Rainbows," and some mishmash of a duet for piano and flute, played too fast by Bertha's granddaughter and a Chinese teenager with an odd haircut.

When the concert ended, I asked Eric for his professional opinion, and he called the numbers "old warhorses." And what was his opinion of the artist?

"Capable technically, but a long way to go before she masters more depth. That may come later."

I felt inadequate, not ever having learned to play any instrument or even read a note of music. There was nothing worthwhile to add to his comments, but perhaps he could sense he had found a kindred spirit or at least one who knew enough to keep quiet when music played.

"I began on the piano," he said, "at the age of five. My mother had been a well-known coloratura. She was my first teacher, and then a gifted friend of the family took over." He looked far off in the distance, as if he could see them coming toward us, and informed me he planned originally to be a doctor and was accepted at medical school. "But music won out, and I found myself at the New England Conservatory of Music."

My heart beat a little faster. "Are you from Boston?"

"We lived all over. My father played trumpet in the big bands, eventually with Artie Shaw." He looked at me with genuine interest. "You?"

"Sorry, no musical background."

He attempted a shrug. "You listen. That's all that matters."

I told him that Braddock, Pennsylvania, was my hometown. "Not many symphonies there."

"Iron Belt?"

"Used to be." It was hard to continue. As usual, my voice evaporated fast, and so did his, dissolving, fainter and fainter.

I strained hard to remain audible. "My parents had a bakery. They were both born in this country."

"So you're second generation," Eric said in a friendly way. "I am too." He bent forward as if he wanted to hear more.

"My mother died when I was in the first grade," I said. "Later we moved to Harrisburg, and Dad and my stepmother opened a bake shop. Went to a high school across the street from it."

The program had ended; most of the audience had gone. He glanced at his watch. "Late," he said, "for me anyway."

"Your walker. I'll get it for you."

I hurried to retrieve it, a compact, three-wheel vehicle with the storage compartment that converted into a seat. He thanked me and then laboriously hauled himself through the open double doors of the empty auditorium. He said he lived around the corner on the ground floor and wished me good-night.

"Thanks for your company," he called over his shoulder. I could barely hear him.

Like me, Eric doesn't talk much or often. When he does, his words seem pounded down, as if a mortar and pestle had been at work on them. Parkinson's may cause that; I don't know. Jake said Eric had once sung every leading bass/baritone role in opera, including his favorite, *Don Giovanni*, which I've never seen. Aaron wasn't wild about opera.

Since that concert featuring Bertha's granddaughter, Eric and I have sat together twice at SVM concerts. Next week I'll go again and hope to meet him there. It's peaceful; we communicate even with our voices in absentia, no idle chatter. He hasn't told me what's wrong with his vocal cords, and I haven't offered any clinical explanation of mine.

One morning recently Eric did wonder out loud why, after attending a musical event, he never hears residents discuss it. Jake offered his usual cynical explanation. "Because right away they forget it. They just drop in to kill time anyway."

Eric suggested that the elderly may have few pleasant memories, and these are quickly crowded out by pill taking, doctors' appointments, and physical therapy. I wanted to add (but didn't) that sometimes people can't manage spoken words. Like me. Jake said again the other morning, "You're not a big talker, are you?" I shrugged. It wasn't worth the effort to introduce spasmodic dysphonia into the conversation. That would only confuse everyone.

While walking away, I overheard Fritzi's condemnation. "She gives me the willies."

And Lydia the Encyclopiddia said in a delighted voice, "The willies! I haven't heard that slang word in a while."

In my hasty retreat, I forgot my pocketbook and went back to retrieve it. Jake was holding forth on Lydia's remark. "Just how long is a while? Time is one thing that's hard to measure. It may collapse like an accordion, but it doesn't expand like one."

Renee Richmond complained that she couldn't take any more of his freaking pessimism and went to have her nails done, but he continued. "There used to be a congenial group across the room, three veterans, and the wife of one of them. She always had a grin on her face. Remember them, Sid?" Jake addressed the question to his closest buddy, Sidney the Savvy Salesman, who often joins us at the table.

"Yeah," he said. "She was married to that heavy guy you used to call Reuben the Rotund. Every time I'd ask, "How're you doin', Reuben?' he'd answer, 'Fan-tastic!' Some days he looked like hell, but he always said, 'Fan-tastic!' And in a single month, all three guys were gone, one by one. Now the wife walks alone outside every morning and never cracks a smile. Guess she has nothing to smile about."

Nor do I except when Eric comes to breakfast. Minus wrinkles and jowls, he looks younger than most of us, possibly less than eighty. Diana, Goddess of the Hunt and ever hopeful, tries to entice him with bubbly small talk, like asking who created his stage makeup. He answered, slightly insulted, that he did his own.

After that Fritzi accused her of robbing the cradle. May I never fall into your mouth, Fritzi Schnell. Sitting with Eric at SVM concerts doesn't automatically stamp a scarlet letter on my purple cardigan. Does it?

## CHAPTER 6

———•———

"A JAZZ BAND PLAYED HERE last night," Bertha said, cutting into her maple-syrup-drenched waffle.

"How was it?" someone asked.

"Too loud. Willa, can you pass the artificial sweetener? No, the pink one."

"The dinner menu last night was hilarious," said Harriet the Happy Housewife. "Under side dishes, it listed a choice: *cholent* or Potatoes O'Brien.'"

"What's cholent?" Renee Richmond asked, as she bit into a cheese danish.

Sidney shook his head in disbelief. "You're Jewish and you never heard of cholent? My mother used to make it for Shabbos, cut-up potatoes, carrots, and onions with a big chuck roast. She'd leave it overnight in the oven so we could have something to eat when my father came home from shul Saturdays. You couldn't light the stove."

"Not us," Renee said. "We were Reform. When my mother came home from Temple, and she didn't go often, we had peanut-butter sandwiches. That's what our maid fixed us."

"Your maid?" Sidney gave an ironic laugh. "Some class to you!"

After Fritzi joined the group, Sidney pushed himself away from the table. He had nothing better to do that morning, but he detested the Schnellbomber and the endless female gossip. His buddy Jake had an early appointment with the dentist.

"Don't do anything I wouldn't do, Sidney," Bertha said playfully.

He cast a dimmed eye in her direction. "We'd all like to, but we can't." Sidney's replacement was Mel the Mechanic, a blunt man who, according to Yetta, embodied the Yiddish expression, what is in the lung is on the tongue.

"Did you know they jammed a catheter into me?" Mel asked. "You think it's a picnic carrying around a bag of urine inside you all the time?"

His tablemates answered that they really didn't care to know about this when they were eating and that anyway they had heard it from him numerous times before.

"So," he said, ignoring their reaction, "I told my urologist, 'I have all my marbles, but I'm losing my cookies.'"

"I used to bake the most delicious sugar cookies," Harriet said.

Mel the Mechanic shook his head. "Cookies? I got diabetes. Anybody here interested in an old-fashioned Sugar Daddy?" The Ha-Ha Table, now deserted, would have been in stitches, but the women at his table didn't want to encourage him. Without enlivening the conversation further, he downed a cup of decaffeinated coffee and headed outdoors for an early-morning cigarette, one of the many he had lit for the past sixty-five of his eighty-three years.

As if Mel had never spoken or even walked the earth, Fritzi made one of her world-shaking announcements. "I have the most loving children," she said. "They call me on the phone every day, knock wood." She pounded the table for five seconds.

A heavily made-up woman identified by Jake as Flo the Faux Blonde shook her head. "I never hear from mine. They made me move from my beautiful home in Wilmington to be near them, and now I never see them."

Fritzi raised her voice in triumph. "Mine call twice a day and come visit at least three, four, five times a week unless I go to them, which I do maybe twice a week. Don't your kids come often?"

"My older son used to live ten minutes away," Bertha said, "but he took a job all the way across the country in Texas. I have a daughter in California, a son in Canada, and a daughter in Israel. Now only my younger brother and his family live nearby. I see them but not my own grandchildren."

"That's sad," Fritzi said cheerfully. "Mine come a lot." She knocked wood again. "Can't complain."

The others said nothing. Often they had seen Fritzi waiting in the lobby to be picked up. She sat there stranded for hours, but no one ever came. Only the day before, they all had overheard Fritzi when her cell phone rang. She deserted the table to stand in a nearby corner for a private conversation in a piercing voice that carried across the vast distances of the Esther Essenvarg Dining Den.

"You're not coming?" Fritzi said. "I thought you were coming today. I wait and wait, and nobody shows up. It happened three times already. Getting sick and tired of this. So how about tomorrow? Why not? You think I like living here all by myself and not seeing you? All right, maybe next week. What day? Is that a promise? I hope it's a promise. Remember, you promised. All right I'll look for you. Don't forget next time. Don't leave me sitting alone, waiting. What? You always forget and so does your sister. She does too. Don't argue with me. She's even worse than you are. Call me at least, OK? OK?"

When she returned to the table, no one looked her way. "That was my Sharon," Fritzi said. "I wish my girls would stop pestering me to spend time with them. They get on my nerves, you know?"

Willa couldn't take her eyes away from the entrance to the dining room. It was growing late. The waiters had almost finished clearing tables.

"Wonder what happened to that new guy, the singer?" Fritzi said, reading Willa's mind. "I guess he figures he's too hot stuff to sit with us."

Once again Eric did not eat breakfast with them. Maybe all the pointless talk had driven him away. Willa hoped not. She couldn't say why, but she missed him.

———◆———

*Friday, July 12.* How wonderful to stumble across these lines from Holmes that would delight Eric if I ever get up enough nerve to show it to him: "I have been tempted sometimes...to envy the immediate triumphs of the singer. He enjoys all that the praise can do for him...at the very moment of exerting his talent..."

If only Eric would share some of his past triumphs at breakfast. But it could backfire. We're out of his league. On the art of conversation, Oliver Wendell Holmes insists that even when a mediocre person makes a remark bordering on brilliance, it upsets the balance, the social order, and causes ordinary people to feel uncomfortable. Eric may be wise keeping it all to himself. Perhaps he thinks discussing music or his amazing career will damage the equilibrium at our table, such as it is.

Deep down I'm sure he prefers solitude. I think he would love sharing my favorite part of the day. At seven o'clock in the morning, a brisk walk takes me down silent corridors to the deserted Gedalia Ginsfarb Fitness Garden and a daily rendezvous with the treadmill. En route, no one is around except a sleepy-eyed Filipina on her way to help a frail elder manage zippers, buttons, and diapers.

On dark mornings, corridor lights burn with quiet intensity. White paper bags containing pharmacy prescriptions drape brass doorknobs, and morning newspapers slump against locked doors. By eight o'clock, most papers will be painfully retrieved by their subscribers. Bending over takes time, and the thought of having to do it is depressing, not something to look forward to early in the morning.

Only remnants of the Eastern European immigrant generation remain here now, but behind these silent doors, their spirit lingers. It survives and lives again in the twentieth-century-born American offspring, their Yiddish expressions, the deprecating humor, our shreds of Jewish superstitions and folkways.

Like well-trained soldiers, the beige-colored doors stand at attention up and down the hallways. The doors have earned their stripes, black streaks like military chevrons where a walker or wheelchair has gotten stuck or just barely scraped by. From time to time, a swab of paint will blot out the unavoidable markings left behind by those no longer able to clear the door on the first try.

I'm fascinated by each mezuzah nailed in a sloping position on the right-hand side of the doorposts. No two are alike: burnished bronze or gleaming china painted with biblical water jugs, impressionistic tubes splashed with waves of color or no-nonsense Israeli ones bearing tawny modern Hebrew letters burned into balsawood. More to my liking in the mezuzah family are traditional filigreed cylinders, golden or silvery. All are blessed. All contain the required biblical quotations, the beginning two paragraphs of the *Shema* ("Hear O Israel"), from Deuteronomy.

Sometimes there's a mezuzah mounted halfway up a doorpost to accommodate those who can't stand or walk. It's touching to watch Orthodox Hannah in her wheelchair as she taps the mezuzah and then kisses her fingers. She does this each time she enters or leaves her apartment. Although Jake and Yetta consider it old-country superstition, touching the mezuzah is a comfort to believers. I helped Aaron put ours up when we first moved to SVM. It made us feel, not exactly pious, but neighborly.

Important note: I almost forgot to mention that just when everyone thought Eric had left us for good, he returned this morning after participating in a clinical trial at Johns Hopkins Hospital in Baltimore. What a relief! Table conversation buzzed with his recent interview in *The Magilla*, our SVM newspaper. He had been away when it was first distributed.

"They spelled my name wrong," Eric said. If he was upset, he didn't show it.

Diana, Goddess of the Hunt, kept disturbing his meal with inane questions. "According to this article, you sang all over Europe. Why didn't you stay in the US of A?"

Eric gave her a patient smile. "More operatic opportunities abroad."

"You were famous!" Bertha said in awe.

"Opera is not for me," Fritzi said. "Too much screeching, and where does it get you?"

"Eric told me that when he left the stage, he taught music on the university level," Jake continued, giving Fritzi a murderous look.

"And he also conducted orchestras and choral groups," Diana said. She grabbed his arm. "Oh, I'm so proud of you."

Eric acted as if he had met many Dianas in his time. He slightly inclined his head in restrained acknowledgment and then focused on his cantaloupe. The man seems a bit stiff sometimes, perhaps heavily medicated to manage his Parkinson's, but I see flashes of enthusiasm in his eyes and would really like to know him better. Today he dropped a menu on the floor, which I picked up and handed back to him. He was as appreciative as if the menu were a bouquet of roses delivered to him while taking a curtain call after a dazzling performance. And another time when I moved a stray walker out of his way so he could reach the table, he thanked me and placed his hand over his heart, the gesture of a seasoned performer's gratitude to a wildly applauding audience.

Imagine an entire life spent in white tie and tails. In daydreams, I see him departing on a tour to Europe. He wears a black felt fedora, a beige cashmere overcoat draped over his broad shoulders. From the deck of the Queen Mary, he waves to cheering admirers and sails for Paris, London, Rome. His schedule is heavily booked; he juggles invitations for command performances from kings of Belgium and Sweden. I see him onstage at La Scala; he rushes for trains to glittering European concert halls, Berlin, Vienna, Prague. *The New York Times* runs heady accolades about his show-stopping roles at the Met. He sings Verdi, Mozart, Bizet. He vanquishes Carnegie Hall and mesmerizes American audiences everywhere, Boston, Chicago, Los Angeles, Constitution Hall, the White House.

Eric even calls Lily Pons and Lauritz Melchior by their first names. He hobnobs with the rich, chatting in French with King Farouk, the Shah of Iran, Princess Grace Kelly. Imagine mesmerizing the international elite and always top-billing, sell-out audiences, the realm of classical music his royal domain, an entire planet at his feet. All this, and he's even Jewish.

So how could a tall, skinny, bag-of-bones redhead like me possibly reach such an elegant man without appearing boring, pushy, or nauseatingly obvious? Diana has already fluttered her artificial eyelashes at him with an invitation to join her in the SVM Chorus. I could have crawled under the table. He smiled and declined with exquisite politeness.

Music is the best approach. Trouble is, Aaron and I attended concerts maybe twice a year. Albums of vinyl 78s and 45s are still piled on bookshelves along with compact discs we never found time to play. Aaron's obsolete hi-fi is broken, lacking parts they don't make anymore. How can I discuss music on Eric's level when the finer points escape me, the tongue-twisting names of famous artists I should know but don't, that whole confusing mishmash of sharps and flats, the fancy Italian words warning musicians how to play the notes, all that stuff?

My brain needs a complete overhaul, and transformation won't come easily. Reminds me of what Jake said the other day. "Everything changes except change, and even change sometimes arrives too early or too late." Still, if I want to reach Eric, it makes sense to bone up on more than Gilbert and Sullivan.

———•———

## CHAPTER 7

———

OVER THEIR CREAM OF WHEAT, the residents at Willa's table once more engaged in an unscheduled, unofficial game called Why Are You Here? It surfaced periodically, involving nearly everyone. Newcomers felt more obligated to play than old-timers, who had been through it countless times before.

Bertha chose a simple reason. "I came here because I like a hot dinner served to me every night instead of cooking for myself."

"I miss cooking," Harriet the Happy Homemaker said. "When was the last time you made chopped liver?"

"To tell the truth," said Flo the Faux Blonde, "I'm not ready for a place like this. I don't even have many wrinkles."

"Forget about wrinkles," Bertha said. "My motto is, I'm here, I'm alive, I can move. Maybe I can't dance anymore, but I can *schuckle*. I can shake my *tochis* a little bit in time to the music."

Sidney the Savvy Salesman, his mouth still full, entered the discussion. "Why did I come here?" he repeated, chewing between each word. "I didn't want to move in with any of my kids, that's why."

Jake topped them all. "I came here to meet girls."

The Ha-Ha Table overheard that and responded heartily, but most of the people sitting around Willa's table took the conversation seriously.

"Everybody knows why we're here," Flo said in a solemn tone. "Read the writing on the wall." No one spoke. "My sons are furious with me," she said, changing the subject fast, "because I'm not getting rid of the car yet."

Fritzi moved into one of the empty chairs at the table and immediately plunged into the conversation. "You're still driving?" she said. "You were going to donate your Buick to charity."

"Fourteen years old," Flo said, "but it still goes."

"Mine is eighteen," Harriet said in a tone of one-upmanship.

Flo had an idea. "I don't drive too much now, but anybody want to join me some day for a nice trip out in the country?"

Lydia, the librarian, shook her head. "My rule is never to ride in cars driven by seniors. I don't do it on general principle."

"That's why you've lived so long," Jake said. There was a respectful pause after which Sidney refused to let the women dominate the conversation. "Know what's on the menu for dinner tonight? Yankee Pot Roast."

Yetta the Yiddishist frowned. "What's that?" Like Sidney and Jake, she grew up on New York's Lower East Side.

"You don't know?" Sidney said, incredulous. "You never heard of *Yenkee* Pot Roast?"

Yetta sniffed in disdain. "My mother didn't cook anything called Yankee Pot Roast."

Sidney persisted in getting his joke across. "No, no, Yetta, not *Yankee* Pot Roast, *Yenkee* Pot Roast."

Yetta wasn't having any part of making fun of her mother's Yiddish accent. "In our house my parents spoke only *mamaloshen*. I never learned English until first grade."

"Unconscionable," Lydia said. Her father had been a professor of philosophy at New York University.

Sidney said he still didn't believe Yetta never heard of Yenkee Pot Roast. "So tell me; you went to the Workman's Circle School. Did it make a socialist out of you?" he asked.

Yetta raised a bushy eyebrow at him. "Leave me alone, Sidney. I was up all night with acid indigestion."

"Once at my high school," Bertha said, thrusting a tablespoon into her oatmeal, "a bunch of girls who were communists wanted me to join the party."

Sidney perked up. "And did you?"

"No. I didn't like their clothes."

With great difficulty, Eric the Meistersinger, as Jake now called him, approached the table. "Is this seat taken?" he asked in his low voice. Willa made room for him to sit and helped push his walker away from the path of traffic. His smile lit up a face that once must have been magnetic in a Gregory Peck sort of way. The trimmed white beard was superfluous; Willa wondered how he would look clean-shaven.

She strained to come up with a topic worthy of him, something musical, but while she pondered over choosing the most creative way to arrange her words in a voice he could hear, Diana, Goddess of the Hunt, plopped down in a chair on the other side of him and brazenly asked what his horoscope sign was. And the most disappointing thing about it was, he told her.

Willa retreated to her apartment in search of wisdom from the pen of Oliver Wendell Holmes, perhaps another thoughtful zinger she could borrow to impress Eric Revelle the next time.

———◄►———

*Monday, July 15.* This is what resonates from Holmes today: "Good talk is not a matter of will at all; it depends…on a certain amount of active congestion of the brain, and that comes when it is ready, and not before." Biding my time, I've just reread Eric's interview in *The Megilla*, and it's amazing how much almost every line parallels the life story of Dr. Oliver Wendell Holmes. This is an objective list of incredible coincidences in their lives:

1.  Medicine. Before switching to study voice in Boston, at first Eric considered becoming a physician and did well in pre-med courses.
2.  Locale. Both wandered the same streets, passed Bunker Hill and the Boston Common, ate New England clam chowder.
3.  Versatility. Eric, note by note, created a potpourri of characters onstage like Figaro, Escamillo, Faust. He projected his voice into

their mouths. Bone by bone, Holmes constructed funny breakfast-table characters like The Boy and the Register of Deeds and serious ones like Scheherazade, a melancholy female writer. Holmes put his voice into their mouths.

4.  Skill. Conducting a symphony orchestra is akin to what Holmes did in his books, blending humor and philosophy, making discordant characters interact with each other in a controlled way, just as Eric did with musicians, inspiring them to play the right notes at the right time in harmony and with feeling.

5.  Charisma. Each artist knew how to spellbind an audience, Eric in opera, Holmes on the lecture circuit. Adoring fans surrounded them wherever they went.

6.  Academia: Both became professors in Boston, Holmes at the Harvard School of Medicine, Eric later at the New England Conservatory of Music.

7.  Universality. Holmes dazzled audiences overseas, especially England. And what a superb singer Eric must have been to impress cosmopolitan Europeans, this dashing American, alive with energy. If only time reversed itself so that I'd know him only as a young man and hear him sing as he did back then. But as Jake says, in old age you make do with what you have.

Before abandoning hope, I discovered a miraculous twenty-four-hour satellite channel that shows classical videos, bits and pieces of opera stars in past concerts, as well as symphony orchestras, ballets, and Arthur Rubinstein everywhere. For the next two hours, I sat spellbound and hated to turn it off. Right now I'm listening to an excerpt from Mussorgsky's *Pictures at an Exhibition*. Not bad. Here may be an easy way to firm up my dismal musical background. To mimic Emily Dickinson, hope is a thing with sharps and flats. If I watch the program every day and take notes, all this could become a direct route to Eric's heart, provided that's where I want to be.

# CHAPTER 8

―――――――

When Sidney the Savvy Salesman appeared at the breakfast table the next morning, he found Fritzi in Jake's chair. Sidney shook his head in disapproval; it was no secret he didn't care to sit near Fritzi, who had a juicy way with words. For a while he and Jake called her Fritzi the Spritzi, but Sidney, a World War II bombardier in the US Army Air Corps, suggested renaming her Fritzi the Schnellbomber. "Because like those German planes, she's quick to unload, hits her target, and gets away fast," he said.

"Did you miss me?" she called out to Sidney, before he could heave his broad backside onto the plastic chair cushion. "Friday, Saturday, and Sunday I was at my daughter's. My Sharon keeps nagging me, 'So, Mom, when are you coming over? We never see you enough.' I hate to disappoint her, so I agreed to come, but I need time for myself, you know?"

Fritzi continued her monologue, which Sidney ignored as he poured fat-free Lactaid milk into a bowl of Cheerios. "My girls, they're always breaking down the doors to see me, rain or shine, through the biggest blizzards, like last winter. No matter how bad it is outside, they always show up, three, four, five times a week. I'm blessed, I'm one lucky mother, knock wood." Fritzi pounded the table hard four times. The others made no comment.

Yetta the Yiddishist seized the moment for one of her twice-told tales because she thought Willa never heard it before. "My mother had seven children in America. Too many children underfoot. She sent me to first grade when I was four. I spoke only Yiddish at home and didn't understand what the teacher was saying. They held me back a year. I never got over it."

Bertha said, "You told us already."

Yetta paid no attention to her. "I'll never forgive my Aunt Thelma. For years she'd introduce me saying, 'This is Yetta. She was held back.' I'd meet people at a Workman's Circle rally and they'd say to me, 'Aren't you Yetta, the girl they held back?' Years later, after I became principal of a Yiddish school and even wrote a Yiddish textbook, at family weddings and funerals, there were always relatives who'd ask, 'Aren't you the one who was held back?'"

Fritzi made a mental note of this tidbit, gobbled down a piece of toast, and left for her place near the fish tank in the lobby. "I'm running late," she said.

Bertha sniffed hard. "That Fritzi. She lives on my floor and says my teakettle gets on her nerves when it whistles. She complains she can hear it through the wall."

"I like a whistling teakettle," Yetta said.

Harriet the Happy Homemaker agreed. "There was an old song— 'Polly, Put the Kettle On'—remember?"

"Sounds nicer than 'Polly, Heat Up Some Water in the Microwave,'" Bertha said.

"It reminds me of the old days in my mother's kitchen and her *tz-chainik*. That's Yiddish for tea kettle," Yetta said with a heartfelt sigh. "Like another old the song, 'Vuss Iss Gevehn Iss Gevehn'—What Was, Was." There was silence while her tablemates nodded in solemn agreement.

"Where's Jake this morning?" Bertha said. "I have a question for him about Judaism. He knows things like that."

Sidney said he thought Jake had an appointment at the ophthalmologist's. "What did you want to ask him? I went to chader too, you know. It wasn't one of your socialist Yiddish schools, Yetta. Old Mr. Horowitz wielded a nasty ruler to keep us kids under control at the Talmud-Torah." He stared into his coffee cup. "My God, right now I'm older than Mr. Horowitz."

Bertha hesitated. "Maybe it's not a religious question exactly, but it's about Jews."

"Try me," Sidney said.

"You've heard of a Jew's harp, haven't you? Well, what connection does it have with being Jewish?"

Sidney gave her a blank stare. "What?"

"It's a musical instrument," Yetta said. "You play it with the mouth, and there's a metal piece inside that vibrates."

"Yes," Bertha said, "but why a Jew's harp? In my day Jewish boys all took violin lessons, and my girlfriends played the piano. I never saw any Jew play a Jew's harp, did you? Why not a Catholic's harp or a Protestant's harp?"

Yetta took exception. "You're assuming that Jews are only a religion. We're also a people with our own culture and a spoken and written language, Yiddish, which will never die.'"

"I'll bet a professional musician like Eric Revelle knows all about Jew's harps," Bertha said. She addressed this remark to Willa, who couldn't take her eyes from the doorway to the dining room. Eric was nowhere in sight.

Willa put a Centrum Silver tablet on her tongue, took a final gulp of lukewarm tea, and headed back to the comfort of her journal, Dr. Holmes, and the blessed nonprofit channel that provided Classical Arts Showcase, with its video clips of Viennese musicians playing "The Blue Danube Waltz" more often than she cared to hear.

———————

*Tuesday, July 16.* Today at breakfast I stole looks at Eric and wondered what he thinks about all this stultifying chatter around us. Whether it's from disinterest or the havoc of his illness, that Adonis face rarely shows any expression. Like me, he's an avid listener. Maybe, trapped inside himself, he struggles to understand what I'm thinking without my saying much.

Wouldn't it be extraordinary to have him all to myself so that he could tell me more about his exciting past? Face to face, we'd swap soft-spoken words over mugs of jasmine tea, two kindred souls alone in my apartment, cushioned by the spirit of Oliver Wendell Holmes, Chopin playing somewhere in the background. What keeps me from breaking the invisible barrier between us?

Embarrassment. My knowledge of classical music still hinders me. I can identify only a few warhorses like Beethoven's *Symphony Number Nine* and his *Moonlight Sonata.* The Classical Arts Showcase is a godsend. Maybe the TV channel that never sleeps will work magic, but it takes time to eliminate all those gaps in my education.

Eric is steeped in every mystery of music. He has performed in French, German, and Russian more operas than I ever knew even existed, and as a conductor, he mastered intimately the scores of countless symphonies, the nuances, the location of all the buried jewels tucked into sonatas, concertos, preludes, nocturnes. As a highly trained specialist, he must still carry traces of all this inside him wherever he goes.

It strikes me that SVM brims with other specialists, but you'd never know it. My neighbors here were once social workers, public speakers, school teachers, engineers, chemists, certified public accounts, executive assistants, entrepreneurs, contractors, civil servants. Not a peep out of them now about the past life. Perhaps they forget who they were or they avoid casting pearls before swine, so why bother?

Oliver Wendell H. dodged this reality. All he had to do with his book characters was thrust entire essays into their mouths. Every word stayed under the control of the estimable autocrat of the breakfast table while he projected his scholarly thoughts and humorous asides into the mouths of his puppets.

If only Eric could share my devotion to Dr. Holmes! When an opportunity arises at breakfast, I'll mention him and see what happens. It may be difficult to slip the name of Oliver Wendell Holmes into our morning chitchat, but it's worth a shot. And if Eric thinks I'm peculiar to be obsessed by a nineteenth-century writer who brilliantly fills page after page and often doesn't know when to stop, well, too bad. Musicians aren't the most normal people in the world either.

# CHAPTER 9

———◆———

WILLA DIDN'T SEE HER HERO at breakfast for the next couple of days. There were a number of vacant chairs. Sidney the Savvy Salesman had quarantined himself in his apartment with a bad case of stomach flu.

"It's making the rounds," Lydia said.

"And the runs," Jake added, to the delight of the Ha-Ha Table nearby.

Yetta the Yiddishist came by at that moment. "Anybody sitting here?" she asked, pausing at what was usually Eric's chair. Willa motioned in the direction of another empty seat across from her, which Yetta took, first brushing away from the tabletop random croissant crumbs left by a previous occupant.

"This is the *A* table," Jake explained to Yetta. "Atheists and Agnostics only."

"Suits me," she said. "My father had a picture of Eugene Debs hanging in the parlor."

"You had a parlor?" asked Jake. "Some class to you.'"

Yetta, a bushy-eyebrowed woman who rarely smiled, reached for the warm pastry and said, "If this is the *A* table, what's *B*?"

With a tilt of his head, Jake indicated a table near the fireplace. "Believers and Beards," he said. A circle of Orthodox men had just finished their meal and were praying, benching, chanting almost inaudibly as they swayed from side to side.

"Takes all kinds," Yetta said, biting into a danish.

Jake's expression changed. "Ladies, your dream boy is headed this way."

Turning her head, Willa hoped to see Eric. Instead, the man Jake called Howie the Unwholesome Wholesaler headed straight toward the unoccupied place next to her. Howie didn't eat breakfast with them regularly; he chose to circulate and give all the ladies a chance to share his divine presence. Willa moved her chair as far away from him as she could without invading Jake's territory. Wrinkled foreheads around the table grew stonier than usual.

"Acts like he owns this place," Sidney once remarked of him. "And maybe he does." The Unwholesome Wholesaler had made sizable contributions to community causes in hope, everyone said, that charity would redeem him from his questionable reputation among women.

"Howie, why wasn't a swinger like you dancing at the Duke Ellington program yesterday?" Jake asked.

Howie frowned. "I don't dance with ninety-three-year-old women," he said.

After a pause, without a single word uttered by anyone except for a demand by Bertha to pass "that saltless salt," Howie turned to Willa and said, "You're very quiet this morning." She refused to look in his direction and continued carefully slicing a bruised banana into her cereal.

Scathing retorts raged through her mind. Willa had *never* spoken to the man. She avoided the most sterile good-morning and never even responded with a skimpy "You too" when he wished her a nice day. He obviously was up to no good. She proceeded to cut him dead.

Minutes passed until Howie said, "This is a nice quiet table." He leaned toward her with a serious look on his face. "Do you ever get lonely?" Willa didn't answer.

Howie interrupted his pitch to accept granola from the Zimbabwean waitress and then continued.

"Are you dating anyone?" Howie asked her.

"Am I what?"

"Have a boyfriend?"

"My husband died recently."

Not looking at her, Howie returned to the soggy wheat flakes in a bowl before him. "So what else is new?" he said pleasantly, mouth full.

Willa grabbed her handbag from under the table and fled. *So what else is new? So what else is new? Idiot.* The absurdity of the conversation struck her. In the elevator all by herself, she somehow could hear Aaron's voice from far off. He was laughing his head off, and in spite of herself, Willa couldn't resist the smile that formed on her lips.

———————

*Wednesday, July 23.* Howie is not my idea of romance. It's safer to watch Turner Classic Movies. Yesterday afternoon, they showed Ronald Coleman in James Hilton's *Lost Horizon*. Wouldn't it be fun if the SVM bus took us to Shangri-La for a field trip? Not the Himalayas but maybe the Poconos. In my daydream, we check into a health spa there and spend the day guzzling mineral water and eating fat-free Greek yogurt by the gallon.

Afterward, on the bus halfway home, Bertha in the next seat chatters away about her strategy for always winning at Bingo and then lets out a scream. "Willa, my hands!"

I examine her ten exquisite fingers, no longer grotesquely knobby from arthritis; the skin radiant, unmarred by sunspots or bulging blue veins.

"And look, my legs!" Bertha cries. It can't be. Her calves and thighs are slender, perfectly proportioned, like the pin-up girls of World War II, no briar patches of varicose veins, her swollen ankles gone. She grabs my hand and says, "Oh my God, you're not slouched over anymore. Look how flat your stomach is! What's going on?"

"We've been granted a last-minute reprieve from the Almighty," I say in a melodious voice, with perfect diction.

Bertha bounces up and down in her seat. "And your face is growing younger by the minute!"

I whip out my compact. A quick look in the mirror reveals the curly luminous hair of yesteryear and pink cheeks, young but without a trace of the acne I once knew. We both squeal at our transformation. I tell her about the *Lost Horizon* movie scene in which beautiful young actress Margo leaves the hidden land of Shangri-La, and while escaping down the mountain, turns into a shriveled old crone who never heard of sunscreen.

"This trip to the Poconos must be Shangri-La In Reverse," Bertha says, now as blond and gorgeous as Lana Turner.

"Yes," I say, "and we'll all live happily ever after. We'll keep the same bodies and faces of our youth and so will everyone else on this SVM trip, although some of us are better endowed and have more to work with."

We continue on to the Greyhound Bus Terminal in Boston, where Eric, a strikingly handsome young baritone at the New England Conservatory of Music, waits for me. I bound off the bus into his arms. Just like Robert Merrill on TV's Classic Arts Showcase, Eric is singing Franz Lehár's "Yours Is My Heart Alone" in perfect German. He hands me the sheet music to it, and in a silvery lyric soprano, I sight-read the entire piece. It's a magnificent duet; the entire bus station throbs with thunderous applause, and a talent scout for *The Ed Sullivan Show* overhears us and signs up both of us. This is my best daydream yet.

But Eric is no reverie. Seeing him at breakfast makes me feel, not young, because there is no reverse gearshift in life, but young*ish*. It's proof that Reality doesn't have to trounce Romance every single time. Outward appearances be damned; we're both still in the game as long as there's Chopin playing in the background.

So here's my ambitious to-do list. 1. Look up eighteenth- and nine-teenth-century composers in Aaron's 1973 Encyclopedia Britannica; their biographies can't have changed much in the past forty years. 2. List their major compositions. 3. Switch on the local classical music radio station while folding laundry or cutting toenails. 4. Force myself to read un-intelligible music reviews in newspaper. 5. Pay closer attention to good old Classical Arts Showcase, and concentrate on deceased baritones like George London and Dietrich Fischer-Dieskau (Eric's idol). 6. Don't skip grainy kinescopes of Toscanini conducting at midcentury. 7. Jot down names of featured symphony orchestras and conductors who get carried away with emotion. Maybe Eric worked with some of these rare ducks. (Ask!!!)

Absorbing music into my bloodstream will be a lifesaving transfusion. Transfiguration has already begun. A word, "forlana," popped up in the morning newspaper review of a local know-it-all music critic trying to impress readers. The dictionary defines "forlana" as a spirited dance performed by Venetians centuries ago. Although not easy to fit it into the conversation, it was a perfect word to spring on Eric over our pancakes. He had never heard of it, or if he had, he said he didn't remember and blamed his newest medication. He smiled his thanks and seemed quite taken with me.

Yesterday after the others left the table, he asked me point blank, "What's wrong with your voice?"

No one here ever mentions it. Discussing health problems at SVM has always been what's yours is yours and what's mine is mine, and I'd rather talk about mine. He caught me off guard until I looked into the gentle eyes of a person who detects and understands distressed voices.

"Spasmodic dysphonia."

"That's what I thought. I've known singers who had it."

"There are two kinds."

He nodded. "Affecting either the adductor or abductor muscles."

"Mine is the rarer one. Abductor. Harder to treat."

"Botox shots in the larynx?"

"Didn't work. Just have to make do with what I have left."

He smiled. "Music is the best medicine for you."

"Always," I said, and thought of my to-do list.

Bluffing and unadulterated chutzpah is what I'll need until more substance kicks in. An occasional sonata or concerto on that twenty-four-hour satellite channel, Classic Arts Showcase, sounds familiar, but classical music still confounds me. I find myself faced with a ragbag of sounds and emotions spilling over in all directions. My mind strays; I rarely give any thought to nuances. Certain melodies have somehow stayed in my head, but where they come from or what the titles of Italian arias mean or in what musical period the symphonies and sonatas belong, all this remains fuzzy or vaporizes. (Keep looking things up!!!)

The more I see Eric the more I ache to learn how a true artist reaches the heart of his audience. Will he ever share that excitement with me? And I'm too shy to ask if singers are ever haunted by phantoms, ghosts of lost music, melodies that have been written but never played or sung, but that might scare him away.

Every time we meet at music recitals in the SVM auditorium, he seems pleased with my company. Seated next to him, I concentrate hard and try to hear what he hears. We don't strain to speak. Congenial but detached, we aren't a couple, just concertgoers side by side, nothing more. And yet Dr. Holmes writes, "It is impossible to come before a public so alive with sensibilities as this we live in...without making friends in a very unexpected way. Everywhere there are minds tossing on the unquiet waves of doubt. If you confess to the same perplexities and uncertainties that torture them, they are grateful for your companionship." Companionship, so be it. At our age what else is available?

# CHAPTER 10

———

WILLA HAD BROUGHT HER COPY of *The Poet at the Breakfast Table* to show Eric the next day, but he never appeared, and only Lydia remained after the others finished eating.

"What's that you have there?" Lydia asked. Willa handed the century-old book to her and hoped no late stragglers would find their way to the table. The librarian would surely appreciate an antiquarian find like this.

Lydia's fingers trembled as she ran them over the faded maroon cover. "Are you donating this to my Biblio Boosters?"

"No."

"Don't. This is a rare find." Lydia's narrow brown lips produced a wrinkly smile as she read the title page. "How charming. They printed the subtitle in a small Germanic type face: 'He talks with his fellow boarders and the Reader.'" She adjusted the wire-rimmed glasses that kept sliding down her nose and continued reading. "'Published by the Riverside Press, Cambridge, Massachusetts, and Electrotyped and Printed by H.O. Houghton and Company.' 'Electrotyped' is a word one doesn't hear these days. Let's be careful not to stain this treasure with the coffee I just spilled."

Crumpling her cloth napkin, Willa dabbed at a threatening rivulet of brown headed in her direction. "No danger," she said.

Lydia remained entranced by the book. "And the publication date in roman numerals, no less. MDCCCXCIV." She glanced at Willa, holding her breath, afraid the elderly woman would lose her grip on the book and drop it to the floor. Most pages were already loose, some missing. "When I was a girl, I read his earlier two Breakfast Table volumes," Lydia said, "but not this one until years later. As a youngster, I could never have gotten through it."

Willa cleared her throat. "It's my favorite of the three."

"Pardon me? I didn't understand what you just said."

"I like it best."

"Why, Willa?"

"More poetry in it."

"I don't recall that. It's been a while. If my eyes were not ready to give up the ghost, I'd read it again. Makes me wonder how young people today would respond." Lydia gently returned it to Willa. "Thank you. This book never had the popularity of his first, did it?"

"No." That was why she liked it so much, Willa wanted to add. She felt sorry for the author trying to recapture all the readers who had made the first book a success and then deserted the third. Holmes must have been disappointed. She wished her voice would stay audible long enough for her to explain how she felt about the man and his work. Instead, Lydia's Nigerian aide turned up with the wheelchair to collect her frail employer for a visit to the cardiologist.

Before the two of them left the Esther Essenvarg Dining Room, Lydia, in her cultivated manner, called out, "Willa! Come for tea at three thirty this afternoon. Apartment seven forty-two. There's another ghost from the past I want you to meet."

---

*Tuesday, July 18.* Before details leave me, it's important to record on paper my frustration over what just happened at Lydia's. I had prepared a list of topics we could talk about and even brought along the final draft of this latest poem intended for Lydia's eyes only:

## Denial

by Willa Warsaw

These ironside days I cannot love
My counterparts as much as I may try,
I can't admire the beige wallpaper leaves
That line indifferent corridors
And way-less-traveled stairwells.
I shrink from wheelchair-battered doors,
Those noncommittal barricades of wood
Protecting loneliness and musty love;
I ought to show affection
For my wrinkled next of kin
Who share the wires and water pipes.
I hear their shuffling footsteps in the hall
And overhead their barefoot midnight strolls;
Misfit, I will not willingly commit
To this bizarre communal waning.

Lydia and her wheelchair waited in the doorway of her apartment; she welcomed me as if my arrival were the most significant event since John F. Kennedy's inauguration, which she remembered attending to hear one of her dear friends, Robert Frost, read a poem.

"Come in! Neighborly visits don't happen often at SVM," she said, "except for Harriet, who invites her family for home-cooked dinners, mostly on Rosh Hashanah and Passover." She swiveled her wheels and led me into the living room. "Our grown-up children prefer taking parents out to upscale restaurants. The food may be unkosher but more reliable," she added. "I suppose adult offspring have learned the hard way. Aging mothers often omit vital ingredients or double the amount of seasoning in case they don't remember whether or not they included it. And there's always the problem of how long food has languished in the refrigerator. Please have a seat."

She led me to a couch smothered with scratchy needlepoint pillows. "There are a hundred reasons why the elderly may be inhospitable. According to the ubiquitous Fritzi, Renee Richmond once lived in a mansion, and now she's ashamed to entertain guests in her two-bedroom apartment because it suggests abject poverty."

I tried to concentrate on her words as my eyes explored Lydia's décor of heavy velvet drapes, red Persian rug, striped maroon wallpaper, Duncan Phyfe chairs, and tufted love seats. It was like a nineteenth century parlor; dark mahogany shadows lurked everywhere. Next to the front door stood a circular table with piecrust edges. I half expected to see the stovepipe hat of Oliver Wendell Holmes deposited on that table and his friend, Emerson, sipping tea in a nearby Morris chair.

Lydia continued with the classic nonstop sentences that afflict the garrulous old. "Some people," she said, "are terribly torn about downsizing when they move. That's why they fill their apartments with beloved but oversized furniture from their houses, and there's no space where visitors can walk or even sit. I heard Bertha say to Harriet yesterday at breakfast, 'I'd invite you over for lunch, but first I have to get rid of two fireside chairs and three lamp tables.'"

Lydia's aide appeared, carrying a silver tea set and filled my Wedgewood cup. After shifting into a black wooden armchair painted with a golden American eagle, Lydia tilted herself forward, beaming at me.

"So you are a fellow devotee of Oliver Wendell Holmes," she said. "One can't read him without delighting in his Yankee sense of humor. Is he your guiding light?"

I nodded. "My mentor, very nineteenth century."

"Just as Holmes looked to Samuel Johnson, who was very eighteenth century." She accepted a cup of tea from Vida and stirred gently with a filigreed silver teaspoon. "Willa, behind that pretty face of yours, I detect an English major."

"An excommunicated one." My throat tightened, forcing me to ration words. An enormous swallow of tea scorched the roof of my mouth. I tried not to flinch, but Lydia didn't seem to notice. She inched forward to hear me better. "And so you ran away to Paris to savor the bohemian life just as I did once."

"No, I married early, just out of State U." My lack of breath pared the sentence down. Lydia responded by pointing to a fluted silver tray piled high with biscotti. "Try those. They're marvelous," she said. "And then what did you do?"

I hadn't come for a job interview. This encounter with Lydia on her home grounds was going nowhere. My words, lacking sound, died in my mouth. Giving her my poem wasn't a good idea. Not now. It involved too much explanation. I had sacrificed an afternoon nap to be there. At breakfast she said she wanted to show me something. What was it?

"My husband's father ran a small advertising business," I said. "Aaron took over when he finished college."

"But what about you, Willa?"

It was difficult for me to answer because the biscotti pieces refused to dissolve; I burst into a coughing spell when a few tiny pieces lodged in my throat.

"Oh my goodness," she said. Her aide poured me water from a massive cut-glass pitcher on the marble-topped coffee table. "Are you all right?"

I nodded and tried to answer as if nothing had happened, but the voice seemed badly shredded when it finally came out. "They took me into the family business as a copywriter."

Lydia gave me a sympathetic old-lady smile. "But you really aspired to become Jane Austen." I shook my head. "Worse. Elizabeth Barrett Browning." Would this be a good time to bring out my poem? Probably not.

"When I left New York University," Lydia said, "I wanted to become a lexicographer, embrace words, compile dictionaries. But there were no opportunities for females. I married well, an older man, a friend of my German Jewish parents. My dear husband had inherited considerable property in Manhattan. Unfortunately, he passed away too soon."

"Sorry."

"So I dedicated my life to the card catalogue and the Dewey Decimal System. I hired nursemaids to care for my twin girls, both of whom unfortunately died of pneumonia. I held my job a long time; the library's switch to computers ended my career. The technology was too complicated to master. And too impersonal. More tea? No?" She dabbed her lips with a lace-trimmed linen napkin. I didn't know what to say, but fortunately Lydia continued. "Well, now that you've confessed your infatuation with Oliver Wendell Holmes and *The Poet at the Breakfast Table*, here's something else you'll like." She raised a gnarled finger to summon the aide. "Vida, please bring that book on the lamp table. Willa, are you familiar with *Over the Teacups*?"

My hands trembled as I turned the stiff, yellowed pages. This was the book of his old age, finished when Holmes was in his late seventies. I had meant to place a special order for it with Barnes and Noble and never got around to it. The faded cover was decorated with a border of golden flowers and tendrils, and the title stood out, etched in roman letters, all capitals, with the *U* of "Teacups" turned into a *V* and the *O* of "Over" dotted in the middle with a gilded daisy.

"You'd be amazed at what the Biblio Boosters hath wrought," Lydia said. "Every week we sort through an avalanche of donated paperback romances and murder mysteries. Parents die, and their children like to unload everything as quickly as possible." Lydia noticed my awed response to the old book. "Want to borrow it? As an aficionado of Holmes and his work, you'll take good care of it, won't you?"

Before I could thank her, someone knocked on the door. "Is it the pharmacy delivering my amlodipine?" Lydia asked as her aide went to answer.

A familiar figure with a shaggy haircut and unkempt beard entered. He didn't take time to look at me. "I need advice," he said to Lydia. "Got a minute?"

"Jake! How nice! Come have a cup of tea with Willa and me." She turned to me. "It's our Jewish autocrat of the breakfast table."

He nodded to me in his brusque way. "They want an answer soon as possible," he said, "and if I can't, they have another guy on the list who's willing, but I know that schmuck, and he'd be a disaster."

"The lecture series?"

"They already bothered me twice about it. Can't decide. Why let myself in for any more agony in my life?" Jake stuffed his mouth with biscotti and chewed loudly. "Mmm, nothing like good mandelbrodt."

"How can you refuse?" Lydia said. "Willa, here's what's happening. Abe, I don't know his last name, that volunteer Abe, the one who used to do biweekly talks on Jewish topics, had to quit. He's having dreadful stomach problems. The activities director wants Jake to take over. I agree; he's perfect for the job."

"But every Wednesday night? Do I want to commit to that again after spending so many years on the road?"

'When Jake was contributing his column to a half dozen newspapers," Lydia said, "the Jewish Lecture Bureau in New York listed him in their speakers catalogue."

"Up and down the East Coast, Hadassah chapters, sisterhoods, adult-education groups," Jake said with pride. "They paid a pittance and all the danish I could eat. Publicity handled by volunteers was always anemic."

"You'd be outstanding in this," Lydia said.

"Those were the days." He grabbed two more biscotti. "I had my share of mothers who wanted to introduce me to their eligible daughters. And too many rides in the dark to suburban places without sidewalks. Not to mention all the one-night stands or morning bookings when the audience consisted of a few old guys who showed up at the synagogue for the minyan. They stayed for my talk because the rabbi begged them to." Jake sank into one of Lydia's green and white brocade fireside chairs. "Give me that tea now, Lydia," he said, "but only with a slice lemon. And in a glass."

"Of course," Lydia said. She motioned for her helper to go to the kitchen while they continued to discuss Jake's dilemma. I wandered over to a huge mahogany china closet, resting on four legs that appeared to be American eagles cast in brass. Behind a locked glass door, the shelves offered Morocco-bound nineteenth-century classics from Louisa May Alcott to Thomas Carlyle to Walt Whitman. In the center next to Thomas Hardy's novels and poetry stood three books that needed no introduction: *The Autocrat of the Breakfast Table*, *The Professor at the Breakfast Table*, and *The Poet at the Breakfast Table*.

"So I should tell them I'll do the lectures?" Jake looked at me for the first time. "What do you think, Willa?"

I was angry. He was usurping my time, devouring all the minutes that should have been mine. Lydia's cozy invitation, at which I had planned to discuss Oliver Wendell Holmes and his place in American literature, had now disintegrated into the neurotic monologue of this bitter, sloppy, brash, thoroughly unattractive man whose rantings I listened to every single morning. I lost the nerve to haul out my sad little poem. Not the right moment. Not with Jake in the audience.

"I have to pick up eye drops at the pharmacy," I said to Lydia. "Thank you for lending me your book."

Jake yanked it from my hand. "What book is that?" He studied the cover. "Teacups? Is this what they call chick lit these days?" He turned the fragile pages. "Lydia, buy yourself a new copy. This one is falling apart." Then he noticed for the first time the author's name. "Ah, Oliver Wendell Holmes. Why should a Supreme Court justice write about teacups?"

"Not Junior," Lydia said gently. "Holmes Senior, his father, the man who helped start the *Atlantic Monthly* and gave it its name; isn't that correct, Willa?"

I would have answered, but Jake cut me off. "I know, I know," he said, handing it back to me. "Just joking. Couldn't help myself. And so, Lydia, it's settled? You think I should take on a whole lecture series?"

By this time, I was halfway out the door, Lydia's precious volume under my arm. "Thank you so much," I called out, but neither of them could hear me. I returned to my apartment and ripped to pieces that stupid poem in my handbag.

The only satisfying part of the afternoon came after I picked up mail in the lobby and found myself in the elevator with Eric, gripping his walker as if his hands were duct-taped to it. In seconds I grew giddy as a sixteen-year-old and simpered, "Alone at last." I've never simpered before in my life.

He almost grinned. "We'll have to do this more often," he said, "when I'm not running late for physical therapy." The elevator doors opened and we went our separate ways, but all evening long as I watched Classic Arts Showcase videos with baritones George London, Thomas Hampson, and Gérard Souzay, I imagined Eric performing in their place. Odd, I've never heard him sing on stage and never will, and he has never read my poetry, and perhaps he's better off, but this unshared past gives us something in common that could bring us together.

## CHAPTER 11

———◆———

FUMING AND OUT FOR BLOOD, Fritzi Schnell sat waiting for a larger audience to assemble at the breakfast table. Willa dragged herself to her usual chair. Her eyelids drooped, and she uttered an inaudible good-morning to all because she had been up half the night reading *Over the Teacups*. Lydia hadn't appeared yet, and Willa didn't want to mention the remarkable book to anyone else.

"I heard that yipping and yelping again this morning," Fritzi said. "Still can't figure out where it's coming from. I reported it to the front desk twice already, and the receptionist said they'd check, but nobody came."

Willa ducked while Fritzi sneezed on an uneaten hard-boiled egg in front of her. "I told them my allergies are acting up because of that animal." She turned to Willa. "You're on our floor. Did you notice a dog barking?"

Willa shook her head, but she remembered a strange noise in the hall lately, a high-pitched squealing sound that lasted about thirty seconds, stopped, and repeated itself a few more times.

Fritzi insisted she would get to the bottom of it and demand that management evict whoever owned the illegal dog. "I stood outside every apartment on our floor and listened to what was going on inside. Ida, the one with the sign on the door that says Please Knock Loudly, said she hadn't heard anything. I told her to wear her hearing aid for a change. But the harder I listened, the less I heard." Willa could picture Fritzi methodically pausing every few steps to press her ear against door after door.

"They told me no dogs allowed here," Harriet said. "Before leaving Boca, I had to sell our golden retriever, Myron. It broke my heart."

Bertha had an idea. "Maybe it's a parakeet."

Fritzi looked indignant. "I know a bark when I hear one. My ex-husband once owned a pet store, and people brought their kids for fun, like it was a zoo, but nobody ever bought anything. I warned him we wouldn't do much business in such a poor neighborhood, but it was like talking to the wall. We lost our shirts. So one day my husband walks out and leaves me with cages to clean, unpaid bills, and my two girls to support. Left me flat—why I don't know—deserted me with all those grown-up dogs that weren't cute puppies anymore and had to be carted to the dog pound to be put down."

Harriet took a deep breath as if she could suggest a half dozen reasons why Fritzi's marriage hadn't worked, but the opportunity vanished when Jake arrived in a foul mood, late because the carrier didn't deliver his *New York Times*. "I dialed the circulation department for twenty minutes straight and kept getting the busy signal," he said. "It turned out I had copied down the wrong number to call, and then I couldn't remember where I put the right number." As a courtesy to him, Fritzi felt obligated to backtrack and recite her dog story from beginning to end.

"And I said to my daughters yesterday, 'Either that dog goes or I move back with you again, six months at Sharon's, six months at Sheila's.'"

"That's the spirit," Jake said. "Nothing like threatening the kids. Pass the Splenda, Bertha."

Fritzi bristled at his dry tone. "My girls always tell me, 'Mom, anytime you want to move in with us, it will make a real difference in our life.'"

"You have devoted daughters," Flo the Faux Blonde said, without enthusiasm.

Fritzi beamed. "Whenever I talk about moving in with them, they argue something awful about who will get me, but you can't do everything your children want. And right now for me the important thing is to figure out who smuggled that animal into the building."

The others wanted to know what kind of person would be so cruel to keep a poor little dog trapped all day in a studio apartment. "Somebody should call the humane society," Bertha said.

Fritzi pursed her lips in a virtuous way. "The police should take out a warrant and search every apartment on the floor."

"Don't be ridiculous," Jake said, and added under his breath, "if that's possible in your case."

Fritzi's sallow face turned a faint red. "Ridiculous? How can you say that? I'm sneezing myself silly from that Mexican Chihuahua."

Jake stroked his unkempt beard. "I comprehend. I comprehend. And you're allergic to dog fur?"

"For years."

"Then it's not a Chihuahua. They're hairless."

Fritzi sputtered and gave an extra sneeze to attract sympathy. Willa tried to remember whether Oliver Wendell Holmes had ever been an animal lover and promptly left the table to seek an answer in his books. She had no reason to remain. Eric Revelle had missed breakfast again, and no one knew why.

———

*Thursday, July 25.* The classical music station on FM is now playing Bach's lovely Toccata and Fugue in D Minor. These days as soon as the announcer identifies any piece, I jot down the name and composer for future reference. After breakfast today I also looked up Holmes on animals but found only a reference to an imaginary humane society located in heaven and the desperate need for organizing a similar haven for the spirits in hell. No help there.

I hope Eric isn't ailing somewhere. I miss his musical puns, still another similarity to Oliver Wendell Holmes, who pretends to be offended by puns and mockingly begs the reader's indulgence: I know most conversations are all together above such trivial details, but folly will come up at every table as surely as chickweed and sorrel will come up in gardens.

The last time Eric joined us at breakfast, cheese frittata was on the menu, and he told the young Eritrean waitress he wanted Bach's Frittata and Fudge in D Minor. She didn't understand what he was talking about and neither did anyone else, except me because I'm doing my homework. Our eyes met across the table, and we sent each other a secret smile.

The following morning, when he became more serious than I had ever seen him before, he told me he had experienced a two-hour muscle freeze the night before. He couldn't move and had to stay put, he said. "I feel that I'm in a box within a box."

I searched for a soothing comment to let him know he wasn't alone in his agony. "It's the discordant symphony of aging," I wanted to say but didn't. Too pretentious. Besides, Lydia thinks the word "aging" is over-used. "I'm not aging," she insists, "I've already aged."

It would help if I could speak Eric's language, and it's worth a try. In the library a book of musical terminology helps me appreciate Eric's puns. He referred to his Parkinson's as a score written in a tremor clef. And I said at SVM there seem to be more scores written on a bass clef because old-timers at breakfast try to prevent newcomers from stealing their seats, their home base.

"Those people," Eric said, "are called bass clef-to-maniacs."

"That's good," I said, and he answered, "But not Gudenov."

Giggling at his atrocious puns, I'm probably nothing more to him than a faded version of admirers waiting at the stage door, that vanished army of youthful females battling for his attention. But is he aware of his most loyal fan? To me he's more than a man burdened with a disease that doesn't respect intelligence or talent. The illness attacks his coordination; it doesn't erase his personality, his history, his triumphs.

Not to get too soppy about it, but for me Eric is the sum total of every operatic role he has ever sung, each concerto, sonata, overture he has conducted. He is all the magnificent European concert halls, the chandeliers glowing with lights, the eyes of thousands upon him. Eric is every stage he has walked upon to thunderous applause, every bow he has taken, every backstage item that speaks of theater, props, costumes; he is even the makeup box, the cold cream, the black liner pencils, the fake noses and beards, and all the curtain calls of a lifetime. He's the throat-clearing sound of musical instruments tuning up en masse before a concert; strings, woodwinds, harps, pianos, brass, percussion, blending together in the miracle known as a symphony orchestra.

Ugh, that reads like a gushing schoolgirl's diary. Eric would probably hoot at all that. He's more down-to-earth than I am. The other morning Jake, while describing a visit to the urologist, added, "As usual, I peed on the doctor." Eric gave one of his half smiles and said, "Me too." Both men snickered, two mischievous little kids. Dr. Holmes may not have cared for such impropriety in mixed company, but alone, cloistered in his study, he would have chuckled. Or perhaps not. Doctors must be peed upon frequently, and I don't think they care for it.

Strange. Eric and I hardly know each other, and yet I grow anxious, watching him maneuver the dining room, sometimes even without his walker. It doesn't make sense that his well-being should worry me this much. There's no basis for any romantic feelings on his or my part, but why hasn't he come down to breakfast lately?

# Part Two

---

*It is safe to assume that intimate relations would spring up between some members of our mixed company; and it was not rash to conjecture that some of these intimacies might end in such attachment as would finish as hints, at least, of a love story.*

OWH

# CHAPTER 1

———

AT LAST FRITZI SCHNELL AT breakfast announced she knew who owned that menacing dog. "People will be surprised what's going on right under their noses," she said. Jake and Sidney remained gloomily silent. Lydia had advised them that she would move to another table unless they behaved and stopped referring to their tablemate as Fritzi the Schnellbomber.

"Nobody else complains about the dog," Bertha said, her voice rising with irritation. She had confided in Willa earlier that her bowels were giving her trouble, and she was in no mood to tolerate Fritzi's wild accusations before noon.

Although Willa didn't enter the conversation, she also had detected odd sounds in the corridor each morning. There must be a valid reason. She turned away and was delighted to see Eric approaching them, with great difficulty, having returned at last from wherever he had been for the past week. All seats were occupied; the women moved with unusual agility to make room, and Diana, Goddess of the Hunt, motioned for a waiter to bring another chair. "You all know Eric Revelle," she said, as if she had invited him as her personal guest of honor.

Renee gave him an engaging smile. "Revelle?" she said. "Is that your stage name?"

Willa thought he looked tired as he rolled his walker aside and gingerly settled into place. He probably hadn't slept well the night before, and now these inconsiderate women would exhaust him. With effort he studied the menu before giving his breakfast order to a server from Mali and then looked up.

"Sorry?" he said.

"Is Revelle your real name?"

The waitress poured him a cup of coffee, and he took a tentative sip and said, "My grandfather's fault. He left Lithuania for America to escape serving in the czar's army."

Willa leaned toward him and whispered, "Mine too." The others ignored her, all eyes on the man who had been an opera star.

"See," Bertha said. "I told you he was Jewish."

Willa dared to ask the next question. Her voice wavered, but he could understand her. "What town in Lithuania?"

"Radvilisik."

Willa gasped. She had sensed a connection with Eric the first minute she saw him. He continued in his pianissimo voice. "At Ellis Island, they asked my grandfather's name, but he thought they wanted to know where he came from and answered, 'Radvilisik.' The official didn't know how to spell it, so he wrote down 'Revelle.'"

Willa glowed in the morning light. "Radvilisik!" She had never heard anyone on the planet except her grandmother mention that place.

Eric took her reaction rather calmly, she thought, as he buttered his toast. "My grandparents landed here in 1900."

"Mine too," Willa said in wonder.

"Maybe your families knew each other in the old country," Bertha said. "You could be cousins." She was so struck by the coincidence, she forgot about her intestinal problems. "Fate. It's *beshert*. You were destined to meet again here at SVM."

"Who can say?" Eric said, entertained by his effect on the women. Willa stared at him without blinking.

"Can't I be a cousin too?" Diana said. "You and I both have blue eyes."

Willa didn't laugh. This could have been a deliciously private conversation between her and Eric, and now every woman at the table was contributing her inane two cents.

Harriet the Happy Housewife interrupted with apologies. "Excuse me, my son is taking me to be measured for new orthopedic shoes," she said in her exit line.

A pause in the conversation, and Fritzi seized the moment. "Eric, have you recently heard a vicious dog barking in the building? Yipes and yelps?"

"Eric has an ear for music, not dog barks," Bertha said.

It was more than Willa could endure. She pushed aside her empty cereal bowl and searched for her handbag under the table.

"Do you have a minute?" a newcomer named Shirley said, sliding into Harriet's place. "The Emma Lazarus Literary Legion meets at ten today, but I'd like to hear what you all think first." Willa knew about the writing group but made it a point not to join, never, even if it meant being evicted. She stared at Shirley, slim in tight jeans and matching short denim jacket. The lively brunette seemed to carry her years better than the others, and even worse, spoke with a confident air that revealed two years of experience in the Toastmaster's Club.

"I call it 'Undercover,'" said Shirley, whose unlined face still harbored dimples like the child actress for whom she was named. She immediately charmed Jake and Sidney; until this point they had concentrated only on wolfing down their lukewarm pancakes before they could turn into cold fried dough.

Shirley cleared her throat and began. "Will the current president of the United States wash his own underwear? Harry Truman did."

"I didn't care for Bess," Bertha said.

Shirley continued reading. "The man from Missouri was taught by his mother never to assign that job to a flunky, no matter what. It's a wise man who knows his own intimate apparel intimately. Our presidents can learn from Harry a valuable lesson in folksiness as well as in soft-soaping Congress."

"Here, here!" said Sidney. Encouraged, Shirley charged ahead. "Underwear has been an issue in the news. But barely." She paused briefly to let it sink in and continued. "Do Congress members ever go on fact-finding junkets to Frederick's of Hollywood?"

"Frederick *who*?" Bertha said. "*Who* did she say?"

Shirley pretended not to hear. "Is there a Department of Underwear at the cabinet level? And what about unmentionables and the federal deficit? Politicians shy away from all that, even though it's creeping up on them."

Shirley raised her violet-colored eyes from the paper. "I like that part," she said to no one in particular and returned to the text. "Older values have been washed away, gone with the Woolite."

Bertha felt she should intervene. "Shouldn't that be 'gone with the wind'? Nobody says gone with the Woolite."

"Read on, Shirley," Jake said. "Everybody here is a critic."

Bertha frowned. "She's talking so fast, I can't understand a word she says."

"Sorry. I'll try to slow down."

"Good," Bertha said. "Shirley, if you want to be a successful writer, you have to learn how to read out loud better and with more expression."

"And talk louder," Fritzi said.

"I'm almost finished," Shirley said, with a pleading note to her voice. "The centuries produced noble undergarments that shaped ancestors of both sexes. Clothing depended on support systems like whalebone farthingales, panniers, hoops, and horsehair crinolines. Underwear stood for something in those days"—she gave a theatrical pause—"suffering!"

The women shrugged and said, "Very nice," but Sidney applauded and wouldn't stop. Jake seized Shirley's hand and kissed it. Entirely unnecessary, Willa thought.

"Brava!" Eric called out, full of genuine admiration. Willa would have given anything to receive that kind of "Brava" from him. She was stunned by Shirley's success at the table. Obviously, a dangerous rival for Eric's attention had entered the scene.

---

*Friday, July 26.* Some say the way to a man's heart is through his penis, but once he hits eighty, a pun works better, and Shirley recognizes this truth. The way to a man's heart is not through groaning at his puns, no matter how awful they are, but to laugh as if his pun is a work of art delivered by the wittiest person in the world. I welcome Eric's musical puns, and it would be unfeminine of me to top them. Oliver Wendell Holmes pretended to loathe any play on words. Although addicted to the practice himself, he said a pun shows contempt for the listeners. In fact, he called the habit total depravity and once wrote a magazine essay on "A Visit to the Asylum for Aged and Decayed Punsters."

Even with her shallow cleverness, Shirley may self-destruct. Holmes put it beautifully: "People that make puns are like wanton boys that put coppers on the railroad tracks. They amuse themselves and other children, but their little trick may upset a freight train of conversation for the sake of a battered witticism."

If Shirley's puns overshadow Eric's, so much the better. Men don't appreciate puns that are better than theirs, especially from women. Her talent will backfire on her, but right now she derails my talks with Eric at the breakfast table.

Jake, also no slouch at puns, has fallen under her spell too. What irritates me most is that he now refers to her as Shirley the Schreiber, which according to Yetta the Yiddishist, means Shirley the Writer.

In my opinion that name is not justified. Whenever she joins the table, she hauls out her tasteless drivel and reads it aloud to Eric. He always faces in her direction these days, not mine, and slightly bends forward to hear every word. His fickleness doesn't come as a surprise. After all, he's a child of show business, a wandering minstrel who probably fell in love with all his leading ladies, all the fiery mezzos he encountered in his worldly travels, all the beautiful young coloraturas in the chorus. Shirley's only endearing quality is her tentative plan to join her recently divorced daughter who lives in Alaska. At last, climate change has its advantages.

This afternoon I consulted my beloved 1973 Encyclopedia Britannica Atlas to locate Radvilisik, Lithuania, on the map. A computer would come in handy now, but I don't intend to waste my leftover years welded to the Internet. Tracking down Radvilisik wasn't easy. Over time the name changed from the Russian version to the Lithuanian, and most likely, it's now Radviliskis or something worse. Lithuanians have a tendency to over-work the letter *s* in their language.

I still marvel how two people whose forebearers came from one tiny, obscure Eastern European town could find each other in America so many generations later. Fate? Speaking of which, practically every time I watch Classic Arts Showcase on TV, somebody is belting out arias from Verdi's La Forza del Destino. It makes me wonder what Holmes thought about the power of destiny. His medical education steered him clear of such an unscientific topic. *The Poet at the Breakfast Table* contains only one refer-ence; he defines destiny as a force that determines where everybody sits at the breakfast table.

Nothing can determine for us who appears at breakfast each day or where they find seats, but if I can manage to land near Eric, it could kindle results. We'll engage in lengthy conversations about Radvilisik, although I don't know what more we'd say about it. Lydia made a sharp observation today about our restraints on vocabulary. "Old age," she said, "slaughters adjectives, but as long as your verbs are intact, you can still function."

Meanwhile, the mystery continued about Fritzi's phantom dog who yelps, yaps, and also yipes. As I entered the elevator yesterday, the doors, opening and closing, made an ungodly noise, and if I shut my eyes, the squeakiness duplicated the barking of a miniature dog with laryngitis. I reported to maintenance that those doors badly needed oiling, and as of today, the noises have stopped. Fritzi must find another noble cause.

Shirley the Schreiber's competition no longer stymies me. Dr. Holmes to the rescue! I'll do what he does in his books—bring my poetry directly to the breakfast table, even though it doesn't belong there. If heartfelt verses landed on Eric's breakfast plate, it would appeal to his poetic side. What hinders me is the ghastly reality of baring my soul before critics like Jake, Bertha, and Fritzi. Perhaps to begin I could borrow the admirable announcement Holmes made every time he introduced his poetry at the table: Those who wish to leave may do so now.

The following poem has remained on my desk for months. Bring it for Eric next time?

### The Breakfast Beguine
by Willa Warsaw
We, the ancients, gather at the starting gate,
Proud early-risers first to dip a spoon,
Foot soldiers in the fight for cream of wheat,
We stand behind the double doors of Time,
One leading in, the other leading out,
Authorities on the ticking of the clock,
But who can say how wisely or how well
We pass our genes to babies yet unborn?

No. Throwing myself to the wolves is folly. Better regress a little. Like a bashful ten-year-old passing notes in class, I'll sneak it to Eric under the table and quickly dash outside to join the other kids at recess.

# CHAPTER 2

———◆———

ONCE AGAIN THE TOPIC UNDER discussion at the breakfast table centered around the behavior of Howie the Unwholesome Wholesaler. The residents insisted on ignoring him on purpose when he paused behind Renee Richmond's chair and lifted two forefingers above her head to create donkey ears.

"No seats available," Bertha said. "We're saving this for a friend."

Howie brightened. "Consider me a friend."

"Howie, you have no friends," Jake said. That took care it, and Howie selected another table populated only by women.

"I knew that bastard in high school," Renee said, picking at her dish of honeydew melon cubes. "Our families belonged to the same country club."

"Country club?" Jake said. "Some class to you."

Renee always overlooked Jake's incipient attempts at class warfare. "Even after we both were married to other people," she said, "Howie never missed a chance to corner me alone in a telephone booth."

With her paper napkin, Fritzi dabbed at a blob of grape jelly fallen into her lap. "I always tell new ladies not to sit too close to him at meals and watch out if he says he's looking for a dropped spoon."

"Exercise time," Bertha said, rising to leave. "I signed up for the Walking Club, doctor's orders. Wish I could hire an aide to do it." She was immediately replaced by Flo the Faux Blonde, who informed them that she just bumped into Howie on the prowl.

"He's always bumping into women," Fritzi said. "He plans ahead."

Flo the Faux Blonde reached for the juice pitcher and filled a plastic glass. "Willa, were you and Eric at the French class they offered here a few weeks ago?" she asked. Willa cringed, while Fritzi, hearing their names linked together, narrowed her ferret eyes in disapproval.

"Wasn't there," Willa lied. She knew exactly what was coming next.

Flo continued her story. "The instructor, Madame LaVamme, retired last month from Community College. She's the dignified professor type. So Howie turns up for the first class to let everybody know what he learned in France when he was in the army during World War II. And right off, Howie raises his hand and announces to Madame LaVamme, 'I speak real good French already.'"

Jake let out a groan that could be heard six tables away. "I can imagine."

"So then he asks her, '*Voulez-vous coucher avec moi ce soir?*'"

Fritzi frowned. "I don't know what that means." Renee told her in graphic terms.

"So then she cuts him dead with a cold stare and goes on to explain how to modify masculine and feminine nouns. Howie waits a minute or two and wanders out."

"Why not? He got the attention he aimed for," Jake said.

Flo agreed. "And he never came back. The class fell apart anyway after two weeks because bingo was scheduled for the same time."

Willa wasn't listening. She concentrated on Eric, who approached his breakfast companions more slowly than ever. Taking a long time to settle down at the table, he accidentally tipped over a glass of milk. It was mopped up by a burly Haitian, who added a few guttural comments no one could hear after Eric apologized softly in fluent French.

Willa found it difficult to establish eye contact with him. "Everything OK?" she said.

Eric nodded, preoccupied. After the others finished and left the table, he gestured for Willa to remain behind. "Your voice sounds stronger this morning, Willa."

"I slept pretty well last night," she said, touched that in spite of his own problems, Eric cared enough to take notice of her. More out of indifference than delicacy, no one at SVM ever bothered to ask questions about the whispery way she spoke.

"Spasmodic dysphonia plays ugly tricks." He gave her a gentle smile. "Especially if you're shy to begin with."

"SD is the condition that won't quit," she said. "Sounds like the beginning sentence of a fund-raising letter." She felt at ease with him, although the Parkinson's often made his own remarks inaudible. They had much in common, straining for words and almost grasping them, only to have them escape without being spoken. With this compassionate man, she didn't worry about the ups and downs of a wayward voice.

Her relaxation didn't last. Fritzi Schnell stood nearby, her head cocked over to one side, soaking up whatever passed between them. How long she had been there, it was hard to tell.

"What's the matter?" she asked. "Are you sick, Willa? I always thought you had something wrong with you."

"Nothing fatal," Eric said.

"What does the doctor say, Willa? Will you need an MRI? When are you going under the knife?"

"A voice disorder. Had it for years."

"That so? I never could tell to look at her." Fritzi's head had been switching from right to left and back again between Willa and Eric, but now she was talking to him as if an ambulance had already spirited Willa away to St. Luke's. "She never said much, did she? Not much of a talker."

Eric shifted from his chair to an uncertain standing position. "Excuse me. I have an appointment with the podiatrist." He grasped the handles of his walker.

Fritzi's sharp gray eyes moved back and forth from Eric's expressionless face to Willa and then returned to Eric. "That article about you in *The Megilla* said you used to be a big singer."

He did not seem flattered by her interest. "Sorry. I have to leave now." He moved himself from the table with determination, his face flushed with strain.

Willa watched the tiny, hesitant steps of Eric, who managed to make a safe exit in spite of dodging a bowl of Quaker Oats spilled on the carpet. If she hurried, she could catch up with him. Fritzi chose to continue her questioning. "Is what you have contagious?"

"No."

"Maybe you should be quarantined. Want me to get the front desk to call 911?"

"Not necessary."

With Fritzi on duty, it wasn't the right moment to be seen running after Eric. "The Breakfast Beguine" by Willa Warsaw remained undelivered in her pocketbook.

———◆———

*Sunday, July 28.* Brainstorm. Saturday during another sleepless night, I put together this explanation of spasmodic dysphonia for the uninformed, which is just about everybody in the world.

### WILLA'S PECULIAR CONDITION: SPASMODIC DYSPHONIA (SD)

1. Spasmodic Dysphonia is a voice disorder that affects the muscles that allow the vocal cords to open and close, regulating sound. 2. There are two kinds of SD, one affecting the adductor muscles and the other, the abductor muscles. 3. Numerous treatments exist: voice therapy, Botox injections into the larynx, oral drugs, or surgery, and Willa Warsaw has tried most of them. 4. For the past thirty years, she has suffered from the rarer, whispery kind of SD, less likely to respond to Botox and other remedies. 5. Doctors don't know what causes SD, for which no cure now exists. 6. You positively can't catch it from Willa.

The office secretary kindly ran off a dozen copies of the above and supplied apartment numbers of all who eat with me. I got up before dawn to slide the papers under doors. Most people still won't understand what it is. I don't either.

In other news developments of the day, Jake has agreed to enlighten SVM residents with further lectures on topics of Jewish interest, and Renee Richmond told him to remind her not to attend. At that point he called her a self-hating Jew. I'll not soil this pristine journal with what she called him in return.

Eric has been away all week. That leaves only Dr. Holmes to shore up my drooping spirits. I've always preferred his humorous verse over "The Chambered Nautilus," a serious poem I never read in college without falling asleep. Maybe it would make more sense now. Holmes thinks the best talkers are poets who never write poetry. It follows that the worst talkers, victims of SD, should be poets. At least it lets everyone know we still walk the earth.

Each young lover is an innate poet, according to Holmes, but what about old lovers? Do romantic clauses and phrases get lost somewhere around the start of middle age and abandon us altogether in our seventies and eighties? Do moldy syllables struggle to be aired? One day an aspiring archaeologist of language will launch a campaign to excavate forgotten words from the silted brains of the very old. Poetry may rise again.

Throughout the Breakfast Table series, my man Holmes scatters a shameless amount of verse. His first book runs only seventeen pages before he can't help himself and hauls out a poem. Once the invasion starts, there's no stopping it. The difference is that readers couldn't get enough of poetry back then; there wasn't much else doing. Today, even if I tried writing literary-magazine-type poetry again, who would read it? Lydia's eyes are bad; she's a slave to talking books. Jake and Yetta the Yiddishist would roast me for not including enough Jewish content. Only Eric, a fellow artist, would appreciate my efforts. Of that I'm sure. Why doesn't he return from wherever he went?

Not much going on. Last Friday night before I recited my weekly Kaddish for Aaron at Shabbat services, Reuben, a rabbinical student whose grandmother lives at SVM, gave a sermon about dysfunctional families, based on the story of biblical Joseph and his brothers. I had never given Joseph much thought. Most girls of my generation didn't learn Hebrew or study Torah.

The young rabbi emphasized the passion of blood relatives, and it brought back memories of growing up in Braddock, Mom's early death there, and Dad, who wore himself out to send me to college. My mind wandered; I saw him up at three in the morning to fill the ovens with the day's supply of fresh bread, and Bubbi Friml mixing batter for apple cake in the tiny kitchen she later shared with Adele. Bubbi never had a good word to say about her new daughter-in-law. Time has blotted out most of the ugly details; I don't recall much about those years except that Adele kept her distance from me and concentrated her attention on her own two girls from a previous marriage. I do remember asking Dad why they were so jealous of me, and he answered, "Because you're better looking than they are. Sweetie, you're going to be a knockout someday." Someday?

But I also remember how Bubbi would scoop out the flour from the Pillsbury bag with a huge tin measuring cup and use a knife to scrape off excess flour. In that soothing grandmotherly way of hers, she always insisted that bad memories vanish if you live long enough. Time levels off the lumps. Maybe. Once my energy returns, I owe them all—Mom, Dad, Bubbi Friml, even my diffident stepmother and her snotty daughters—a visit to the place where they're buried a hundred miles away. The Hebrew name of the cemetery slips my mind; it's hell to reach by public transportation, and anyway, there's no one left to go with.

In those years when Dad drove us to visit the graves, he never failed to deliver his baker's dozen of platitudes en route. "Do what you're supposed to do," he said, "when you're supposed to do it." I've always tried to follow his advice, but who determines what you're supposed to do and when to do it? Sometimes it's a disaster and sometimes it turns out better than expected.

At the agency, when Aaron first drafted me to supply lyrics for singing commercials, I convinced myself this was terribly beneath me, but since he expected me to do it on deadline, I forced myself to juggle around rhymes set to songs like "Oh Susannah" or "Camptown Races." I was amazed that the words blossomed without effort, delivered on short notice. It became a way to let off steam, light verses, unorthodox parodies, dancing in my head, and it still works.

Last night when insomnia struck full blast, I found comfort in scribbling down these lines based on that young rabbinical scholar's tale from the book of Genesis:

### Brotherly Breach
#### by Willa Warsaw

"I dreamed a dream," young Joseph bragged,
"The universe I owned;
The sun and moon bowed down to me."
"Good grief!" his brothers groaned.

Since Joseph was Pa Jacob's pet
("My Joe can do no wrong"),
The brothers trapped him in a pit
And sold him for a song.

No doubt they felt a guilty twinge,
And there'd be hell to pay,
But taking all into account,
They did it anyway.

A lesson in this Bible tale:
Pay heed to children's quibblings,
And never underestimate
The rivalry of siblings.

These days my competitive hackles are raised only by pushy souls like Shirley the Schreiber. Eric is absent from SVM so often, she says, because he's participating in a new clinical trial at a New York hospital.

"People with Parkinson's," she added, "lose control of their muscles when the neurons in the brain deteriorate and don't make enough dopamine. Eric said it ranks second only to Alzheimer's in neurodegenerative diseases. He suggested I write an article about it."

Although I didn't say anything, my blood pressure soared. Why did he confide in Shirley but never talked like that to me? I hate her.

# CHAPTER 3

———

BERTHA WAS HOLDING FORTH ON one of her favorite breakfast-table topics, the abundance of food accidentally spilled down her ample front. "No matter what I pull out of the closet, there's a stain on it. Last week I wore a new dress to my grandson's fancy wedding. I looked down and found a big fat stain right in front where everyone could see."

"Spit happens," Renee Richmond muttered under her breath. Or something like that.

Bertha let Renee's vocabulary roll by. "So I had to stop everything and run to the ladies' room to wash the stain off. If you rub with a paper towel, it makes the stain worse."

"I wouldn't know," Renee Richmond said, who had just described in full detail her daughter's recent trip to Rome, where she had been mugged by gypsies and her airplane ticket stolen. "My aide takes care of laundry."

"Borsht is the worst," Bertha said.

Harriet the Happy Homemaker nodded in sympathy. "Once you spill beets on yourself, you're marked for life."

"I have a good system. If the stain doesn't come out," Bertha said, "I sew a button on it."

"She must have buttons in peculiar places," someone at the Ha-Ha Table said, and they all chuckled significantly.

Willa sawed off a sizable chunk of waffle and bolted it down without syrup. She took three quick swallows of Lactaid skim milk and slathered a slice of cold toast with strawberry jam. The faster she finished breakfast, the sooner she could get back to the sanity of Dr. Holmes.

She would have left, but Jake appeared with news that he planned to deliver future talks at SVM on Jewish topics, subjects to be announced. "If I give them the title in advance, nobody will show up," he said, taking his usual seat near the window overlooking the parking lot.

Lydia, always ready to boost his confidence, objected to that remark. "Jake, your series will be glorious. I can feel it in my bones."

"That's your arthritis acting up," he said. "Pass me the extra spoon over there," he said to Willa, and added, "Lydia tells me you are a devotee of Oliver Wendell Holmes."

"*Who?*" Bertha said.

Willa sensed that her tablemates were staring at her, and she felt betrayed that Lydia had discussed such an intimate subject with Jake.

Fritzi Schnell picked it up at once. "You're seeing another man so soon after...?"

Flo the Faux Blonde stepped in. "Oh, for heaven's sake. Holmes was the famous Supreme Court justice."

"That's his son," Jake said.

Bertha carefully poured a minute amount of whole milk from a Styrofoam cup into her bowl of Cheerios. "If I get this on myself, I'll have to change all my clothes. I can't stand the smell of sour milk. Even if I sew a button on it, it smells sour."

Jake changed the subject. "Seen our friend Eric around lately?" he asked Willa, who shook her head.

"I live across the hall from him on the ground floor," Bertha said. "Maria, the cleaning woman, told me he fell down in his apartment two days ago, and the rescue squad took him to St. Luke's."

Willa tried to breathe deeply.

"Too bad," Jake said. "Eric has no family, only a niece across the country, Washington state, Oregon, or some other godforsaken place in the wilderness. Did he break anything?"

"Nobody knows," Bertha said.

The breakfast table entourage continued chewing and swallowing. Willa pushed her chair back from the table, collected her handbag from the floor, and stood. "Excuse me," she said in a small voice, less audible than usual.

"You're leaving?" Bertha said. "You didn't even finish your waffle."

"Notveryhungrythismorning."

The breakfast brigade looked confused. "What did she say? Can't understand a word that woman says." Willa didn't care. At least now she knew where she could find Eric.

———————

*Tuesday, July 30.* I call this prose poem "Melancholy Anthem for an Ambulance": Bedeviled, much feared / monster first responder, we meet again, / your siren in full voice / your blinking devil-red eyes /greedy with anticipation / your mouth eager for another bite of my generation served up a la carte / Blessed are you / holy of holies / sacred to the aged / fruit of phone calls to 911 / blessed is your digestion / as another dear one lies / prostrate on your mobile altar.

My concern for Eric kept me up all night producing the above garbage. I slept late and didn't bother with breakfast or the Gedalia Ginsfarb Fitness Garden this morning. Later an afternoon walk took me outside through bland suburban streets, where July sunshine burned through my anxiety. The trick is to remain upright and keep moving; it lightens our cares, or so Oliver Wendell Holmes opines: "I do not deny the attraction of walking…I concede therefore that walking is an immeasurably fine invention, of which old age ought constantly to avail itself."

Holmes explains that three powers work all at once: the will, the muscles, and the intellect. As I understand it, when we walk, the will and muscles are so accustomed to working together with not much energy wasted that the intellect is left free. This explains the mental pleasure in walking and appreciating the power we have over our moving machinery. When the intellect is free, the doctor insists, it can make the walker powerful, but it just exhausts me. And lately, so does he.

Walk on, walk on, he advises, and I do, pondering the limits of friendship in old age. How much worry should we allot to our contemporaries? In our latter years what do we owe those we love or think we ought to love? And what happens if the will falters at the same time strength dissolves? The choices grow skimpy when a person finds herself the last leaf on the tree.

I don't remember studying "The Last Leaf" in college. If so, the poem made no impression on me, but it damned well speaks to me now. Unknowingly, Holmes foresaw his own future when he wrote it during his twenties. Wouldn't it be gratifying to leave behind such perceptive verses instead of a drawer heavy with forgotten lyrics of singing radio commercials? I wonder how the author felt about these mournful lines when he reached his eighties?

"They say that in his prime / Ere the Pruning-knife of Time / Cut him down / Not a better man was found" and then Holmes describes the old codger's cane and "his feeble head…a melancholy crack / In his laugh." (Sounds like happy hour at SVM.) Holmes has confessed elsewhere that the poem describes someone he knew, a soldier of the Revolutionary War "in the old three-cornered hat / And the breeches." It occurs to me that nineteenth century Americans looked upon these heroes in the same detached way young people today regard vanishing World War II veterans like Jake and Sidney.

Critics considered the poem one of the best Holmes created. It ends:

> And if I should live to be
> The last leaf upon the tree
> In the spring,
> Let them smile as I do now
> At the old forsaken bough
> Where I cling.

Nothing like a hearty dose of self-pity to make a person feel worse!

What's wrong with me? Someone I deeply care about lands in the hospital, and here I sit scribbling about a dead writer most people have forgotten or never heard of, and if they do recognize the name, they think it's his son. I'm getting another one of my great-dismal-swamp headaches. This one arrives accompanied by dark, elongated shadows hanging in midair. I should make an appointment with the ophthalmologist. Eric's visit from me must wait.

# CHAPTER 4

———➤———

FRITZI HAD BEEN SAVING ANOTHER unsavory bit of gossip for a morning when Jake and Sidney would be away attending the B'nai B'rith men's breakfast, but it had been postponed, and she couldn't hold off any longer. She would have to tell her story in mixed company. Not looking at the men, she directed her remarks to Willa, who did not appreciate the favor.

"See that aide, Margaret, who just passed by the table?"

"The slightly zaftig one taking care of Shmuel, the Holocaust guy?" Jake asked.

"Right," Fritzi said. "She's from some place in Africa. I don't think they called her Margaret over there. So when I was walking down the hall yesterday morning about ten o'clock, I saw her knocking hard on the door of Shayna, with the pinkish hair, the one who sits at the table opposite us and pretends she doesn't know me."

"Can't imagine why," Jake said, his mouth stuffed with Froot Loops.

Fritzi ignored him. "So anyway, this aide is pounding away, and Shayna comes to the door and..." Fritzi lowered her voice. "Guess what?"

"What?" Bertha asked.

"Shayna was not—I repeat *not*—wearing any panties."

"Some people can be so forgetful," Bertha said.

Although Jake remained quiet, he seemed more intrigued by Fritzi's conversation than usual.

"She was also wearing a string of blue beads she made last week in art class," Fritzi said. "So then Shayna says to Margaret, who goes around singing hymns in the elevator all day—"

"I know her," Sidney said. "She does my laundry. Nice lady. Faithful churchgoer. One of my favorites."

"So Shayna says to Margaret, 'I hope this doesn't offend you,' like it's the most natural thing in the world."

"What was her apartment number again?" Jake asked, winking an eye at Willa, who refused to wink back. "Sidney might want to pay her a visit."

Sidney, who choked on a swallow of grapefruit juice, began to cough so hard he could barely take air into his lungs.

"Need a *klopp*?" Jake used his boney fist to pound on his friend's back.

Sidney wheezed loudly. "Thanks, buddy."

"Nothing like a good klopp between friends." The two old men smiled at each other.

Fritzi refused to let them sidetrack her. "So, 'I hope this doesn't offend you,' Shayna says to Margaret. 'No, no,' Margaret says. 'You need any help?'

"Shayna says, 'I'm OK,' and slams the door. Now Margaret and I walk down the hall together, and then Margaret says to me, I swear, she says to me…" Fritzi paused for dramatic effect.

Bertha glanced at her watch. "Hurry it up. I have an appointment at three this afternoon."

"'Naked butt.'"

Sidney thought he hadn't heard right. "What?"

"Naked butt. I mean, really. What can you answer when someone says 'naked butt' like that to you out of a clear blue sky?"

Jake smirked. "Butt out?"

Fritzi looked annoyed at having to share the spotlight with him. "And then Margaret says, 'These people. You ask if they need help, and they say no.' So I just nod, and then she says it again, like she can't get over it. 'Naked butt.' Then she spots a man she knows, one of her landsmen, going into the supply room. 'Naked butt!' she calls out to him, and they both start talking in African."

"Maybe what she really said was, 'Sacred gut,'" Bertha suggested brightly.

"Why would she say 'sacred gut'?" Sidney asked. "That doesn't mean anything."

Bertha seemed miffed at being put on the defensive. "Maybe it does in her country."

Sidney, the World War II veteran, had a better idea. "If this story is true, you heard her wrong, Fritzi. What she probably said was, 'Aching butt,' like we used to say in the service. 'Oh, my aching back!' Only she's a foreigner and pronounces it "Oh, my aching butt.'"

Fritzi, with a dissatisfied look on her face, prepared to take her story to a more appreciative audience. She started to leave and then turned around. "By the way, the singer, what's his name, Eric, didn't do himself much damage when he fell. I heard he's out of the hospital already. He'll spend a few days at Verdant Valley Rehab before he comes back here."

"Good for him," Bertha said.

"Just thought you'd like to know, Willa," Fritzi said, with a genuine sneer, and looked as if she might have added, "You tramp!" but didn't. The Schnellbomber had struck again and moved on. But at least Eric would return soon. Willa knew the time had come for action.

———◆———

*Tuesday, August 6.* Eric didn't rejoin our breakfast beguine right away. Jake went to see him in his apartment and informed us that a neurologist had tried out a new medication on Eric that resulted in hallucinations and poor balance. That's why Jake thinks he fell.

"They should be more careful about giving an experimental drug to an older person," Jake said. I agreed. After Aaron's long ordeal, I have no regard for any doctors except my author of the Breakfast Table books. Holmes always had the good sense to blast quacks and charlatans peddling questionable patent medicine of little or no value. He recognized how primitive medicine was in his time. Following Jake's mention of hallucinations, I reread Holmes on the subject of homeopathic prescriptions. Holmes unleashed his ridicule on gullible souls who believed small amounts of untested, potentially dangerous potions and powders could cure any ailment. Not much has changed.

I take deep satisfaction from his attacks on the public's accepting attitude toward dangerous medication: "There is a class of minds which is more ready to believe that which is first incredible, and because it is incredible, than what is thought generally reasonable."

My breakfast table crowd imagines they suffer from every ailment described in the health magazines. Bertha has blind faith that the latest over-the-counter products can perform wonders. Having worked in advertising, I know the bigger the lie, the more likely it will be accepted. The following advice of Holmes should be posted in every retirement community, hospital, and nursing home to prevent the horrors of self-medication:

> ...those who know nothing of the natural progress of a malady,... its duration,...its liability to accidental complications,...the signs which mark its insignificance or severity,...or how little is to be anticipated from remedies, those who know nothing...of all these things, and who are in a great state of excitement from...zeal for a new medical discovery, can hardly be expected to be sound judges of facts...Medical accuracy is not to be looked for in the florid reports of benevolent associations, the assertions of illustrious patrons, the lax effusions of daily journals, or the effervescent gossip of the tea table.

Or the breakfast table.

When Eric finally returned a few days later to the Esther Essenvarg Dining Den, females greeted him like a long-lost explorer. Even strangers who never sat anywhere near our table stopped to welcome him back. I didn't realize he had so many lady friends. Luckily, I didn't react to his recent fall like a moonstruck schoolgirl, dashing off to the hospital every day with flowers and love poems, although the idea did occur to me.

It makes me wonder how many sweethearts he left behind him at the nursing home. If I had more nerve, I'd ask him if he ever performed the song "When I'm Not Near the Girl I Love, I Love the Girl I'm Near." Sinatra once recorded it, but I haven't heard it lately.

Passivity gets me nowhere. My obvious solution was to invite Eric for lunch at our café right here in the building, everything out in the open, not a clandestine tryst that could fire up more of Fritzi Schnell's vitriol. So when Eric and I met by accident checking our mailboxes, I asked him on the spot. He accepted right away. "I've never eaten before at the exotic SVM Café," he said.

If it's difficult for him to maneuver among the tables, chairs, and walkers, he can depend on me to hack our way through the rain forest. I canceled my appointment with the ophthalmologist, and we set a date for the witching hour of 11:30 a.m., early to avoid the lunch crowd. On that fateful day, I skipped both treadmill and breakfast, devoured a Power Bar, rested all morning, and dressed in slimming black velour pants and my bluest silk blouse. Men like the color blue. Even my salon-enhanced auburn hair looked more enticing than usual. I was glad to be rid of the Brillo-gray, although Bertha says the shade of the hair doesn't matter as much as the amount left.

I expected the date with Eric to be a turning point, a milestone. For conversational fodder, I collected newspaper photos of a Korean violinist scheduled to play at State U, also two write-ups of *The Magic Flute* and *Carmen* performed by a local opera company, and a *New York Times* interview of a renowned French countertenor of whom I had never heard. I stuffed all this into a Fresh Foods shopping bag and arrived at the café twenty minutes early.

According to plan, our tête-à-tête would float as gracefully as Offenbach's "Barcarole." Eric would worry about the survival of classical music today, and I'd ask about prizes he had won, his greatest triumphs on stage, and early disappointments when auditions didn't go as planned.

He would repeat scandalous stories about other famous baritones and the impossible conductors he had encountered. We'd laugh in a sophisticated way and once in a while stop to gaze longingly into each other's eyes, but no handholding over the table in case Fritzi Schnell should be lurking under it.

Alone at the circular wrought-iron café table, I watched residents, their aides, and staff members arrive, order, devour spaghetti and meatballs or soggy chicken salad sandwiches and leave. I eyed the clock often and waited an hour and fifteen minutes. Eric never came. Over a cup of green tea back in the apartment, I marveled at my composure. Our aborted meeting seemed less devastating than if it had happened to me say, sixty years ago. No bitter tears, no outrage, no weepy phone calls to sympathetic friends. A sense of calm enfolded me.

That's how it goes. Once more Reality had outwitted Romance, and all it boiled down to was a woman in her eighties disappointed by an elderly friend for any number of reasons: forgetfulness, fatigue, muscle spasms, headache, misplaced keys or glasses, indigestion, nausea, or merciless diarrhea. Perhaps after a restless night, Eric experienced an equally bad morning and felt too tired to dial my number. Or he planned to come, but his medication played tricks on him again and the date slipped his mind. Or he received a rare phone call from his niece in Seattle and hated to hang up. Or Jake had dropped by unexpectedly and Eric couldn't get a word in edgewise to escape.

Tomorrow morning I'll greet Eric pleasantly, hand him a copy of "The Breakfast Beguine," and to avoid upsetting him, not even mention our ill-starred lunch. For him, it meant nothing. Our appointment hadn't registered with him and therefore left no mark. But the awful truth remains.

*He stood me up!*

## CHAPTER 5

———

ERIC DIDN'T APPEAR AT THE breakfast table the next morning nor the days following.

"Absent without leave," as Sidney put it. Later in the week, Willa found herself alone, eating with irritable Jake, furious over having been served a cup of lukewarm decaf tea. As was his usual custom, he tapped his teaspoon loudly against an empty juice glass to attract the attention of their overworked Sierra Leonean server. Noticing the weary disapproval in Willa's eyes, Jake gently laid the spoon next to his plate. "Some days, little things get to me," he said.

"It's all right."

"No, Willa, it's not. I should be able to control myself better. Never could."

He leaned closer to her and lowered his voice. "Want to hear the story of my life?"

"I don't care."

"You don't care about much, do you?"

"No."

"Good. I'll tell you a thrilling tale, what our friend Yetta the Yiddishist would call a *mysa*. If she were a Galitzianer, speaking the dialect from Galicia in Poland, she'd call it a *monsa*. So do you want to stay and hear this story or not?"

"No."

"Excellent answer. Sit down."

Willa felt trapped but couldn't escape. "Once a long time ago," he began, "there was an eager young scholar named Yaakov who dropped out of rabbinical college although he was knowledgeable and articulate and borderline melodramatic. He swore to himself he'd never become cynical or negative, no matter what. So far, so good, right? Pass the salt. These hash browns are cold and have no taste whatsoever, no *tahm*."

Willa handed him the salt shaker. "Sugar?" she said, reaching for a plastic bowl of paper packets.

He shook his head. "Don't interrupt. On a trip to Florida, Yaakov took a detour through Georgia and Alabama, where he discovered a small congregation, not rich, not poor, but the main thing was, he talked a blue streak, and they liked him so much they hired him to conduct Rosh Hashanah and Yom Kippur services."

"Why would they do that?"

"The real rabbi had left to take a job with a bigger congregation, and they were desperate."

"I really have to go."

"Sit. You're making me nervous. Yaakov never returned to rabbinical school. Although synagogue politics disgusted him, and he decided to become a newspaperman instead. Those years you didn't need a degree from a fancy-schmancy journalism school. But try as he may, he couldn't crash into the world of city newspapers, many of which were still not hiring Jews."

"Not even in New York?"

"Too much competition. Instead, he dedicated himself to Jews scattered throughout the Deep South. He taught Hebrew to the children of isolated dry-goods merchants and lonely grocery store owners. From town to town, city to city, he went, writing for Jewish newspapers and directing Jewish youth activities. He was hired as a fund raiser for Zionist groups. And so, the years passed while he danced the hora for little money and an indifferent clientele."

Jake broke off the narrative. "Your eyes are glazing over, Willa," he said. "Should I stop? Am I making you uncomfortable?"

Willa shook her head. Although she didn't want to hurt Jake's feelings, Eric's continuing absence upset her. The morning had slipped away; she missed those tranquil moments with Oliver Wendell Holmes. That obsession would be hard to explain to Jake, who would want to know if Holmes was good for the Jews, and she had never given it any thought.

"Is your story true?" Willa asked. She didn't know how to answer an agitated old bird like Jake; she preferred to dodge the whole thing.

Jake put his finger to his lips to silence her. "But no matter how Fate treated him, Yaakov would not go gentile into that good night." He paused, waiting for her to laugh.

Willa sighed at the pun. Dylan Thomas. "Gentile?"

"Yaakov was angry but not enough to convert."

"What happened to him?"

"He took the advice of that famous nineteenth century Jewish journalist, Horace Greenberg: 'Go in de Vest, young man, go in de Vest!' So he left Old Dixie and continued his glorious career in Texas as a rolling stone, a tumbling tumbleweed…a Judaic pitchman. In the meantime, he married twice, divorced twice, fathered a couple of kids whom he didn't like and who didn't like him, and led a double life as a professional gambler in his spare time."

"I'm sorry."

"Don't waste your sorryness. Yaakov had a bachelor uncle named Mendele who started with a horse and wagon and parlayed it into a fleet of cabs. Meanwhile, he saved leftover soap slivers plus every dollar he ever made. End result: all his money was left to Yaakov, a professional Jew without a profession. And that's how I can afford to live out my years at luxurious SVM. And now I'm signing off."

Jake raised the saltshaker to his lips as if it were a microphone and deepened his voice to imitate the host of a long-departed radio program. "For Mercury Theater, I remain…your obedient servant…Orson Velles."

Orson Welles? Willa moved away from Jake as soon as she could manage. Never would Oliver Wendell Holmes allow at his breakfast table such a *mishuganer*, such a madman. She stashed away Jake's renegade confession in a distant corner of her mind. In twenty minutes the Somalian cleaning woman would crystalize at her apartment door with vacuum cleaner and clean garbage bags in hand. Jake had robbed Willa of extra time to shovel out her messy living room and make sure there was nothing embarrassing left behind in the bathroom.

———◆———

*Thursday, August 15.* In *The Autocrat of the Breakfast Table*, Oliver Wendell Holmes describes a young unmarried Victorian woman, a character overly careful not to arouse gossip in the closed society of the boardinghouse. According to Holmes, "She was…troubled with the thought that…she was doomed to be the…prey of some of those corbies who not only pick out… eyes, but find no other diet so nutritious and agreeable."

Thank you, Dr. Holmes. That's an ample warning about ravens like Fritzi. I hope I didn't overreact when she gave us some good news today for a change. After Eric's brief stay at Verdant Valley Rehab, Medicare wouldn't cover any more physical therapy, and he's now back home at SVM.

Consequently, I've thrown all caution to the Canada geese feasting on the garbage of a nearby McDonald's and executed a daring move. After breakfast, I took a dozen deep breaths, applied a rare dollop of mascara, and took the elevator to the ground floor. Once at Eric's door, I glanced furtively from left to right and wondered why I felt like an elderly hooker on assignment.

Aside from living with Aaron for fifty-five years, this counted as the first time I'd be alone with a man in his apartment. Eric is not threatening like Howie the Unwholesome Wholesaler, or at least I don't think he is, but appearances count. My consuming fear is the devastation Fritzi the Schnellbomber can leave in her wake. Because of her gossip, poor Diana, Goddess of the Hunt, has become the laughing stock of SVM for her flirty antics, real or imaginary.

Under my arm I carried a box of gourmet brownies, bundled in royal blue paper found on sale at CVS and tied with a glittery ribbon saved for a worthy occasion like this. Nothing was too good for Eric, probably accustomed to gifts of fabulous diamond cuff links from smitten heiresses all over the world. Now when it matters most, where are all those fickle glamor girls jostling each other to touch his sleeve and whisper outrageous invitations in his ear? Who remains except one last leaf on the tree? Me.

It was impossible to find him an appropriate card. The drugstore kind featured obnoxious puppies that barked inane messages like, "Get well, doggone it." You don't get well from Parkinson's. Less desirable greetings included coarse references to flatulence, the mention of which women of my generation prefer to ignore and for good reason.

With tremendous effort Eric opened the door, held tightly to the brass knob for support, and appeared surprised. I told him it felt strange being alone with him in his apartment, and he answered quite seriously, "Nobody cares. We're old people." Somehow that put a damper on a possible romantic moment. Somehow I felt disloyal crossing the threshold without a husband to cushion the impact and ease the flow of conversation.

"I'm ruining my beautiful reputation," I said in an abandoned manner, blinking my scarcely evident eyelashes. I was flirting with him. Well past eighty, I had turned coquettish with an attractive man I scarcely knew. He smiled when he heard my remark. Time for me to flip the subject to music and the cheerful news of opera companies going out of business.

I sat on a metal folding chair and examined his barren efficiency apartment for traces of his fabulous past. The décor reflected only the indifference of a male living alone with no female available to shop for curtains or tack Picasso prints to the walls. No piano in sight, only an electronic keyboard, which he said he hadn't played lately.

Almost forgotten was the gift in my hand, but I couldn't recall whether or not he had diabetes. "Can you eat this?" I asked, and he said yes, of course, but he didn't want to open the brownies just yet—he'd rather chat—and so instructed me to put them on the kitchen counter, which he could reach easily. A lag in our conversation provided a good opportunity to hand him "The Breakfast Beguine."

"It was written for your eyes alone," I said. It wasn't exactly true but sounded dramatic.

"Intriguing title." It sounded like the no-nonsense pronouncement of the college professor he became in his later years. "Humorous?"

"Not really." Maybe the light verse about Joseph and his siblings would have been better. "I'm working in a more serious vein now," I said. We exchanged understanding smiles. "Your own versatility inspires me."

He seemed pleased at that remark but added no comment. I chattered on to fill the silence. "Many authors can be both funny and serious, just like composers who can write comic opera one day and majestic symphonies the next."

"Mozart," he said.

It was a perfect opening for me to introduce my favorite subject. Speaking a total of six syllables on one breath was not easy. "Or Oliver Wendell Holmes."

Eric sent me a questioning look and didn't respond. Then I took the plunge and began a verse once memorized in sixth grade. "Have you heard of the one-hoss shay?"

"Sorry?"

I repeated the first line of my favorite Holmes poem, "The Deacon's Masterpiece." "Have you heard of the wonderful one-hoss shay..."

Eric raised his head, whitened magnificently at the temples, and recited in a low, but unmuffled tone, "That was built in such a logical way / It ran a hundred years to a day."

He knew the poem! I picked it up from there. "I'll tell you what happened without delay / Scaring the parson into fits / Frightening people out of their wits..." My voice was strained, but the words, all vowels and consonants, came through as well chiseled as New England quartz.

"Have you heard of that, I say?" Eric finished, looking proud of himself. At breakfast he sometimes apologized for what his medication did to his memory, but now he recited Holmes, letter-perfect.

Our hands touched in the most sensual high-five ever delivered. I was ecstatic. "Did you learn it as a child?" I asked.

Eric explained that during his student days at the New England Conservatory, he and his roommate had the wild idea of writing an opera based on the life and work of Oliver Wendell Holmes! I couldn't believe it, Eric and I on the same wavelength. He explained how they planned to set Holmes to music, dramatizing the struggle in his mind between two competing adversaries: medicine and literature.

"Was Holmes a tenor in your opera? I read somewhere he had a high-pitched voice."

"Bass/baritone of course," Eric said. "I would have played Holmes."

"You would have played?"

"Nothing came of it. Contemporary operas weren't in great demand. Audiences preferred Verdi, Bizet, and Wagner. Still do. We dropped it and concentrated on our singing careers."

"If only you had finished that opera," I said. My disappointment was showing, but all wasn't lost. "Maybe you still can. I mean, these days who wouldn't want to buy a ticket to see an opera about Oliver Wendell Holmes?"

Eric gave me a patient look and, to indicate that the discussion had reached its finale, quoted the last lines of the poem. "End of the wonderful one-hoss shay / Logic is logic. That's all I say."

It was almost dinnertime. Before I left, he thanked me for the brownies. "Come again," he said in a courtly way. "You look lovely." He took my hand. "Come again."

I must have blushed; do women over eighty blush? How long has it been since any man told me I looked lovely? "No," I said, "let's meet at the breakfast table. Then I'll know you're better."

Passing his barren kitchenette, I glanced at my gift offering, the unopened box of brownies. My package looked forlorn; the cheap paper wrinkled, the gold-colored ribbon shabby and wilted. It didn't do Eric justice. In the corridor three highly vocal females appeared from nowhere and watched me exit Eric's apartment. One pair of eyes belonged to Fritzi Schnell. Not knowing what else to do, I gave her an innocent smile.

## CHAPTER 6

———◆———

EARLY-MORNING ANNOUNCEMENTS OVER THE SVM intercom created no excitement whatsoever. Certain residents made it a policy not to pay attention to any information not in writing or delivered verbally in person. Others didn't wear their hearing aids that hour of the day or had been busy with noisy electric toothbrushes, and the din of water running full force blotted out messages of all kinds. Most were unaware of the announcements. Or they forgot whatever it was that the front desk wanted them to know and waited for further notice, possibly a flyer with extra large print.

That's why when Kathy, an energetic young volunteer in a T-shirt that read "Kiss Me—I'm Jewish," stopped at the table, she found tenants less than enthusiastic.

"Does everybody know about the contest?" Kathy asked. She gave them a tolerant smile. "Want to win a cash prize and a free coupon for a supersized package of paper towels from CVS?" Flustered by their empty stares, the young woman continued. "It's a What's-in-a-Name contest And most important of all, the prize winner gets—"

Jake was ready for that one. "To change his name?"

Lydia put a hand on his arm. "Jake, let the young lady tell us," she said. "If you treat her badly, she won't ever come back." Lydia gave her a loving nod. "Please go on, dear."

Kathy consulted the notes in her hand and then continued. "People always say, 'S-V-M, what do those letters stand for?'"

"I've asked that myself," Bertha said.

Kathy brushed a strand of her long blond hair out of her eyes. "There you go. SVM. What does it mean to you?" She didn't wait for an answer but continued reading from a script, her voice rising up and down in a sing-song pattern. "It ought to be pleasant and inviting. Something inspirational. Something to attract future residents to the best kosher retirement establishment in the East."

Bertha applauded. "You did that very nice, honey. My granddaughter Millicent gave the graduation speech at her high school. She's very intelligent and recited it from memory. She didn't need notes, like you."

Harriet had a question. "So what do we have to do, Kathy?"

"You make the letters, SVM, stand for something. Three initials, *S*, *V*, and *M*. You supply words that begin with those letters, three good words that describe this place."

"Kathy, dear, give us an example," Lydia said in her gentle way.

"For instance," Kathy said, "SVM could stand for Sincere-Valuable-Management."

Sidney had another idea. "I dedicate this one to you, Jake. How about Sloppy-Vicious-Misfit?"

Jake almost smiled. "That's me! Too bad Diana's not here. Here's one for her: Seeking-Vigorous-Men."

If Eric turned up, Willa thought, he'd suggest Schubert-Verdi-Mozart. But she didn't think it was worth mentioning.

Kathy decided to give it a rest. "If you think of anything, write it down and bring your contest entries to the front desk," she said. She turned and nearly bumped into Diana, firmly gripping the hand of a bewildered gentleman who had signed his lease only the day before.

"Just showing him the ropes!" Diana shouted as they passed by.

"I'll bet you are," Sidney said, and the Ha-Ha Table responded a bit weaker than usual because two of their company, the most raucous laughers, were out of town attending the weddings of grandchildren.

Five minutes later when Fritzi Schnell arrived at the table, she sat next to Willa, who had saved that empty chair for Eric but didn't want to make a fuss about it, especially now that Fritzi had seen her leaving his apartment.

"Diana and her latest catch," Fritzi said, with obvious relish. "Some women just can't live without a man around, can they?" She darted a glance at Willa. "Her new fellow is a widower from Raleigh. I saw him moving in yesterday. He has emphysema and a whole rack of nice suits, which I can tell you right now he's not going to wear here. They'll wind up in the Goodwill bin."

With Fritzi at the table, Jake and Sidney finished their breakfast at high speed.

"Why are you two leaving so soon?" Fritzi asked. The men didn't answer her, muttering unpleasantries to each other. "And I'm not crazy about you either!" Fritzi yelled after them. She turned to Willa. "They're not friendly. Most people here think the world of me. Right?"

"Right," Willa said, hoping to avoid being inscribed in Fritzi's catalogue of fallen women.

The others vacated their chairs one by one. Eric had skipped breakfast again, but Willa thought it unwise to leave abruptly. Fritzi was sensitive to any perceived slights. Willa watched her take a final sip of coffee. It wouldn't do to abandon Fritzi now; why make things worse? They would leave together like good friends. As the two women parted, Willa forced a weak smile, and Fritzi ordered her to have a good day.

"You too," Willa said, and then concentrated on Fritzi's final words. They swooped down like predatory birds. "You move too fast. You're running, running, always running. Where are you running?"

"Wish I knew," Willa whispered, but Fritzi couldn't hear her.

———◆———

*Monday, August 19. Old age is like an opium dream. Nothing seems real except what is unreal…*

So wrote Dr. Holmes in his *Teacups* book, but how would an upright Bostonian like him know about such things? Who sets the limits on what's real and what's not? Last night I slept and fell into a limbo dream, the kind you know is fake and can't escape. Eric and I breakfasted on a Caribbean terrace hung with fuchsia and pink frangipani. Freed from eavesdropping tablemates, we had no inhibitions about speaking. Tropical magic turned straw into gold; our voices, melodious and clear, floated through the sunshine.

"Remember that opera you never finished?" I said.

"How can I forget?" He raised a Bloody Mary. "Here's looking at you, kid," he said, echoing the hero of a favorite Turner Classic Movie.

"You were a triple threat: composed, conducted, sang. You might have become famous even earlier if you hadn't abandoned Oliver Wendell Holmes."

His handsome face grew serious. "Why are you fixated on him? Holmes is not exactly a household name these days."

(My warped dream continued, and I'm trying to remember and record here every single word we spoke. Otherwise if not on the record, it's subject to forgettery.)

"Don't be jealous, Eric. My feelings for him are scholarly, nothing more."

"I'm relieved to hear that." Like Paul Henreid in "Now Voyager," Eric debonairly lit two cigarettes in his mouth and offered one to me, a non-smoker all my life. I handed it back to him. "Holmes reminds me of lost opportunities," I said.

Eric wrinkled his unlined forehead. "Sorry you're so troubled."

"Holmes became one of the most popular American writers of his day. Even as a doctor, he was remarkable. In his time, although childbed fever was widespread, he was positive it could be prevented."

"What's that have to do with you?"

"For years after our marriage, I suffered one miscarriage after the other. I'm sure Holmes would have been more sympathetic than my modern obstetrician, who just advised me to keep on trying and later insisted on a hysterectomy that knocked me for a loop."

"Doctors make jokes about their patients to other doctors the way singers make jokes about their audiences to other singers. What makes you think Holmes would have spared you?"

"Not when all around him young women were dying from childbed fever."

"I wouldn't know about that," Eric said. "In grand opera a soprano dies, the curtain closes, and then she takes curtain calls."

His detachment puzzled me. "I thought you would understand, Eric."

"Why? Childbed fever is the one ailment you don't get in old age."

"No, but it could pop up again for young women, the way other diseases have come back when we thought they were wiped out."

Eric poured himself another Bloody Mary. "Wasting your life on Holmes gets you nowhere."

"Don't you see? He was a nineteenth century whistle-blower. In his professional papers, he exposed unclean medical practices. Because of him later generations avoided infection and lived to see their babies grow up. What other American author did that? He was very sanitary for a writer."

"You think of everything," Eric said with admiration.

And now the pivotal moment arrived in this dream of mine. "Tell me more about your Holmes opera," I said.

He gave a deprecating laugh. "Hard to remember. I think we opened act one with 'The Deacon's Masterpiece.'"

"That poem hooked me on Holmes when I was twelve. Go on."

"My music had a galloping rhythm to imitate a horse pulling the one-hoss shay." With a butter knife, he beat out the clippety-clop gait on the breakfast table.

Our intimate little chat headed in the right direction. "Such a simple story line," I said, "but meaningful. The deacon's unpretentious horse and buggy lasts a whole century. As a child, I loved the way all parts of the carriage were built of equal strength so it would never break down. And then pop! The bubble bursts. The shay disappears all at once, nothing last and nothing first."

"Not like people," Eric said, sipping his Bloody Mary. "We fall apart piece by piece."

I charged ahead. "Eric, why not resurrect your opera? Finish it."

He stared hard, as if he were considering me for an audition to his master class. I felt timid under his stern gaze. It was beyond me how I had summoned the chutzpah to suggest such a wild idea to him, but a dream is not an unlikely place to juggle Romance and Reality. For women my age, it's the only place where Romance has a chance.

"Who would direct it?" Now he was humoring me. "And where would you find professional singers willing to work long hours without a paycheck?"

"Plenty would do anything to appear before a live audience."

"You expect me to work with amateurs?" He became mischievous. "Let me ask you something," he said. "Can you define the word 'glottis'?"

I knew the answer from thirty useless years of visiting countless pathologists and speech therapists. "The area between the vocal cords and the upper part of the larynx."

Eric shook his head. "No, it's when you sing and don't get paid for it. That's when a performer works glottis." He received no response. "It's a singer's joke," he said.

I didn't expect bad puns at a time like this. Oliver Wendell Holmes had it right. Puns derail a conversation beyond repair. But what truly mattered now was persuading Eric to spend some precious time together with me.

"The SVM chorus would do it glottis," I said recklessly. Since this was my dream, not his, why not be positive? As for casting, had Eric forgotten the miracle of stage makeup? The SVM chorus would drench themselves in it and act young against all odds.

"In act two you could compose a show-stopping trio sung by Holmes, Emerson, and Longfellow."

"Who'd be your soprano?" Eric asked. "Susan B. Anthony?"

I got carried away. "And I'll even write the libretto and direct if we can't find anybody else."

He lost patience with me. "You don't have the vaguest idea of what goes into staging an opera!" he yelled.

*Wake up. Wake up at once. It's turning into a full-blown nightmare headed nowhere.* My eyes remained glued shut and wouldn't open. Eric glanced at his watch. "Time for lunch." He reached for his walker.

In one last desperate try, my voice no longer melodious, I screeched, "Leonard Bernstein did OK with *Candide*. Holmes would be a lot easier to set to music than Voltaire."

"*Candide* closed after fifty-three performances," Eric said. "This turkey wouldn't last that long."

*Oh, for the love of Pete, wake up,* I commanded myself. *End this. Slap your cheeks. Bulge out your eyes until the lashes are forced apart. Open sesame! Wake up!* And then I found myself staring at the gold-framed wedding picture of Aaron and me on the wall next to the walnut chest of drawers and heard my voice audibly croak, "Wake up! Wake up and sing!"

All was lost. I had overdosed on Judy/Mickey fantasies via Turner Classic Movies. Hey gang, let's all get together and do Wagner's *Ring* cycle in our garage! Stage an opera? I can't even read music. Then I caught myself. All this never happened. A dream. Relax. Eric needn't ever know about it.

My brain cells refused to quit. Really, why not resurrect Eric's opera about Oliver Wendell Holmes? We'd become celebrities, a pair of venerable artists demonstrating to the world how talented we still are. We'd astound the critics. "Here's to the remarkable vitality of two gifted souls in tandem," they'd write. Only one thing holds us back, one ironsided obstacle. What stands in our way? The gray truth landed, and I was awake at last. *We're too damned old.*

Hello, Reality! You're really good at booting dreamers out the door and tossing our baggage after us. But one thing puzzled me. Eyes open for business, fully awake, why had I blurted out, "Wake up and sing"? It's the title of a Clifford Odets play. One weekend Aaron and I drove to New York for a revival of this Depression-era show, well acted but melancholy and dated. *Wake Up and Sing!* Lights over the marquee. Now Playing for a Limited Time Only: *Wake Up and Sing!*

En route to the Gedalia Ginsfarb Fitness Garden today, I couldn't lose that phrase. Alone among the spidery Nu-Step machines, I mounted the treadmill, and the four words reverberated along with the rumble of the moving pathway underfoot. Wake up and sing. Sing and wake up. I dimly recalled a peppy song of the 1930s: "Wake Up and Live." My mother would play the record on the phonograph while polishing brass candlesticks for Shabbos. My father even owned Dorthea Brande's self-help book with the same title. But as he used to say, what does this have to do with the price of beans?

Wake up and sing. From some distant place, a free-wheeling idea had floated down to me. Of course. Why hadn't I thought of it before? It could lead to a major victory of Romance over Reality. It would be one for the books.

# CHAPTER 7

———•———

THE NEXT MORNING FLO THE Faux Blonde confronted the breakfast-table entourage with an unsettling philosophical question. "When did 'rouge' become 'blusher'?" she asked. "They don't call cosmetics 'rouge' anymore."

"What difference does it make?" Sidney muttered.

Flo refused to let yield the floor. "I mean, did they think young women today were too dumb to know French, so they changed it to 'blusher'?"

Jake shrugged. He was wearing a borsht-stained sweater that, he said, dated back to the Iron Age. "Ask the copywriter," Jake said, nodding in Willa's direction. "What's your take on it?"

Willa shrugged. "No comment." She watched the dining-room entrance for Eric and hoped they could manage a private interlude in which to share her momentous idea that could bring them closer together.

Flo expanded her weedy patch of opinions. "And what ever happened to compacts? Young women today don't even know what they are."

"A compact is a small car," Sidney explained.

Flo ignored him. "I use to buy Lady Esther face powder, the loose kind, and shake some into a compact to keep the shine off my nose."

'My husband, Meyer, may he rest in peace, once gave me a silver compact for an engagement gift, sixty years ago," Bertha said with a sigh.

"Now," Flo said, "you buy pressed powder in a crummy little plastic case that falls apart right away, and you throw it out and go to the drugstore to buy another one that'll do the same thing in a couple of weeks. What good is that?"

Jake frowned over his cantaloupe. "Helps the Chinese get richer. What happened to my napkin?" He bent to search under the table and muttered, "Even laps don't work the way they used to."

An African woman glided by, pushing a crumpled little man in a wheelchair. Erect and graceful, the aide wore a magnificent black-and-gold turban and a flowing purple robe trimmed with sparkling green vines, the material draped to perfection around her slender hips. Only Jake and Sidney watched her pass; the females interested themselves in their scrambled Eggbeaters.

Willa hoped Eric would arrive soon. If he were sitting across the table now, they could exchange amused looks at the conversation or roll their eyes in perfect, exasperated sync.

"It's hard to buy cosmetics anymore," Flo said. "At the drugstore I asked where they kept their foundation, but the girl didn't know what it was."

"That's the trouble with the world these days," Jake said, his mouth jammed full of bagel. "No foundation." He brightened. "Well, here he is!"

Willa glanced up from her pumpernickel bagel spread thickly with nonfat cream cheese and smiled a secret smile. Eric, leaning hard on his walker, was back for the first time that week.

Everyone dawdled longer than usual just when Willa needed to talk to him alone. While the others drank their coffee refills, Lydia tried to rid herself of a Styrofoam dish of stewed prunes. "I didn't order this," she said. "Here, Jake, have some."

Jake shook his uncombed head. "I don't do prunes."

"Never look a gift horse in the mouth," Lydia said.

Bertha disagreed. "In the *face*! The saying is, Never look a gift horse in the face." Willa and Eric sent each other amused looks.

Lydia stood her ground. "If you do the proper research," she said, "you'll find it's never look a gift horse in the mouth. When you look only at the horse's face, you can't tell what condition the teeth are in."

Good-natured Bertha raised her scanty eyebrows. "What do I know? I'm from New York."

"You can't help it," said Flo, who grew up in Cleveland.

"I had a lousy dream last night," Sidney said.

Jake frowned. "Me too. Must have been that lemon custard at dinner."

"I dreamt," Sidney continued, "I still had my car, still driving. The keys were in the ignition, the motor was running, but I couldn't open the door. I tried and tried, just couldn't get in. I'd wake up, go back to sleep, and I was still locked out of the car."

"I always carried an extra key with me," Bertha said. "That way you can always get in."

"Not in a dream, you can't," Sidney said darkly.

Bertha turned and called out to a passing stooped-over woman dressed in a navy-blue suit and matching beret. "Have a good time, Gussie!"

"Going to a funeral," Gussie said. "Belle on the fifth floor died yesterday."

Bertha took it in stride. "I knew she was sick but not that sick."

"Well," Gussie said as she continued on her way, "now you know."

Willa made up her mind to finish the cup of Wissotsky tea and leave. She couldn't have a private talk with Eric in this chaos. Wake up and sing. Maybe she should forget the whole preposterous idea. Before she could rise from her chair, The Centenarian approached, and four people at the table remembered doctors' appointments they hadn't mentioned before. The stampede out of the Esther Essenvarg Dining Den left the table to Willa and Eric.

The Centenarian paused behind Eric's chair. "I'm a hundred and one years old," he said, "and I don't believe in anything."

Eric murmured something the very old man couldn't hear, and Willa joined in with words equally inaudible.

"The hell with it," The Centenarian said, and hobbled away.

Willa moved into the empty seat next to Eric, still eating in a tentative way. His hand gripping the coffee cup trembled more than usual.

"Must ask you something," Willa said. She forced her voice to a higher pitch that startled him. He turned away from his scrambled eggs and gave her a smile that melted her heart.

"Good," he said.

Willa took three long breaths, so deep the air filled her toes. "Remember when we talked about spasmodic dysphonia and you thought some part of my voice was left; it wasn't all gone?"

"It's not. I hear you now."

"A couple of days ago when leafing through an old book…"

"By Holmes?"

"No, someone named Arthur Lessac."

"Good man. Wrote *The Use and Training of the Human Voice*."

"Stuck in the pages of the book was a yellow newspaper clipping I saved once."

"About the Lessac System?"

Willa shook her head. "About a music teacher who gave singing lessons to adults with voice disorders. They learned to use muscles they didn't know they had, and somehow it helped them speak better."

Eric stopped eating and listened. Willa inhaled another three breaths that came this time, she thought, less from the diaphragm and more from depths of her soul, if she had one. "Would you be interested in teaching me to sing so maybe I can improve my speaking voice?"

As soon as she asked, she regretted it. Eric moved sideways in his chair to get a better look at her. She steeled herself, expecting a negative answer, and had a ready answer waiting. She'd simply respond, "It's OK, Eric, I understand." Surely, an opera star, an artist of his rank, wouldn't demean himself by spending time on her wayward vocal cords. He would never waste limited energy on a health problem not his own.

Eric didn't hesitate. "Of course," he said, pleased.

"What?"

"I'll do it."

The answer made her heart pound, and she committed the sin of not inhaling enough air to sustain any sound. "I…I have no training." Additional words stopped, stranded somewhere down in her throat.

He leaned forward to hear her. "Sorry?"

"You want to think it over first?"

Businesslike, he touched a napkin to his lips. "I've taught many students to sing. When do you want to start?"

Willa hated herself for underestimating him. "Let's check our calendars," she said. It would take a while to absorb the miracle that just happened. "We'll talk again."

Grasping the handles of the walker, Eric struggled to an upright position on unsteady legs. "No," he said in an even tone that didn't reflect the physical strain he was under, "we'll sing."

---

*Tuesday, August 20.* My chutzpah astounds me; I'm euphoric! If Eric can summon my voice from wherever it has been all these years, I'll never stop talking. "My dearest Eric," I'll say, "you've proved that elderly people can be wild cards. Old age is not monolithic; one size doesn't fit all, and there's no valid reason for us to parade in lockstep."

And then in full, round tones, I'll ask Eric, "Ever see those slick handouts distributed at senior health fairs? Pages sparkle with color photos of elderly models breezing around on bikes or a cluster of fifty-year-olds imbibing cocktails next to a stone fireplace. Meanwhile cheerleaders proclaim we can do anything if we put our minds to it. That's the spirit, the American dream, an equivalent of awarding prizes to every kid at the birthday party. It's a cinch to age gracefully when you arrive at this time of life healthy and accident-free and possess the right longevity genes, money, education, responsive government, and a handful of buttons to hide the stains.

"You've noticed by now, Eric, that whatever we do at our advanced age must fit between standard goal posts. Question: who sets those parameters? Who calls the shots? In an entire lifetime, we never fully understand ourselves, and certainly not each other. So how can the youthful experts of the old age industry figure us out? And if an elderly person deviates too often from the curriculum, will she be diagnosed as a danger to herself and others? When do the benign adjectives 'quirky' and 'eccentric' spill over into the realm of dementia? At what point does Romance prostrate itself in front of Reality?"

If my voice ever returns, that's what it will say to Eric. Granted, the physical stress of voice lessons could overwhelm both of us, but we won't know until we try. Right now I'm absolutely goofy over our upcoming date on the calendar; our limitations don't matter. Eric agrees to take on my badly shredded voice and mend it. He wants to do this, I can tell. It's not just to indulge me. Against the odds, he'll renew the excellence within himself. No longer an anonymous old man living out his days among the forgotten, he'll become the renowned Eric Revelle one more time.

And even if he can't lift my voice out of the dark hole of Calcutta it has inhabited for years, so what? With Eric as maestro, I'll slave away under his direction in spite of obstacles. Spending time with him is better for me than a phalanx of doctors and speech pathologists and a thousand electrical shocks to the larynx. Just like in my crazy lemon custard dream, we'll transform ourselves into two vital young people again, working together, savoring whatever life sets before us.

# CHAPTER 8

———

THE FOLLOWING WEEK, AFTER A hefty new resident dared to invade the sacred territory of their breakfast table, Lydia complained that Jake's pet names went too far. "It's unkind of you to call that new woman Minnie the Matzo Ball," she said. "Please stop."

Jake pretended not to hear. The blacker his mood, the more inspired he became, referring to a poor soul with allergies as The Thespian Sneezer, also known as The Show Off, not to be confused with The Cantorial Cougher. On a humid morning at the end of that dreary week, he remained at the table after everyone had left except Willa, depressed by another of Eric's unexplained long absences. Jake made a feeble attempt to entertain her.

"I didn't win the What's-in-a-Name contest," Jake said, spreading cream cheese on his second bagel. "Know what they picked? SVM: Superb-Valiant-Managers, probably submitted by one of the superb valiant managers." He took a substantial bite out of his bagel. "Mine was more to the point. Want to know what it was, Willa?"

"No."

"SVM: Salivating-Violent-Mongels, and I signed Fritzi's name to it."

"You didn't."

"I also entered one for Diana: Seeking Virile Menfolk."

"You're making this up."

"Of course. Nobody knows what the initials stand for. And who cares?" He finished his bagel and reached for a danish. "Too bad about

Eric's relapse, but they say he's out of the hospital again and back at good old Verdant Valley Rehab. I went to see him yesterday. It may take a while, but he'll return."

Willa nodded. Tears came to her eyes. Good-bye to the voice lessons that never began.

"What did you think of my talk the other evening?"

Willa tried to look enthusiastic and failed. "Fine," she said in a semi-whisper.

"Just fine? I mean, you'd expect second and third generation American Jews not to give a damn, but what some of these first-generation oddballs know about our culture and history couldn't fill a book of matches. They apologize and claim they were always too busy making a living and raising the kids. Now at last, with time on their hands, they attend lectures on Jewish topics and forget everything the minute they leave the room." Jake stirred real sugar into his tea. "*Nu?* This is what we've become. We're all Jews, but we don't share the same values. Maybe when our parents were still living, but not now. So what remains of that great foreign-born generation? This place is loaded with grandmothers, grandfathers, great-grandmothers, and great-grandfathers, and old age is the only thing we have in common, plus the universal consensus that we don't belong in a place like this." He squinted to get a better look at her. "You're a good listener, Willa."

"Am I?"

"Getting old doesn't automatically transform us into a people we never were, does it?"

"No."

Jake leaned forward to hear better, but she didn't add to her remarks, and he continued. "It's my next lecture. 'We Can't Be More Jewish than Our Backgrounds.' Great title, don't you think?"

Willa shrugged. "It's OK."

"My point is, if they didn't absorb anything basic from their earlier years, it's hard to learn at this time of life. Really, what's Judaic about them now? A preference for matzo balls and blintzes? Am I wasting my breath?"

Willa found it difficult to concentrate on Jake's convoluted ideas. She took another pointless glance at the doorway. Eric was not in good enough condition to start her voice lessons now, probably never. There was nothing left for her to do but escape from Jake's histrionics and flee to the wisdom of Dr. Holmes for medicinal purposes. Passing the lobby bulletin board, she noticed a flyer about a professional string quartet concert scheduled to play a baroque program at SVM that evening. She would go by herself and listen with Eric's ears.

———◆———

*August 23, Friday.* Doreen, that young woman who works in the Esther Essenvarg Dining Den, is reaping a lot of criticism lately, and she's losing patience with us after trying to start our day with mimosas. She did better this time than with the bloody marys, but there still was a rumble of criticism about serving alcohol at breakfast. Meanwhile, Fritzi has begun a campaign to keep Doreen from wearing tight sweaters and form-clinging skirts because, so Fritzi says, "she wants to stir up the men." The other morning Doreen broke into a little Irish dance and Fritzi denounced her for inappropriate dancing and showing off in front of people in wheelchairs and walkers who could no longer dance. "It's very mean of her," Fritzi said.

"All of a sudden she's Mother Teresa," Jake said.

A fine concert took place here last night, although it's tiresome to sit alone through Handel and Bach all at one gulp. And it doesn't erase my guilt over neglecting Eric at Verdant Valley just when he needs me. Classical Arts Showcase is no longer enough either. Instead, I continue to lose myself in the wonders of *The Poet at the Breakfast Table.* Holmes had the guts to mix serious pronouncements with lightweight chaff, and that takes courage when you have a reputation for writing humorously. Deep down he knew readers wouldn't choose to slog through his heavier meanderings without comic relief.

What riles me is how easy it was for him to spout on and on about aging in his earlier books. What was he then? In his twenties, thirties?

That's when he blithely wrote, "But the disease of old age is epidemic, endemic, and sporadic, and everybody that lives long enough is sure to catch it." Big joke. Much later in life, Dr. Holmes realized how lucky he was to enjoy a life span longer than his writer friends like Whittier, Lowell, and Longfellow. At one point he almost gloats when he lists the ages of these men at their funerals. Anyway, what the nineteenth century considered "old" doesn't apply today. Holmes fills his pages with remedies for treating the condition. Unsophisticated readers of the time must have found hilarious his descriptions of aging as a "disease" and "a malady." What a wag! It's not funny when you're coming down with it. Eric, of course, does have a serious condition and so do others here burdened with cancer, heart disease, or diabetes, grim ailments that don't lend themselves to humor. Still, unpleasant old codgers like Howie the Unwholesome Wholesaler or The Centenarian don't have much physically wrong with them. They're just odious.

I've located a lesser-known poem of Holmes's. Titled "The Old Man Dreams." It begins, "O for an hour of youthful joy." Why not "The Old Woman Dreams"? We could use a youthful joyride ourselves. Today I drained two full mugs of caffeinated coffee and acquired the nerve to ask the front desk about Eric's status at the nursing home.

"Have they switched him to long-term care for good?" I asked.

The receptionist rifled through some papers. "Still at Verdant Valley Rehab," she said. "That's all I can tell you." Although relieved, I wonder where all this is leading. In my head Romance argues with Reality and demands, "Why don't you let me enjoy myself?" And Reality answers, "That's not how I operate."

"Eric keeps asking for you," says Jake after each visit. Although he offers to drive me to Verdant Valley, he can't see worth a hoot, and besides, what's romantic about appearing with Jake in tow? I'll go by myself, even though it means facing alone whatever awaits at the end of that familiar sterile corridor. It's unkind to abandon Eric like this, but my reasons make sense to me. Aside from not wanting to relive memories of Aaron's last days, I'm concerned that Fritzi will learn where I'm heading and spread her latest fable about me. She disapproves of anyone who finds a purpose for living after the loss of a spouse.

Right now I'm clinging to Chopin, especially his Etude no. 12 in C Major, Opus 10. Must tell Eric that Oliver Wendell Holmes was a music lover too, one who faithfully attended open rehearsals of the Boston Symphony Orchestra. Speaking for me, he writes this:

> I have but a superficial outside acquaintance with the secrets, the unfathomable mysteries, of music...I do not even pretend that I can appreciate the work of a great master as a born and trained musician does. Still, I do love a great crash of harmonies, and the oftener I listen to these musical tempests the higher my soul seems to ride upon them...Take a music-bath once or twice a week for a few seasons, and you will find that it is to the soul what the water-bath is to the body.

That does it. Tomorrow I'll visit Eric at Verdant Valley, bring him a CD of Hayden's "Water Music," and hand in hand, we'll frolic in the surf.

## CHAPTER 9

LYDIA THE ENCYLOPIDDIA BEGAN THE breakfast conversation on a high note. "I have a pet peeve: the careless use of the word 'icon.'"

Jake couldn't help himself. It was his cue for, "Sometimes I con, and sometimes I con't." When his audience didn't respond, he added, "Well, you can pun, but you can't hide."

Lydia held her ground. "The media use 'icon' and 'iconic' to mean highly appreciated or celebrated. But 'ikon' simply means a sacred image or representation on display in the Greek church."

"I've always considered myself an iconoclast," Jake said to Willa, in an attempt to draw her into the conversation. "It's my singular charm. What's yours?"

Willa shrugged. Although she had made up her mind to visit Eric, she hoped she wouldn't have to. Instead she whispered to Jake, "Is Eric back yet from Verdant Valley?"

In his booming voice, Jake directed the question to the company at large. "Anyone seen Eric lately? This lady wants to know."

"They haven't discharged him from rehab yet," Fritzi said. She and the others at the crowded table surveyed Willa with a disapproving light in their eyes, or at least that's how she interpreted it.

Lydia bit into a slice of toast spread with jelly. "Perhaps next week," she said.

A blob of blueberry jam, the size of a quarter, dripped on the front of her white, dotted Swiss blouse and left a purplish stain, but she didn't seem to notice. Bertha pointed to it. "If that doesn't wash out," she said, "sew a button on it."

"I'm giving two more talks next month," Jake said.

"In Yiddish?" asked Yetta the Yiddishist, but Jake, his mouth full of cold scrambled Eggbeaters, shook his head, and Yetta continued. "Sometimes I teach these African aides Yiddish words just for the pleasure of teaching again."

"So what did they learn from you?" Bertha asked.

Yetta pointed to an aide two tables away. "That Nigerian woman with the magenta head wrap, see her? I taught her to say good night...*gute nacht.* Now every time she sees me, she yells out, *'Gute nacht!'* even if it's nine o'clock in the morning."

Jake looked up from his emptied plate and noticed that a sprightly woman in a pink baseball cap was approaching them. "Ah," he announced with a sweeping movement of his good arm, "Madam President! The radiant Penina Dubansky."

Penina, a Sephardic eighty-one-year-old director of the SVM tenants council, clasped a stack of yellow papers to her scrawny chest. "We stuffed the mailboxes with these flyers for our What's-in-a-Name contest," she said, "but we're still waiting to hear from everybody. How about some good ideas on what the letters SVM mean to you?"

"Didn't we do this already?" Jake asked.

"Only three people participated," Penina said, "and that includes an entry from a Catholic kitchen staffer. She suggested Sacred-Virgin-Mary."

"Wait," Flo said. "How about So-Very-Modern?"

Penina pointed an unbendable forefinger. "See? This is a smart table. Give me more suggestions."

"About what?" Bertha asked. She resented unfamiliar ideas, even though the staff had posted numerous notices about the contest and made announcements about it over the public address system every day for two weeks.

Penina's voice sounded weary. "What do the letters SVM stand for? In other words, what does SVM say to you?"

"Is this some sort of contest? Is that it? What are we supposed to do?" Bertha said, confused. Penina handed her a flyer. "Read this."

Bertha shook her mousy-gray head. "My reading glasses are upstairs."

"Here's what you do, Bertha. You find a pen and paper," Jake said, "and write down three words. One should begin with *S*, the next *V*, and the last letter, *M*." Inspired, he scribbled something on the back of the flyer. "Here's my entry," he said, handing it to Penina, who read it and shook her head. "I can't give this to the judges," she said.

"What did he write?" asked Lydia.

Jake sounded proud of himself. "*S-V-M*: Surly-Vegetating-Martyrs." He paused. "And that includes me."

"How about something pleasant like Scholarly-Vigorous-Members?" Lydia asked.

Penina smiled. "Now you're getting it."

Flo the Faux Blonde had a brainstorm. "Stunning-Vivacious-Models!"

"Where?" Jake asked.

Harriet offered another approach: "Sumptuous-Vegetarian-Menus," and Sidney suggested, "Scarcely-Visible-Menfolk."

When Penina instructed them to deposit their entries in the cardboard box marked "Contest" at the front desk, they all nodded with enthusiasm. After she left, they agreed it was too much trouble.

Willa refused to play the game. It was obvious to her that the SVM publicity department had initiated the contest to locate fresh adjectives for their next promotional brochure. Later that morning in her apartment, she switched on Classic Arts Showcase and found a German orchestra playing excerpts from Schubert's Symphony no. 8, unfinished, incomplete. The music reminded Willa of her own unfinished business, the visit she owed Eric. No more postponement. She must act, and soon.

———

*Monday, August 26.* Although it's now two in the morning, sleep eludes me until I finish recording what happened this afternoon at Verdant Valley.

Eric's room was identical to the one Aaron once occupied, the same impersonal space with the standard warehouse pine dresser, the institutional bathroom smelling of Lysol, the blurry TV screen flashing randomly, a bowl of plastic violets, and a white telephone on a rollaway table next to the bed, made up in regimental hospital style. Straight-backed and stiff, Eric sat fully dressed in jeans and a new yellow sport shirt open at the neck. I had expected to see him lying prostrate in a hospital gown.

We hugged, the first time ever. "Brought you gourmet cookies" was all I could think to say. "Not too sweet." Oliver Wendell Holmes once used the musical expression, *dolce ma non troppo dolce* and translated it as "sweet but not too sweet," but I didn't dare risk speaking Italian before someone who once had played Figaro in "The Barber of Seville."

He said he was glad to see me and thanked me for coming. I felt giddy, babbling with nervous abandon in a hoarse little voice. "Know what, Eric? There was an article in the paper yesterday about a New York theater breaking new ground with an original opera. They call it a whisper opera. The singers don't really sing."

He tried to smile and answered so softly, I strained to hear him. "They whisper?"

"Let's audition for it. You and I could walk off with the leads."

He nodded, amused. "How are you doing?" he asked.

"Let's talk about you. When are you coming back to SVM?"

"I argue with the doctors. They want me to stay, but what do they know?"

"Now you're sounding like The Centurion."

"You mean the Centaur."

We both laughed, and then he told me his niece was flying in from Seattle. "For the second time this year."

"It's a long way from there to the East Coast."

"You'll have to meet her. She's my sister's daughter. Her mother died last year."

I didn't know he had a sister. "Sorry."

"Lucky me. Jake came yesterday, you today, Rochelle tomorrow."

"Eric, I miss you—everybody does at the breakfast table, I mean. They ask about you every morning."

He looked into my eyes with such sweetness that my heart melted like honey in hot milk. "Miss you too. Give me your hands," he said. I leaned across the mobile serving table that separated us, and we sat holding on to each other. "Do you remember," he said, "we talked about singing lessons for you?"

"But then you had another fall that put you in the hospital and now rehab again."

"We can still do it."

"What?"

"A lesson right now."

"Here?"

At that critical moment, a Filipino aide rattled in, her cart loaded with medical equipment. "Blood pressure check," she said in a brisk way. She wrapped his thin arm with the black pad. "A little high this morning," she said, after a short wait. She collected the apparatus, smiled knowingly at the two of us, and retreated, closing the door behind her.

"I'm sorry I raised your blood pressure, Eric."

He knew I was flirting with him. "It's all right," he said, taking my hands again. "Anybody can learn to sing," he began, with an air of authority he had never used with me before. "Put your chin in your hand like this and push it back. Relax. Now sing Ah-h-h-h."

I opened my mouth and waited for something to happen. The sound was a long time coming. When it arrived, my breath escaped with a hissing sound and nothing more.

"Place your voice here; let the sound come through the nose," he said. I was so delighted to be doing this with him that I couldn't concentrate on what he told me. Somehow it was difficult to take his instructions seriously; a thousand flip, facetious comments raced through my head. Making him laugh was not the goal here, not today. What *was* the goal here today?

My voice had been out of order for years. How could Eric coax from me some kind of respectable sound this late in life? The absurdity of it caused me to giggle. Here we were, sitting on opposite sides of a wheeled hospital table in the romantic setting of a nursing home: Eric, an eighty-year-old patient with Parkinson's, and I, an eighty-plus widow, still in mourning, almost voiceless with SD for years. But if he could still teach, I could still learn.

He demonstrated what he meant. "Ah-ah-ah. Run it up and down like the scale. Repeat after me. Ah-ah-ah-ah."

The sound he produced, something I had never heard from him before, was startling, a rich baritone, controlled, vibrant, fully alive, and ageless, the same instrument that had thrilled audiences throughout the states and Europe. At last I could hear it, not in a full opera at the Met or a recital at Carnegie Hall, but a trace, enough to demonstrate the excellence he had once reached. Here was the voice that won prolonged applause and curtain calls and adoring crowds at the stage door. This was a hint of the voice women fell in love with.

"That's it. Good," he said, as I sent forth a feeble little soprano, reedy and thin, a sound from nowhere. "Try it again. Don't force it. Relax. Let it come out."

"Now I can say I studied voice with the great Eric Revelle," I said, laughing but also with a touch of awe, which he seemed to like.

"It's a beginning. You're not Callas or Sills yet."

We tried more exercises, open vowels up and down the scale, and too soon it was time for me to leave. He had a sad, lonely look in his eyes. "We'll do it again," he said.

"Yes. Something to look forward to." I bent over to give him a sisterly kiss on the cheek. Eric would not release me. He pulled me toward him, and our kiss landed where he intended it to be, on the mouth. It was light, brief, almost virginal, but I was swept away.

In the doorway of his room, I paused, turned, raised my hand to my lips, and, stretching my arm out as far as it would go in a grand gesture, flung him a majestic theatrical kiss. It was the gesture of his last prima donna making a grand exit from this bizarre comedy, this unlikely *buffa* opera of our old age.

# CHAPTER 10

———

JAKE, EXPOUNDING HIS THEORIES AT the breakfast table for anyone who bothered to listen, had come up with a new idea. "The ebb and flow of this dining room is symbolic of our entire history," he said over his peeled hard-boiled egg, which he had cut up in quarters and then eighths to make it last longer. He had switched over to his lecture mode. "Look around you," he ordered. "What do you see?"

"A bunch of cranky people," Bertha said. At a neighboring table, Doreen, the embattled assistant manager of mealtimes, listened wearily to the bitter words of two women complaining about the room temperature.

"OK," Jake said to his captive audience, "here's the subject of my next lecture. It's called Now You See It, Now You Don't.

Renee headed for the door, but Jake stood firm. "The living history in this room," he said, "will soon disappear forever. Here we are, the Ingathering of the Exiles. Think of what's collected here all in one spot, our fast-dwindling generation. It's not just the fading World War II and Korean War vets. Look at who's assembled here in one room."

"I'm missing a fork," Bertha yelled to a passing server.

Jake did not relent. "Who is still here? We're mom-and-pop storeowners burned out during the 1968 riots: we're former refugees from Austria and Germany, the lucky ones who escaped as children from the Nazis; we're the last of the Holocaust survivors. We're a Jewish American house of representatives. Once we were salespeople, government workers, factory owners, restaurateurs, cab drivers, nurses, typists, and stenographers.

And we're professionals, more of the men than the women, lawyers, doctors, pharmacists—"

"Don't forget us nursery school teachers," Flo the Faux Blonde said.

Jake pointed to her. "Teachers at all levels, from kindergarten to college professors, and technicians, jewelers, insurance brokers, cab drivers, shoemakers, all occupations. We're descendants of fugitives from everywhere—Russia, Turkey, France, Argentina, Hungary, Poland, Romania. Think about it. Ashkenazi, Sephardic, Orthodox, Conservative, Reform, Reconstructionist, secular humanists, atheists, Talmudic scholars, and know-nothings, the works, all under one roof. And time is running out. Never again will the world see such a collection.

"Any Smart Balance on the table?" Lydia asked, her eyesight not as good as it used to be. Willa passed her a bowl heaped high with tiny margarine containers.

Jake refused to be sidetracked. "What an inventory!" he roared, with a sweep of his hand. "South African, Israeli, Iranian, Yiddishists, Ladino-speakers, Anglo-Saxon Jews from Australia, Canada, the United Kingdom, and the US of A. Hail, hail, the gang's all here."

"*Genug*," Yetta said, breaking open a corn muffin. "Enough already."

Jake nodded in the direction of a recent newcomer limping toward them. "And here he comes, our newest SVM acquisition, our all-American boy. Ladies and gentlemen, presenting that all-time favorite, I give you Marvin the Marginal Mogul!"

Lydia politely wished Marvin a good morning as he took an empty seat, usually occupied by Harriet the Happy Housewife, who was out of town visiting a Philadelphia cousin. According to Fritzi, she had developed shingles. Willa barely acknowledged the new "fellow boarder," a term used often by Dr. Holmes in his books. Preoccupied, she was looking forward to reading *You, Too, Can Sing*, a book she had found in the library. It would make sense to spend her time doing vocal exercises before Eric returned, whenever that would be.

Marvin, reported by Fritzi to be a one-time real estate developer, prided himself on his full head of ecru-colored hair, topped with a battered green skullcap. Jake said the man and his handlebar mustache resembled the Monopoly game plutocrat without the top hat. Marvin's pink cheeks looked as if they were stuffed with nuts squirreled away for the winter, or so Jake observed the morning Marvin skipped breakfast to see his hematologist about increasing his blood thinner. In his absence, Jake had ridiculed Marvin's lumberjack shirts and green suede vest that clashed with whatever he wore and his black linen shopping bag, fat with what Jake claimed were "stocks, bonds, and defaulted mortgages."

"That man may be rich as cream," Fritzi said, "but every day I see him in the Trash Room, and he's rooting through the garbage looking for yesterday's newspaper. He doesn't get one delivered."

"I've watched Mr. Money Bags collect those little cups of artificial creamer from the tables," Sidney said. "Says he drinks it like milk."

Fritzi lowered her voice to convey a truly juicy tidbit. "He also has woman problems."

'He's a cross-dresser?' Jake asked.

Fritzi delivered her punchline. "Marvin has a lady friend."

Jake clapped his hand to his forehead. "He's been here, what, a month? And already he's found himself a woman?"

Unasked, Fritzi obliged with more details. "He lives on the second floor, but there he was at six thirty in the morning, coming down on the elevator from an upper floor when everyone except me was still asleep. I asked him, 'Marvin, what are you doing up so early?' He nodded to me sort of sheepish, and then he winked."

Having arrived that morning at breakfast, Marvin let it be known to all that in November he planned to go to the mountains with his son, Nathan, and his family."

"Why the mountains that time of year?" Jake asked. "It's cold and may snow. You'll be stuck up there with nothing to do."

"I'll go shopping at the outlets," Marvin said calmly.

Jake let out a snorting sound. "You shop at outlets? A man with your money?"

Marvin said he was proud to be a self-made man and always had a dollar in his pocket.

Jake couldn't resist. "And you still have that same dollar."

Marvin stuffed his cheeks with scrambled eggs. He spoke with a full mouth and spit out little pieces of yellow. "Benjamin Franklin said, if you take care of the pennies, the dollars will take care of themselves."

Bertha, fascinated by this conversation, felt obliged to join in. "A dollar doesn't buy what it used to, even at the Dollar Store."

Marvin seemed annoyed with Bertha for intruding on an exchange in which he and Jake faced each other down in an ongoing competition. "I was just quoting what Benjamin Franklin wrote," he said.

Jake made a noise with his mouth that sounded like *Puh!* or *Poof!* "Benjamin Franklin wasn't Jewish."

Marvin smiled. "No, but he was a womanizer. And didn't he have an illegitimate son who was governor of New Jersey?"

Jake addressed his remarks to the women. "See the character of the man he's quoting?" At this point, although he realized the absurdity of a debate that wasn't leading anywhere, he waited for an answer from Marvin, who didn't intend to give his opponent the satisfaction of a response.

Instead he lifted a utensil from an unused place setting. "Is this thing clean?" With his fingernail, he chipped away a microscopic spot on his tablespoon before dipping it into a bowl of milky oatmeal. For Marvin the confrontation had ended, and Jake was the loser.

Lydia felt it her duty to deflect the tension. "Has anyone seen that nice gentleman, Mr. Revelle, these past few days? Is he still at Verdant Valley?"

Jake turned to Willa, who said in her faint voice that she really didn't know where he was.

"Odd," Jake said. "When I called Eric at the nursing home yesterday, he told me you just paid a visit to his room."

Heads at the table strained to get a better view of Willa's stricken face. Fritzi Schnell leaned forward, determined not to miss a single detail. Willa choked on her grapefruit juice, and Jake, noticing her discomfort, tried to cover. "Probably Eric dreamed it. He's on a lot of medication."

The others nodded in sympathy and took to discussing the harsh effect ordinary drugs can have on older people. Only Fritzi remained quiet, smirking as she planned to make good use of what she had learned.

————◆————

*Tuesday, August 27.* My mind refuses to face the possibility that voice lessons with Eric may never happen again. This afternoon, instead of my usual long nap, I headed outside, down a maple-lined street, and wandered into a distant neighborhood lined with anonymous, two-story brick colonials left over from the post–World War II era. It was almost a duplicate of the suburban cul-de-sac where Aaron and I had lived for so many years. After we first came to SVM, I would walk there at least once a week for additional exercise and a kind of clandestine tryst.

On a secluded street nearby, stood a remnant of the previous century; it was a home I would love to have owned instead of the modern, cookie-cutter place that Aaron insisted we buy. My dream house was an authentic Victorian complete with turret, three dormer windows trimmed with gingerbread curlicues, an endless wraparound porch, and a shady yard. Who lived there I couldn't say.

I looked forward to passing the nineteenth-century homestead and especially a rendezvous with a mysterious white rabbit, isolated in a hutch at the side of the house. My plump, bewhiskered friend didn't realize how lucky he was. Penned away, exiled and idle, he seemed oblivious to unending warfare among nations, the melting of Antarctica, the rape of tropical rain forests, gun control, and endangered whales. Nor did he concern himself with racial strife, political hypocrisy, pestilence, or hunger. In freezing weather, although a khaki tarpaulin smothered the hutch to keep out the cold, my languishing lagomorph sat indifferent to fog and drizzle.

What's wrong with me? Why am I thinking about that phlegmatic rabbit when my dearest friend has just been carted off to the hospital? Should I ask Jake for Eric's room number, send a card, order flowers? Or would they both think it pushy, too Jewish motherly of me? Do I know him well enough to shlep over to St. Luke's for a visit? That's getting a little too personal, isn't it? Besides, Fritzi would have a ball if she found out.

No, back to the inscrutable cottontail! Today, when I returned to my favorite out-of-the-way street, I was certain that in my year's absence, Brer Rabbit had survived, season and after season. In the past he always seemed aloof from his gray kinfolk hopping freely from lawn to lawn. I could almost hear their conversations over the chicken-wire Berlin Wall that encased him. Hey, you, in the white velvet suit, what's it like to be a pampered capitalist in a gilded cage? Hey, you, in the gray Walmart wash pants, what's it like being chased by dogs?

Anyway, this time I wanted to cry. That indolent creature had vanished, disappeared, although I had never seen him move so much as an inch before. Even his pen was gone, his prison, his box within a box. We'd never see each other again.

Genug, to quote Yetta. Enough already. No more about that snowy-haired Bugs Bunny. What happened to him eventually happens to us all. And so after saying a warped prayer for Eric's recovery and another one for my dead rabbit, I've decided to avoid any more walks in that neighborhood.

I realize these fantasies of mine must be part of what social workers call the mourning process. The Judaic version is divided into four time zones: from the passing of the loved one to the burial, and then seven days after burial, and then the first thirty days after the loss, and finally the entire year following the death. Where's the workable blueprint for widows like me? Women of my generation don't know exactly what bereavement ought to be. In olden days, widowhood became a full-time career for grieving females of a certain class, but how long we should mourn in the twenty-first century? A day, a month, a year? Is there a celestial timer we can set to notify us when the period of sadness is over? Is it ever over?

And Dr. Holmes does not help much with advice for widows. He's more concerned with how a woman should blend into the life of a man. Herewith: "A woman notwithstanding she is the best of listeners, knows her business, and it is a woman's business to please. I don't say that it is

NOT her business to vote, but I do say that a woman who does not please is a false note in the harmonies of nature."

Granted, Holmes didn't oppose female suffrage when he wrote this more than fifty years before the Nineteenth Amendment, but I don't know what he means by those damned false notes in the harmonies of nature. Is a woman past eighty still obligated to please gentlemen, no matter her age or condition? And what's left for her to offer? Holmes tries to answer that question: "She may not have youth, or beauty...but she must have something in her voice or expression, which makes you feel better disposed toward your race to look at or listen to." And then he finishes with this condescending observation: "Her first question after you have been talking your soul into her consciousness is, Did I please? A woman never forgets her sex. She would rather talk with a man than an angel any day."

It all depends on the sensitivity of the man. Forget about chatting with angels. I'm not ready for that. I prefer masculine talk; Jake's rantings or even inaudible chats with Eric delight me more than hearing Bertha and Harriet debate the wisdom of soaking their feet before a visit to the podiatrist.

But my dear Dr. Holmes, why this? "The less there is of sex about a woman, the more she is to be dreaded. But take a real woman...at one moment she is microscopically intellectual, critical, scrupulous in judgment...and the next as sympathetic as the open rose..."

Isn't that also true of certain men? How could a real man like Eric live immersed in operatic love stories underscored by the most exquisite music ever imagined by the human soul—the melodies day after day, permeating his skin, his eyes, his heart—how can all this happen to him without his ever learning to interpret the true thoughts of a woman?

Eric won't go the way of the white rabbit. Not this time. When he returns from Verdant Valley, we'll resume those singing lessons right away. It may not do anything for my voice, but for both of us, it's a one-way bus ticket to rejuvenation.

## CHAPTER 11

———————

EACH MORNING AT BREAKFAST, BERTHA's nasty habit irritated Jake even more than the insensitivity of Renee or the smugness of Marvin the Marginal Mogul.

"Why do you keep doing this?" Jake said as she selected a fork from a nearby place setting and proceeded to pick her teeth. "That's a lethal weapon."

"I have floss in my bathroom," she said, "but I don't remember to bring it."

He made a disgusted face. "Use those wooden picks I brought you."

"That was real thoughtful of you, Jake."

"So where are they?"

Bertha continued digging away at her incisors with the fork. "My forgettery is working overtime these days."

"Stop it!" Jake said, red-faced and bothered. "You'll stab yourself and drip blood all over the tablecloth."

Willa, sipping her cranberry juice, ignored this little exchange. Bertha left the table earlier than usual for an appointment with her rheumatologist, and her seat was immediately occupied by Ethel, dragging the oxygen canister behind her. Willa remembered her only as someone to be avoided. Somehow she looked different. A thick braid that once hung down her back had disappeared. Her thick hair, now cut short, held a soft curl and seemed whiter than before.

"By the time I reached my regular table this morning, all seats were taken," Ethel said.

"What happened to your long pigtail?" Fritzi asked.

Ethel spoke in short pauses as if her breath had been doled out on an ungenerous scale, scarcely enough to complete more than three sentences at a time. "I donated it to a charity that makes wigs for cancer patients on chemotherapy. By next year I'll grow more hair to give away." She smiled as she unfolded a napkin and spread it on her lap. "It's the right thing to do."

Fritzi felt she had to clarify matters. "Today is OK, but we usually don't have room for newcomers at this table."

"Maybe," Ethel said, "I should wake up earlier and get here before anybody else." She stopped talking and concentrated on her cream of rice. Once or twice she looked around the table as if to gauge the quality of the group as a whole. On one of those glances, her eyes met Willa's, and they both nodded.

Willa wondered what kind of label Jake would attach to Ethel, but instead he welcomed her and introduced everyone by first name only, all except one. "That's Willa the Wordless," Jake said. "Maybe she'll talk to you. She doesn't to me."

"We've met before," Ethel said to her. "I saw you yesterday when I moved to your floor. They've finished renovating my new apartment. You were on the elevator, and we both got off at the same time, and you passed me as you walked to your place."

"Didn't see you," Willa lied.

"I was carrying a huge piece of tagboard covered with my collection of beetles."

"Didn't notice."

"And know what? We're next door to each other. I'm your new neighbor."

"That's nice," Willa said, but couldn't decide whether it was or not.

*Friday, August 30.* It's not a terribly attractive habit that Bertha has, attacking her teeth with a fork. Dr. Holmes would never allow his boarders to do that. Nor did he spend any effort describing the landlady's menu. Imagine three books filled with breakfast table conversations and nothing about what people ate. Two nights ago I leafed through page after page to learn what specific food those New Englanders consumed, and discovered only a vague reference in *Over the Teacups* to the maid Bridget, who was "putting something or other on the table." Obviously, that household wasn't Jewish.

In days to come, when Eric is finally discharged from Verdant Valley, I'll throw a tea party featuring corned-beef sandwiches on seeded rye and garlicky pickles. He'll be my only guest. After he marvels at all the titles on my Oliver Wendell Holmes bookshelf, our precious voice lessons will start again right there on the spot, and it will be one of many, God willing. I wish he were living next door instead of Ethel.

"My hobby is bugs of all kinds," she said one afternoon as she taped on her door a sign with bright-red letters that read, "Oxygen in Use, No Smoking, Non Fumar."

"Did you know monarch butterflies are in danger? But if we give them the right kind of milkweed for the females to lay their eggs in, we can save them from extinction."

She reminds me of a Holmes character known as the Scarabee. A fanatical lepidopterist, he adores insects but is more reserved than extroverted Ethel. On her third day in the new apartment, Ethel dropped off my morning newspaper delivered to her by mistake. I didn't care to ask her in. Entertaining strangers takes too much effort from me, but at least she didn't act hurt. The following day in the elevator she asked if her television could be heard through the walls. Did I want her to turn the volume down? I just had to say the word, and she would. "I don't want to disturb my neighbors," she keeps saying, with that sincere look on her face that tells me she means every word. "That's not the right thing to do."

Ethel has such a trusting air that even when her optimism grates on me, I keep quiet. She constantly struggles with a pulmonary problem and has a tube hanging from her nose like a plastic icicle. Back and forth she shleps that monster of an oxygen canister. "It follows me everywhere," she says, "like Mary's little lamb."

Lydia likes Ethel so much, she invited her to become a member of our breakfast table entourage. Not counting Eric's temporary absences, we have a sudden permanent vacancy. The would-be writer, Shirley Schreiber, has joined her daughter in Alaska. Global warming has its advantages.

Ethel told us she worked as a stenographer at the Central State Penitentiary and cared for her invalid mother because "it was the right thing to do, even though she was pretty grumpy." After battling post-polio syndrome for years, the old woman died, leaving her only child unmarried, alone, and no longer young.

"But," as she informed me when we chatted while picking up our mail in the lobby, "I'm provided for. Dad died of tuberculosis, and Mom worked in a hat factory for a while. We never had much until she inherited a pile of money from my beautiful Aunt Sandra, who married the owner of a luggage factory. Mom wasn't a big spender. With what she left me plus my pension, I can live in this nice place with plants in the lobby and yellow and blue tropical fish to watch. Do you ever stop to look at them?"

"Not really."

"Aren't we lucky to live here?" she said.

That's naïve but refreshing. Yesterday morning after I overslept and missed breakfast because leg cramps kept me up all night, Ethel knocked on the door.

"Are you all right?" she asked, genuinely concerned. "You always pick up your newspaper early, and when I saw it still lying there at ten o'clock, I got worried." She handed it to me and it seemed rude not to invite her in for a moment although I'll not make a habit of it.

In the cluttered living room, Ethel marveled at the floor-to-ceiling bookcases and pointed to Aaron's photograph on the wall. "Your husband?"

"Forty years ago."

She studied it carefully, as if she intended to make a drawing of it. "He has a kind face. You were married how long?"

"Fifty-three years."

She took my hand. "You were blessed to have him that long."

I pulled away fast. For weeks Aaron has been neatly, deliberately shut out of my thoughts, a fugitive from memory. He and I had been happy together, but there was no reason to blather on and on about my marriage to a stranger.

Although uninvited, Ethel lingered. "Were you childhood sweethearts?"

And then for some ungodly reason, the dam broke, my whispery voice took over, unleashed at last, and I described how Aaron and I met as undergraduates, how as freshmen we both joined the staff of *Mushrooms and Martyrs*, our spunky campus magazine, how one thing led to another.

"What fun that must have been working together, two young people in love."

I couldn't stop. My hoarse words ran wild with submerged details, everything from our Girl Scout troop in Braddock to junior year at State U, when *Mademoiselle* magazine chose me for its College Board. "The prize was a month in New York as a guest editor for their annual college issue."

"Sounds exciting, Willa. A paying job?"

"Foot in the door. Winners could meet bigwig publishers and interview celebrities like Agnes de Mille and Carson McCullers. It wasn't all writing and editing. The chosen girls posed as models in good clothes, lots of cashmere sweaters from Scotland and tartan skirts and crepe jersey gowns draped Greek-style, off-one-shoulder."

"You were just the right height for a fashion model, tall, slim."

"The editors gave us assignments throughout the year and contestants were picked from campuses all over the country, mostly places like Vasser and Smith."

"Did you win?"

"No. I was in the top fifty but not the lucky top twenty."

"Still, look how far you got."

"Losing had its bright side. Otherwise I probably would have moved to New York right after college and never married Aaron."

"So it worked out for the best."

"Ever hear of a poet named Sylvia Plath?"

"I'm not a poetry reader."

"She made it. Before they returned home, the *Mademoiselle* college editors were always given the fancy clothes they had modeled. Really expensive stuff. And know what Sylvia Plath did? She spent her last day in New York tossing everything off a skyscraper roof."

Ethel stared at me. "Why would she do a thing like that? I'd still be wearing those things to this day."

"Me too." We both laughed, and then she asked about Aaron.

It hurt my throat to continue talking. "At State U he majored in business and public administration, and afterward worked in his father's advertising agency."

"The family business."

"After college Aaron recommended they hire me as a copywriter. Not much later we married, his parents retired......and do you really want to hear all of this?"

Bedazzled by it all, Ethel insisted I continue. "I loved that show on television about advertising people," she said. "It's so glamorous, isn't it?"

"Maybe in New York, but not in grubby agencies out of town. With Aaron and me it was mostly retail accounts, and I didn't have the knack to go door to door begging reluctant storeowners to run cheesy little ads in the local papers."

Before the famous TV series, Ethel said, she never even thought about anybody actually sitting down and thinking up ads. "And where did you go from there?"

I didn't feel it necessary to mention my three miscarriages. "Kept house for Aaron, wrote unpublished poetry, joined Hadassah. Finally, to get me out of the house, my husband pulled strings and found me a job on the State Arts Commission, reading grant proposals." My voice gave out. "Tea?" I croaked, and she nodded. At the kitchen sink I found two slightly used Styrofoam cups, which I rinsed and filled with enough steaming water to cover a decaffeinated tea bag, and then, never a classy hostess, I slapped two Power Bars on a paper plate.

"There was one great love in my life," Ethel said, "one summer forty years ago on a cruise to Victoria, Sitka, Juneau, you know, the Inland Waterway."

So far my morning of solitude was shot to hell; I gestured toward the badly sagging couch.

With a relieved sigh, Ethel settled into the understuffed pillows. "Mom hated the idea, but I needed a break and hired an aide for her. The trip was sponsored by State U. It had nice lectures by retired college professors about whales, totem poles, even Alaskan bugs." She pulled the oxygen tank closer to her feet and paused for breath. "On board ship a professional string quartet gave chamber music concerts every evening."

"I didn't know you like classical music."

"I don't, but there was a handsome viola player in the ensemble," she said. "We met strolling on deck and had lots in common. Right away I knew Paul was the one. I had just turned forty and never met anyone like him before."

"What happened?"

"Listening to him play made me cry buckets. He became my beau."

I sipped my tea and could imagine Lydia saying, "Beau. Now that's a word you don't hear much these days."

Ethel's voice softened. "He liked me," she said. She finished her tea. The Power Bar lay uneaten on the paper plate. "Where do you want me to put this?"

"Leave it on your TV table."

She wiped her mouth with the paper napkin. "I gave him my heart. The last night of the cruise when we were supposed to exchange phone numbers and addresses, Paul confessed he was engaged to be married."

"Sorry to hear that."

"Don't be. It's an old, old story." She looked into my eyes for verification. Dr. Holmes had it right. Women live to please.

"We keep looking for happy endings," I said, not knowing what else to answer.

"Paul did enjoy my company."

I consulted the digital clock on the TV set. Too much wasted time. Yesterday's laundry needed folding, after which I had planned to watch Classic Arts Showcase on the satellite channel in hopes of finding a repeat performance by baritone Thomas Hampson singing "Lord Randall" with a Scottish burr. There was a sweetness in his upper register, a tender longing, but I was sure Eric could have done it even better.

"Willa, please don't be sad. I'm grateful for those two weeks on board ship." Ethel stood upon shaky legs. "Thank you for the nice cup of tea," she said, swaying from side to side until she established her balance. She moved, tortoise-slow, dragging the canister behind her. Before opening the front door, she paused again at Aaron's framed headshot and ran a pale hand over it as if she were stroking his face.

"I had barely two weeks with mine," she said. "You lived more than a half century with yours." We hugged, and she was gone.

Ethel's Goody-Two-shoes attitude annoys me, and yet somehow we hit it off except for the bug collection. Maybe I'll confide in her about Eric if she can be trusted not to give Fritzi more outlines to embroider.

## CHAPTER 12

———◆———

AT BREAKFAST THE CONVERSATION CENTERED around Howie the Unwholesome Wholesaler. "Did you know he's back from Chicago?" Fritzi asked Renee Richmond, who had just reached the table.

Abandoning her top-of-the-line walker in the direct path of passers-by who could trip over it, Renee pulled out an empty chair. "Cinnamon doughnut and black coffee," she told the hovering Namibian waitress. "Make it snappy. My daughter is picking me up for acupuncture in fifteen minutes." She wrinkled her nose. "In Chicago Howie has a woman he's been living with for years. It's three months here, three months there, and another two in Boca, where he's lined up a whole harem."

Fritzi said she knew a lot about those Florida retirement places. "I heard a story from someone the other day about two men who moved there with their wives and the first day when they were all taking a walk together, a strange woman came up to them, and right there on the spot said she was looking for a man and asked would they be interested. In front of their wives!"

"Too bad she didn't run into Howie," Diana said.

Renee turned abruptly to a passing heavyset man. "Keep your hands off my walker!" Renee yelled. "If you didn't take up so much freaking space, you wouldn't bump into it." The indignant gentleman retreated, muttering, "So don't leave it in the aisle where I can trip and break my neck."

Bertha insisted on knowing why Renee hated Howie so much.

"He ruined my fourth husband's memorial service at the country club."

"How?" Fritzi asked, moving closer.

"Everybody showed up. Even his proctologist and tax lawyers. So there we all are, nobody moves, nobody talks except for the boring speeches. Halfway into the service, Howie wanders in. He looks the crowd over and says in a voice that splits our eardrums, 'So what's cooking in here?'"

"Did he leave when he found out what it was?" Harriet asked.

"No, he takes an empty seat on the front row next to the mourners. Now tell me, who else goes to a memorial service, sits on the front row, and falls asleep, snoring his ass off?"

Willa finished her tea, excused herself inaudibly, and retreated to her journal. Instead of reaching for one of the Breakfast Table volumes, she selected a dusty black book of poems left from an ill-fated college course in American literature. Absent with acute dysmenorrhea throughout the semester, she had missed handing in a term paper and did poorly on the final. She meant to catch up somehow but never got around to it.

Now, flipping the yellowed pages of the old textbook, she stopped at a Holmes poem she had never been able to read all the way through. She slowly whispered the lines to herself as she tackled the five stanzas, line by line, and realized it wasn't half bad. She especially liked the beginning of "The Chambered Nautilus": "This is the ship of pearl, which, poets feign / Sails the unshadowed main..." When she had more time, she might even try memorizing the whole thing.

But before that, she promised herself to outline specific preparations for a memorable visit to Eric in rehab.

———◆———

*Monday, September 2.* Labor Day and nothing's going on. I still haven't been to see Eric yet. Today as we sipped bottled spring water in my apartment, I asked Ethel if she ever daydreams. "Sure," she said, "I think of my shipboard romance and what would have happened if Paul hadn't married someone else."

"And then?"

"And then he would give up the viola for me, and I'd work to put him through medical school. We'd tie the knot first. Although Daddy had been Irish Catholic, my Jewish mother would insist we be married by a rabbi at her bedside. She'd write us an enormous check to make a down payment on a gingerbread cottage in a woods filled with white birch trees and monarch butterflies." Ethel closed her eyes. "How about you?"

I had visions of a Versailles garden, where Romance and Reality, in black velvet waistcoats trimmed with gold braid, duel for my bejeweled hand, unsullied by sunspots. I offered Ethel honey popcorn from an open bag. "My dreams are more reckless," I said.

"Because you're you. I was a clerk-typist for the warden. He ran the entire operation at Central State Penitentiary."

"The top man?"

She nodded. "People considered him a tough boss to work for, but I saw Warden Grosz as an emperor ruling over his enemies in a magical gray-stone castle."

I realized then that Ethel was to the opera born and said, "Sometimes on an enormous stage, I play a gorgeous young soprano half-swooning in distress."

Ethel plunged right in. "Close your eyes. What else do you see?"

"A white chiffon hood frames my blond corkscrew curls." The wordy mouthful made me draw so many deep breaths that my left arm tingled. I resumed whispering.

"Yes," Ethel said in awe, "then what?" Silent in the timeless afternoon, the two of us dug into the popcorn.

My voice grew foggier, but she could understand me. "I'm wearing a hoop skirt, eighteenth century style, like Marie Antoinette. Voluminous sleeves of my sky-blue gown billow dramatically. They're propelled by a hidden wind machine at stage right. Two bearded young men named Romance and Reality draw their swords, parry, and thrust. I flutter about in delicious helplessness."

"What's happens next in your dream, Willa?"

"I plead with my suitors to drop their swords before someone gets hurt."

Ethel entered the scene full blast. "And I'm your loyal nurse and yell, 'Stop! Stop! Or I'll call Warden Grosz and it's a month in solitary for both of you.'" We giggled. "Are they hollering at each other?"

"Singing."

Ethel said yes, she could see it all. "Who's ahead now?"

"Root for the baritone."

In my mind a tenor and a baritone are popping their vocal cords with emotion as they clank swords. Neither expects me to play any role in this battle because they know I can't read music. The fierce encounter ends. One singer lies on the floor, glad to rest from an exhausting duet. The other rushes to embrace me. It's the baritone, who bursts into an aria about his boundless love. My voice doesn't hold up long enough to finish describing all this to Ethel. We open our eyes.

"So who wins?" Ethel asked. "Romance or Reality?"

"Don't you know?"

"Never did." Ethel looked more drained than usual. "I ought to take a little nap before dinner," she said with a quick glance at her watch.

"That was my best daydream ever."

"Mine too, Willa." She stood, readjusted the tubes in her nose, and gently pulling the oxygen canister behind her, hobbled out the door.

Ethel has convinced me. Romance never quits. Even that crusty New Englander, Holmes, thought so too, when he left this lavender-tinted passage for my eyes to read a full century and a half later:

Once in a while one meets with a single soul greater than the living pageant...This was one of them...sorrow had baptized her; the routine of labor and loneliness...were before her. Yet, as I looked upon her tranquil face, gradually regaining a cheerfulness which was often sprightly...I saw that eye and lip and every shifting lineament made for love, unconscious of their sweet office as yet, and meeting the cold aspect of Duty with the natural graces which were meant for the reward of nothing less than the Grand Passion.

Holmes goes no further. Grand Passion? What kind of prescription is the doctor handing me?

# PART THREE

---

*It is in the hospitable soul of a woman that a man forgets he is a stranger, and so becomes natural and truthful, at the same time he is mesmerized by all those divine differences which make her a mystery and a bewilderment.*

OWH

PART THREE

# CHAPTER 1

———•———

THE NEXT MORNING OFFERED A popular breakfast treat, french toast, bountiful plates heavy with glistening fried challah bread oozing cinnamon. Fritzi arrived late, found a vacant chair next to the wall, and dragged it over to the table, already at full capacity.

"Willa, I forgot to tell you," Fritzi said. "That singer who used to eat with us? After he left Verdant Valley Rehab, he returned here for a day, and now he's back in the hospital."

Willa made no comment. She continued swallowing and pretended to enjoy the treat everyone raved about. A piece of gooey bread slid from her fork into her lap.

"Did Eric fall again?" Bertha asked.

Fritzi shrugged. "My friend Lena lives two apartments down from him. She overheard the rescue squad in the hall but didn't even open her door. Some people have no curiosity."

Willa dabbed her napkin at the stickiness on her jeans. Fritzi continued to observe Willa with steely, judgmental eyes.

Jake chose that moment to introduce a favorite subject. "What happened to Eric illustrates our compromise with God."

Yetta the Yiddishist, brought up in the Workman's Circle socialist tradition, corrected him. "With nature. Some of us don't believe in God."

"Let me finish, woman," Jake said, an annoyed look on his face. "OK, so we bargain with Grandma Nature and tell her, 'Go ahead. Sabotage my body. Ruin my face. Just let me live a few years longer.'"

Renee Richmond slammed her napkin down and stood on uncertain legs. "Jake, you're too freaking morbid. Besides," she added, "you never heard of getting a facelift or going to a first-class spa for a makeover?" She yanked her walker toward her. "I'm moving to that table where those idiots laugh all the time." Renee left, pushing her way through a thorny nest of parked walkers.

"That one has got a mouth on her," Bertha said, and turned to Jake. "What's your next talk about, Jake?"

"I call it Outstanding Jewish Thinkers Most Jews Never Heard Of," Jake said, deadpan.

Bertha moved her plump body closer to him. "For instance?"

"You never heard of them," Jake said. Willa smiled. She hadn't until this moment realized that Jake had such a dry sense of humor.

"You're so religious," Bertha said. "Always talking about God."

"Wrong. Ever hear of spontaneous combustion?"

"Why?" Yetta said.

"My lectures aren't Orthodox, Reform, Conservative, or Reconstructionist. I call myself a Recombustionist."

"What's that, you mishuganer?" Yetta asked.

"Like in that old Ink Spots song. I don't want to set the world on fire. I just want to start a flame in their hearts. After that, it's up to them."

Willa slumped in her chair after the others left the table. Eric had fallen again, and she didn't know what to do. She should make a list of options. Combing through her handbag, she found neither pen nor paper, only a well-worn eyebrow pencil and a return postage paid envelope from AARP. She felt a hand on her shoulder.

"I waited in the lobby for the ladies to finish their meal," Jake said, parking next to her and turning off the scooter switch. "Relax," he said. "Last time Eric fell, his niece came from out of town. She's probably here again with him now."

"He hasn't anyone else?"

Jake shook his head. "Don't take it so hard. In a place like this," he said with a gentleness he rarely showed, "you have to observe the rules of the Professional Old Persons Society. You begin with detachment. That means setting up boundaries, like a doctor or a nurse. People like us should get involved in other lives only so far and no farther."

"Hard to do."

"It's OK being sympathetic, but don't go overboard. Because it can destroy you. The Talmud tells us not to grieve too long; that's selfish and arrogant. In our grief it's impossible to compete with God. Do you think we're more compassionate than the Almighty?"

"You said you can't believe in God anymore."

"Sometimes you con and sometimes you con't." Jake gave her a broad wink and consulted his watch. "The cleaning woman comes at nine thirty. My place looks like a tsunami just struck. Got to bulldoze before she gets there. Listen, Willa, it's sunny outside. Go for a walk and clear your head."

He inserted a dangling key into the lock, revved up his scooter, and exited fast, leaving Willa in what Holmes called "passive cerebration," which she considered a more dignified way of saying "a blue funk." The garrulous Bostonian would have made a good copywriter except for his large vocabulary. His literary colleagues said he could write to order on deadline, whatever the occasion demanded, a birthday poem, a wedding toast, a moving eulogy.

Willa fixed her eyes on a trail of spilled coffee leading nowhere. Although it made the cavernous dining room seem more livable, it didn't show her which way to go next.

---

*Tuesday, September 3.* Returning to the apartment, I switched on Classic Arts Showcase, where a young Yehuda Menhuin was playing Mendelssohn's Violin Concerto in E Minor, Opus 64. The first movement obliterated my demons and inspired a to-do list full of promise:

1. Call hospital to make sure Eric hasn't checked out yet for Verdant Valley Rehab. 2. Don't buy flowers or plants; he has allergies. 4. Prepare sparkling conversation, search newspaper for concerts in town, and include

nasty review of Mostly Muzorksky program at Performing Arts Center. 5. Bring gourmet cookies (something foreign) from upscale supermarket. 6. Wrap package in red and gold paper bought last year at CVS after-Christmas sale. 7. Reread Dr. Holmes on nineteenth century hospitals, and reassure Eric that modern ones aren't that dangerous anymore. 8. Do not mention drug-resistant superbugs that cause infection in elderly patients.

I still haven't summoned the energy to call a cab and drag over to St. Luke's on the other side of town. My two feet, bulging with twin bunions, won't take me in the right direction. Not yet anyway.

It's too soon to relive those months of running back and forth each day to watch Aaron dwindle down to less and less of himself. Am I ready for a return engagement, trudging through deadly hospital corridors and greeting the same medical employees with a martyred half smile, my face aching with the strain of putting on a brave front? I detest the clinical metronomic pace, the mechanical dirge of announcements over the loudspeakers, and doors left ajar with raw heartbreak in full view.

When I confide in Ethel, she hugs me and says if I phone, the hospital won't give out specific patient information because I'm not a blood relative.

"But you can see for yourself how Eric is getting along. Visit him!" Ethel says in her gung-ho, cheerleader voice. "It's the right thing to do."

Meanwhile, time evaporates. My restless inner voice murmurs, "Call St. Luke's. Find out if he's still there." And what if he's neither there nor at Verdant Valley? He didn't give me his niece's address in Seattle. If we can find a phone number somewhere, Ethel offered to call her. My voice fights me whenever I pick up the receiver. For the simplest call, I must write down each word ahead of time and read it like a play script. Even then, strangers don't understand what I'm saying, and hang up.

As I told Ethel yesterday when she dropped by, "I'm not an outgoing person. Introverts like me should never develop spasmodic dysphonia. It's even too difficult to pronounce."

She grinned, reached into her canvas bag, and handed me three tangerines. "You said a mouthful, kid."

"Spasmodic dysphonia has seven whole syllables, Ethel. Count them."

"That's nothing. Pulmonary hypertension has nine."

"Why can't every sickness at least be easier to say? Like 'piles' or 'mumps.'"

Ethel's smile illuminated the gray morning. "Or 'shingles,' two measly syllables."

Chatting with her always calms me down. Later, the classical music station soothed me further with the soaring notes of Chopin's Etude Number Four in C Sharp Minor, a familiar piece, but until now, I never knew the name. It's more important than ever to dig deeper into good music; that way I'll be better prepared for Eric's return when we can resume our musical fantasies together.

A relaxing nap before dinner has convinced me that his accident was minor, nothing to worry about. Besides, opera singers learn in their acting classes how to fall on stage without breaking anything. He'll be OK, back home soon. Of that I'm certain. Silly me.

After dinner I revisited *Over the Teacups* and found this: "I must have my paper and pen...to set my thoughts flowing in such form that they can be written continuously...There are authors...who can compose and finish off a poem or a story without writing a word of it until, when the proper time comes, the copy...they carry in their heads."

But not Holmes and not me. Later, at 3:00 a.m., a mass of disjointed lines expanded inside my head and put an end to any sleep before daylight. The sonnet didn't exactly tumble into place; a Petrarchan rhyme scheme is tricky, but by 6:00 a.m., the following had risen to the surface:

### Retro
by Willa Warshaw
First Love, the hypochondriac's disguise,
Turns sick at heart, and in a moment well,
Its puppy symptoms, only time will tell
What malady, or where the fever lies,
Or if the ailment dressed in healing sighs

And stimulated by the frenzied bell,
Are more than worldly prophets can foretell
Or less than youthful couplets analyze.
Much healthier are lovers near the close
Of life, who shun the bittersweet malaise,
The vertigo of lips and sun-kissed locks;
More circumscribed by calendars and clocks,
The hale survivors wink at languid days
Before the doggerel gave way to prose.

Into the mail with it! Eric should receive it at St. Luke's, but if they've discharged him, the hospital may not forward it to Verdant Valley Rehab. So maybe I should wait and save my energy. I'm a wreck today. Working all night on the poem has left me in no condition to raise up a fallen comrade. Hope no bug has hit me.

## CHAPTER 2

———◆———

THE BREAKFAST TABLE BUZZED WITH serious talk for a change. A frail, osteoporosis-ravaged woman named Clara had done something awful to herself, so spake Fritzi.

"I heard a commotion in the hall and cracked open my door. Standing around were four people from the County Rescue Squad plus Dr. Patal from the medical office plus the new social worker lady, all outside Clara's place."

"How can you remember all that?" Bertha asked. "You must not have a good forgettery like me."

Fritzi continued. "Next came two men pushing her on a gurney. When I tried to follow them and ask what happened, the social worker lady told me I should respect Clara's privacy and go back to my apartment."

"But naturally you didn't," Jake said, his mouth full of hash browns.

"Nobody tells me what to do. I grabbed my shopping cart and rushed down the hall behind them so if they told me to go back, I could act insulted and argue that I always do my shopping at this time on Tuesdays."

"What was wrong with Clara?" Harriet asked. "We're supposed to have lunch together tomorrow at the diner."

Fritzi took a deep breath. "Her aide, Lola, keeps medicine bottles on a high shelf in the kitchen so Clara can't reach them. And when Lola left for a few minutes to collect a package from the front desk, Clara climbed up on a chair."

Bertha gasped. "She fell?"

"The aide didn't know exactly what happened. Clara was unconscious. She either grabbed the wrong pills or took too many. They pumped her stomach and took her to St. Luke's in the ambulance."

Jake shoveled a forkful of Eggbeaters into his mouth. "Change the channel, ladies. It's none of our business." He sounded more irascible than usual, swallowed recklessly, and broke into a major coughing spell.

"Your new cough medicine isn't working," Bertha said.

"Ever notice," Flo the Faux Blonde said, "the more dangerous the drug, the smaller the print on the package? They may put 'warning' in bigger and darker letters, but the part that explains why we should be careful is teeny tiny."

"It should be king-size so older people can read it," Bertha said.

"What I hate," Flo said, "is when commercials show what happens later after they take the stuff. Everybody looks too happy."

"That's right," Harriet said in wonder. "They're laughing and digging in their gardens or patting cute dogs."

Flo agreed. "And exactly that's when the announcer lists the side effects or warns not to take the medicine in the first place if you have this condition or that condition."

"Those happy faces distract you from worrying about how dangerous the drug is," Jake said. "Otherwise the pharmaceutical plutocrats won't rake in the profits."

Jake noticed that Willa had leaned forward to hear better. "C...copywriters must be c...careful," she said. She looked surprised by her own comment and an unexpected stammer. The others stopped eating long enough to stare at her.

"What?" Bertha asked. "What did she say?"

Jake felt he had to intervene. "Ads never claim a drug cures anything. The company could be sued. They only suggest what the product can do. Then they build on the customer's imagination with pictures of happy-go-lucky idiots strolling on the beach. Commercials never show someone having a bad drug reaction. That'll be the day, right, Willa?"

Although she tried to crawl back into silence by merely nodding, Jake pressed on. "You seem to know something about it."

"My son-in-law Larry worked for an advertising agency in New York, and it was crazy," Bertha said. "One time when he was working late—"

Jake cut her off. "We know all about your son-in-law. I want to hear what Willa has to say." All eyes turned to her. Her throat muscles tightened; her breath wasn't working the way it should have, and she paused between each hard-earned word. "We owned the Aaron Warsaw Agency."

"Really?" Jake said. "Their clients ran ads in a couple of the Jewish newspapers I wrote for. What was that swill they tried to unload on the naïve public?"

A painful subject. Willa tried to smile. "Samaria Wine."

"Foul-tasting concord-grape stuff. And they also had a lousy slogan."

"Don't remember," she lied, standing, escape on her mind. The last thing in the world she wanted to discuss was her dismal slogan for a lucrative account she had massacred. When Aaron gave her the chance to handle it, she botched the whole campaign. She should have known better than to try to sell winos that cheap bilge by quoting passages from Edward Fitzgerald's *Rubaiyat of Omar Khayyam*. Aaron often defended her choices, until the clients walked out, taking their business with them.

Jake clapped his gnarled hands together. "Got it. 'A loaf of bread, a jug of wine, and thou...Samaria Wine...Sip Some More of It.' Haven't thought of it in years." He frowned. "And I'm a better man for that. So were you in the business with your husband?"

A sweaty flush colored Willa's forehead. "Copywriter."

"Mom-and-pop agency?"

"Yes." She pushed her chair away from the table. "It didn't work out for me." She was straining hard to be heard, and the effort exhausted her.

Fritzi wanted to know more. "Why not?"

The entire table stopped eating to listen. Words came out of her in an almost inaudible whisper. "We wanted to have a family." She hadn't meant to say that. Nobody's business.

"I didn't know you had kids." Fritzi sounded resentful as if she had been deprived of air or water. Willa wiped her lips with a blue linen napkin and reached under the table for her shoulder bag.

Fritzi pushed ahead. "So how many children do you have?"

"None." Willa stood. "I've things to do," she said, and walked away fast before anyone could ask more questions.

"Tomorrow my daughter drives me to St. Luke's for blood work," Bertha said, raising her voice so that it could reach Willa's ears. "Plenty of room in her car if anyone wants to visit a friend!"

———◆———

*Wednesday, September 4.* Never again will I let strangers root around in my personal life. And I'll accept no uncomfortable rides to the hospital with inquisitive outsiders. If I do decide to spend private time with Eric, nobody has to know, and I'll take a cab.

Then why put it off? Aaron used to say that procrastination is a terrible thing to waste. All right, I'm a coward. Besides, tonight Rosh Hashanah begins, and the next two days are not a good time for hospital visits, when my thoughts should center on deciding how to live the rest of my life. Eric will be out of St. Luke's before we know it. Also my throat feels scratchy; no point carrying germs to the hospital. It has too many already.

Jake, who saw Eric yesterday, gave us a full report anyway. Our patient will be discharged as soon as they knock out an infection he developed from scraping his ankle when he fell. He'll go to Verdant Valley Rehab for a short stay before he returns here. Why exhaust him with an endless stream of visitors?

The main thing is that when he comes back, I'll entertain him with quotes from Holmes and theories about his split doctor/author personality. I'll ask Eric specific questions about his glorious career too. The operatic roles he performed, his love of German lieder, his favorite orchestras and conductors, his adventures touring on the road. There's a ton of subjects we've never explored, and I feel cheated. What was he like as a younger man, at sixty, forty, twenty? How did he spend his time when not rehearsing; what efforts went into memorizing scores in French, German, and Italian? And what famous performers appeared with him on stage? Who are his favorite singers?

So much to talk about. With his voice limitations and mine, we've been able to give each other only tidbits of ourselves. He must have received my Petrarchan sonnet by now, but can he read it? His eyes have been troubling him for months. I'm sure he will want to resume our voice lessons as soon as he can. Perhaps he'll even ask, "But was Oliver Wendell Holmes good for music?" I've already discovered this answer to that question: "Some...people will perhaps find that they have a dormant faculty which is at last waking up, and that...they are listening (to music) with a newly found delight. Every one of us has a harp under bodice or waistcoat, and if it can only once get properly strung and tuned it will respond to all outside harmonies."

That's charming but dated. Try hiding a harp under your bodice and getting past airport security these days. Today I skipped breakfast again. Headachy and not very chipper.

# CHAPTER 3

———◆———

DURING THE HIGH HOLY DAYS, absentees at the Esther Essenvarg Dining Den outnumbered the handful of residents not spending that time with their families or preparing to attend one of the four religious services held at SVM. The nonobservant celebrated the birthday of the world by just watching it pass by. Jake attended an Orthodox synagogue near the VA Hospital. "Contrary to the theme song of that old TV show," he said, "I like to go where nobody knows my name."

Fritzi, who claimed she had turned down three or four invitations to spend the holidays in Florida with wealthy friends, continued her updated reports on Clara, Bertha's friend, who remained at St. Luke's under observation because the doctors concluded she hadn't overdosed by mistake.

"You mean suicide?" Flo asked.

"Maybe," Fritzi continued, "and Eric Revelle is back at Verdant Valley Rehab now."

"Where's Willa?" Jake asked. "She'll be glad to hear it."

"I'll bet she will," Fritzi muttered. There was no reaction from the others, and Fritzi seized the moment. "Has anybody seen her or Ethel around anywhere?"

"They never came to holiday services," Lydia sighed. "I missed them both."

"There's something untidy about Willa," Jake said. "I like that in a woman."

Fritzi wasn't going to mention names, but she could swear a certain man and a certain woman at SVM were having an affair. "And everybody knows."

"They do now," Jake said.

Fritzi continued. "The whole place is talking."

"Only if you distribute flyers about it. The man in question suffers from a chronic condition and spends a lot of time in the hospital when he's not in rehab," Jake said. "That's some hot romance."

"My guess is she's with him right this minute," Fritzi said.

Jake launched into a favorite topic. "The sages tell us it's a sin to spread gossip. Guard our tongues from speaking guile. Sound familiar? Do me a favor, Fritzi. Take a break and start the new year right."

"Haven't you ever watched them looking at each other?"

"When you face somebody at the same table," Bertha said, "there's nowhere else to look."

The others disappeared for a session on the Nu-Step machines in the Gedalia Ginsfarb Fitness Garden. Jake waited until only Lydia remained. "I'm concerned about Willa," he said.

Lydia daintily raised a tiny square of cantaloupe to her mouth. "Our dear friend Ethel is watching out for her."

Jake propped his elbow on the table and rested his chin on folded arthritic hands lined with bulging veins that looked like a grid of superhighways merging into each other. "I've seen strangers come and go in the last three years. Occasionally, when two people of the opposite sex meet here, they hit it off and become a couple."

"Yes. That's enchanting, isn't it?"

"Is it? A woman can become attached to a man in worse shape than she is, but it rarely happens the other way around."

"Men want to be pampered, Jake."

"Well, a man isn't attracted to a sick woman he has to take care of. On the other hand, certain women may realize what they're getting into but become entangled anyway. Do you get what I'm saying?"

"I recall a line by Edna St. Vincent Millay. 'Pity me that the heart is slow to learn / What the swift mind perceives at every turn.'" Lydia stared into space, remembering more than what she recited.

"The real question is why should Willa get so involved with him at this time of life?"

Lydia patted Jake's hand. "A man in need stirs up the maternal in a woman. Or he reminds her of her departed husband. Or he's the opposite of the man she married long ago when she was young, and that charms her. A multitude of beautiful reasons."

"Senile infatuation."

"Love."

Jake shrugged his boney shoulders. "Love through the courtesy of low vision and impaired hearing. I remember another couple here. The woman mothered the guy. She pushed his wheelchair to meals and took him for walks outside. She also made phone calls for him and knew the names of his children and grandchildren."

"Perhaps she enjoyed worrying about him, Jake. It gave her something worthwhile to do. She was useful again."

"The guy welcomed it. Didn't cost him a penny. He flattered her and gave her compliments all the time. Her own health went downhill. You could see she wanted to end the whole thing but couldn't. One time I overheard him begging her not to desert him."

"Who can refuse a cry for help?"

"So she wore herself out for a person she scarcely knew. The man passed away. She was left alone in worse shape than he ever had been."

"You have no romance in your soul, my cynical Jake."

"She could have avoided the whole thing."

"And deny herself love and companionship?" Lydia touched his shoulder gently. "I have to go shopping for bedroom slippers with softer soles. The ones my son bought gave me too many seed corns on the bottom of my right foot." She neatly folded her napkin into a triangle. "Thank you for this provocative discussion," she said. "I'll remember your words the next time I meet an attractive man."

After a Namibian aide took Lydia away in her wheelchair, Jake sat a long time alone, looking at Willa's empty chair. He missed her silence.

———

*Wednesday, September 25.* Too many blank pages. I'll try catching up today. Three weeks ago I woke up one day with a dull headache and slight nausea, worsened by the prospect of an eye doctor's appointment looming ahead at ten thirty that same morning. My voice wasn't up to the strain of dealing with the receptionist who never understands me on the phone. I debated with myself over what to do until Ethel yelled through the door, "You missed breakfast. Everything all right?"

"Getting dressed," I called, reaching for a bra on the floor. "Appointment with Dr. Rosen today. Must go."

She advised me to cancel it. Her words, usually soothing and thoughtful, did nothing to chase away my anxiety. Something I couldn't explain was happening to me, and I didn't know whether to be cautious, worried, or terrified.

Denial is a human art. Caregivers excel at it. With Aaron ill, I trained myself to ignore the condition of all my body parts, especially the eyes, which had already begun playing a spooky game of now-you-see-it-now-you-don't. Each day the fuzziness increased, and the effort to read even the shortest newspaper articles left me with monstrous headaches. It also threatened quality time spent with Oliver Wendell Holmes.

I had already missed Rosh Hashanah and the Yom Kippur yizkor memorial services at which I intended to recite Kaddish for Aaron. On those days the headaches worsened, and my misery increased. The appointment with Dr. Rosen was worth keeping; I pulled on jeans, unearthed a wrinkled blouse from the laundry hamper, grabbed a broken umbrella, and trudged blindly through a chilly drizzle to a nearby street corner.

Traffic worsens on rainy days; once I boarded the free ride-on bus for senior citizens, we barely crept along. I noticed one lane of the street blocked off with orange cones. A touch to my hot, sweaty face convinced me I should have crawled back into bed instead of running to catch this exhaust-filled, overheated bus, but it was too late to turn back.

Another compromise with God, a choice between submitting to flu or saving my eyesight, select one. On a shabby avenue of rundown stores, we came to a dead halt in front of a theatrical costume shop called Pop's Props and Play Things. Strange, I never noticed it before.

In the store window an undulating black shape drifted into place. It looked like what Dr. Rosen would call a floater, one of those squiggly things you sometimes get from eyestrain, only an enlarged version. He'd most likely prescribe new glasses for me.

What followed continues to astound me. Even though I may take all night, it's important to record here exactly what happened. On the elevator ride to the doctor's office, that dark whatever-it-was from the costume shop stood next to me, elongated, swelled to human size, and accompanied me to the sixteenth floor of the medical park office building, where an army of patients, mostly old people recuperating from cataract surgery, waited to see the doctor. That odd, shadowy aura hovered over me until a disembodied voice called my name and invited me into a suite of tiny offices, one tucked inside the other like Russian dolls.

Dr. Rosen's Asian medical assistant resembled Gail Sondegaard, a Caucasian Hollywood villainess who led the innocent astray in creaky 1930s B-rated films set in Chinatown. The inscrutable technician beckoned to me with her sharp, jade-green nails and challenged me to guess the contents of a blurry chart. She squirted drops into my eyes and led me to a secluded chamber with dimmed lighting, obviously an opium den. Although I expected to find Peter Lorre and Sidney Greenstreet conferring at a table under a ceiling fan, the room was empty.

"Dr. Rosen is busy with an emergency," she said. "You may have to wait a longer time than usual." She gestured toward a chintz-covered sofa that had seen better days but not recently. Seated there alone, I knew my dilating pupils would transform the entire room into one indelible smear. Nothing like several hours at the eye doctor to help us appreciate the numb beauty of time and space. The words floated in and out of my mind like unpowered boats.

Time and space. Once, they were sacred mysteries until the evil of advertising led the way in a massive takeover. At the Aaron Warsaw Agency, we ordered them as if they were apples or onions from a corner grocery that delivered: space by the column inch and time in thirty-second commercials. Infinity was ours. What a crime against humanity we committed in the name of business. And the civilized world believed only Einstein could play around with space and time. The world never can see clearly.

Still exhausted from the bus trip, I rested, determined to save energy for my chat with the ophthalmologist, whose technician had detected traces of cataracts in both my eyes. The peaceful interlude didn't last. A slight man in a heavy overcoat with a crushed velvet collar materialized in the doorway and chose to sit next to me, although an entire row of empty seats lined the wall closer to him. The newcomer made me so uneasy I snatched my handbag from the floor and moved to a chair across the room. The man faded in and out of my sight; my eyelids drooped, and a wave of chills swept my body. Eyes closed, I tilted my head back against stiff cushions and nodded off.

When I woke up, the same strange man occupied a seat immediately to my right. In his boney hands he held a book with a faded green cover frayed at the top, strands of thread dangling from a well-worn spine. The binding appeared to be loose, the pages ready to fall out, obviously not a recent best seller hot off the presses. He sat hunched over, concentrating on his book and turned the pages fast, as if he had read them all before.

He might have been in his early fifties, not tall, perhaps five feet four inches or so. Most striking was the black, double-breasted frock coat that reached down to his knees and flared out like a skirt, an outfit like what actors wore in that old Turner Classic Movie about Abraham Lincoln in Illinois. After SVM showed it the previous weekend, everybody at our breakfast table raved about Raymon Massey and refused to believe he was Canadian.

The odd gentleman moved closer to me than was comfortable. The skin above my eyebrows felt sweaty, feverish. On a nearby wall, two anemic watercolors seesawed up and down, up and down. It was much too hot in the room for that man's heavy winter coat. As if he read my mind, he struggled out of it to reveal an even more outlandish costume underneath.

He wore a black woolen suit and an ebony satin scarf tied under his chin in an elaborate bow. Two top buttons of his vest were fastened, the rest left open for a dangling watch fob, a gilded chain that looped under his waistcoat to a gold pocket watch that he consulted and then thrust into an inside pocket. His shirt collar stood up as if it were cut from poster board. Why was he dressed like that? And then I remembered the theatrical costume shop we passed in the neighborhood. Maybe he had stopped there on his way and found an outfit he couldn't resist.

My companion glanced up once, a reserved smile on his lips, and returned to his book. Those eyes, large and thoughtful, resembled whose? From my research, I recognized the clean-shaven face, the short dark hair slicked down, combed away from a side part, and the tapering sideburns. Then I remembered. Bostonians often referred to him as "the little doctor," and one even described him as "bristling with eyes, collar, and ears."

He didn't speak, unusual for a garrulous soul like him. I wanted to ask him impressive scholarly questions. Somewhere I read that his friends called him by his middle name. "Wendell," I'd say, "what's Herman Melville really like?" Or more important, "Does Walt Whitman know that same-sex marriage is legal now in America?"

A better idea hit me. Holmes enjoyed classical music. I should inquire about illustrious nineteenth century composers of operas. Eric would love getting a firsthand report.

"What do you hear from Verdi and Puccini?" I asked.

He gave me an enigmatic smile. "One thing more," I said to him, "would you do us the great honor of joining our breakfast table at SVM? We could use a better brand of conversation."

Before he could answer, someone else entered the room and took me into Dr. Rosen's office, where he diagnosed me as seriously dehydrated, forced me to drink eight ounces of water, and scolded me for having exposed his other patients to whatever I was coming down with.

"It's rather odd," I said. "I'm seeing spots." Spots hell, I had just seen a full-blown ghost, circa 1860.

By the time we finished the eye examination, at which Dr. Rosen recommended future cataract surgery, Oliver Wendell Holmes had dissolved back into the exclusive hereafter, a Saturday Club reserved for literary gods of bygone days and creative-writing professors. The worried medical assistant put me into what looked like an orange rickshaw, which carted me back to the old homestead. I fumbled with some bills in my wallet, stumbled through the SVM lobby to the elevators, and succumbed to a massive gastronomical earthquake in the bathroom.

Still fully dressed, I collapsed on an unmade bed and sank into a blurry dream that banished me to an overheated Victorian room with pulsating stained-glass windows and swirling Tiffany lamps. All three hundred of my SVM neighbors sat munching bagels around a legless mahogany table. Jake, positioned at the head, kept shouting, "The only thing any of us have in common at this place is we don't think we belong here." In my chair next to him, I pondered whether or not to inform that motley crew about having run into Oliver Wendell Holmes at the eye doctor's.

I decided to give it a go, and they peppered me questions. "Is he a specialist?" Bertha asked. "Can he give me something for my constipation?" And Jake merely said, "Jewish people don't see ghosts unless they're Isaac Beshavis Singer." And Flo asked, "Didn't Woodrow Wilson appoint him to the Supreme Court?" And I cut her off with, "*No, that was his son, you nincompoop!*" And Lydia marveled, "Nincompoop. Now that's a word you don't hear much lately." But then Jake felt he had lost control of the breakfast conversation and banged a spoon loudly on the table as he roared, "Let's have some Jewish content at this meal."

Opening my eyes, I discovered someone was pounding on the apartment door.

My voice sounded like a very old lady's. "Sick as a dog!" I croaked. "Go away or you'll catch it."

"Never," Ethel answered, perpetually cheerful. "If I haven't already, it won't get me. Open up. I baked cinnamon buns."

"Ethel, the last thing I need right now is cinnamon buns."

"Have it with tea when you feel better. Let me in. Maybe I can do something for you."

"I look horrible. Massive diarrhea. Apartment smells from you-know-what."

"Smells don't bother me. I worked in a prison, remember? Not exactly a perfume factory."

I dragged myself out of bed and heard her say, "The officers nabbed the bad guys, but I never caught anything, not even the flu. Are you going to open up?"

Although my head floated unhooked from my body, and I shivered, hot and cold at the same time, somehow I let her in. Clear-cut nausea enfolded me as I took a whiff of freshly baked cinnamon rising from the gold-rimmed plate in her hand. One glance at my ghoulish face and Ethel hurried back to her apartment as fast as she could move with tubing up her nose and an oxygen tank dragging behind. She returned, carrying a bottle of Bayer and an old-fashioned mercury thermometer. "Sit down and let me take your temperature," she said. Into my mouth zoomed a glass projectile that reeked of isopropyl rubbing alcohol. "Have you seen a doctor?" she asked.

Counting Holmes, I had been in touch with two doctors that day but didn't tell her. Fever encouraged me to play a trick on Ethel. While she studied the thermometer, I reverted to my childhood as a cranky sick child. She'd be sorry she forced those damned cinnamon buns into my life. "Yes, but he won't call back," I said.

"What's his name?" she asked, shaking the thermometer down. "Wait, lean on me but not too hard or you'll knock me over," she said as I stumbled toward the bedroom. "Lie down after I straighten out these linens." With considerable effort she bent over to smooth the jumble of sheets and spread my moth-eaten wool blanket. "There," she said, "that'll make you much more comfortable."

As best she could, she guided me, monster leg by monster leg, into bed and covered me. "Who's your primary care doctor?"

"He won't come here."

"No, not like the good old days when you could get a house call for five dollars a visit. I'll phone for you. Maybe he'll order an antibiotic from the pharmacy. Where's the doctor's number?"

I laughed fiendishly to myself. Time to shock Ethel out of her complacent good nature. This was what overly helpful persons deserved for wanting to cheer up people who didn't want to be cheered up. "He doesn't have a phone," I said.

Ethel gave me a quick look. "What?"

"Alexander Graham Bell hasn't invented it yet." There. My secret was out. Dear, sweet Ethel would be stunned by what I planned to tell her next. "I guess what's bothering me is puerperal fever," I whispered.

"What?'

"My doctor figured it out a long time ago. Too many women died after childbirth. He tried to tell the guys at the Harvard Medical School what caused it, but they didn't pay any attention. Later they agreed with him, but look at all the women they might have saved if they listened to him ten years before."

"You're dehydrated," she said, dragging herself to the kitchen for a glass of water. She doled out two aspirins. "Take this and get some rest. Is your doctor's name and number written down somewhere?"

"No." My voice fell apart, too tired for any more conversation.

"Who's your doctor, Willa?"

"Dial long distance. Long, long, extralong distance."

"Where's his office located?"

"The Boston Common." I half dozed off at this point. "Ask for Dr. Oliver Wendell Holmes. Accept no substitutes."

She took the empty water glass from me. "I'm calling 911."

That woke me up. "Look, I'm not just another expendable old crock they can shuffle off to St. Luke's. Besides, superbugs in hospitals can make people really sick."

Ethel sighed, too tired to argue. She wearily agreed to wait until morning when she would have more strength to deal with first responders if needed. "A good night's sleep, a gallon of water, and a few more aspirins may do the trick," she said. "You look terrible, but your temperature isn't all that bad, and I'm exhausted." She sighed. "Or do you need 911 right now?"

Another fuzzy thought drifted by. Romance can easily change into Reality. Happens all the time. But can Reality slide into Romance? My blond-oak furniture whirled around the room like a Hanukkah dreidel. If Ethel knew how dizzy I felt, she'd packed me off to the hospital right away—the last thing I wanted. Perhaps Eric hadn't been discharged yet from St. Luke's. Perhaps he'd have a relapse seeing me there. My ghastly appearance as a fellow patient lacked romantic panache. Eric and I would be hospital gurneys that passed in the night, and who wants that?

"No rush, Ethel. Wait till morning." I closed my eyes and slept.

# CHAPTER 4

———

THE BREAKFAST TABLE DIDN'T EXACTLY throb with excitement over the return of Howie the Unwholesome Wholesaler. He had checked out of SVM months before with no advance notice, and everyone assumed that he was either very ill or very dead or moved to his son's house in Rye, New York.

"No," he said, "It was too boring here. I transferred to Gladness Gardens just over the state line. Cutting edge, independent living, sexy women. Everybody drinking cocktails and laughing around the stone fireplace. Or that's what their fancy brochure showed. Pass the rolls, honey," he said to Flo the Faux Blonde, who had moved her chair as far away from him as possible.

"So if we weren't wild enough for you," she asked, handing him the nearly empty wicker basket, "why leave those swingers and come back here?"

"Turns out they were in worse shape than all of you," Howie said. Flo started to laugh, choked on her Cheerios, and couldn't stop coughing.

Howie leaned toward her. "Do you need a klopp?" he asked, one hand at her back and the other zooming in on her heaving chest.

Flo clenched a fist and pushed him away. "Keep your hands to yourself," she said. "I need a lozenge." She reached under the table and groped blindly for her handbag. In her search for the pocketbook, she accidentally grabbed a vital part of Howie. "Oops," she said.

"Quite all right. I consider it an opportunity."

"Well I don't," Flo answered, red-faced, and left the table, her bowl of Cheerios half eaten, her virtue intact.

Although Bertha, Lydia, and Harriet were not amused, Sidney reached over to shake Howie's hand. "Missed you, old buddy," he said. "Not enough guys." He lowered his voice. "Too many yentas."

"Good to be back." Howie hummed loudly as he sawed into a tough piece of pineapple in his fruit cup.

"Some faces are missing," Lydia said.

With care, Sidney poured creamer into his coffee. "Jake went to the VA hospital early for his shots today. Said on his way back he may drop off at Verdant Valley for a quick visit with Eric."

"They didn't discharge him yet?" Bertha asked.

"Complications." Lydia glanced in the direction of the dining-room entrance. "Has anyone seen our dear friend Willa lately?"

"Still sick," Harriet the Happy Homemaker said. She chewed hard on a lactase enzyme tablet before drinking her milk. "According to Fritzi, something's going around. Don't forget to wash your hands."

Howie ran his forefinger over his front teeth for a last-minute cleaning and brushed toast crumbs from his debonair mustache. "Ladies, hate to leave you, but they're cleaning the wax out of my ears today. My son's on his way to drive me to the doctor."

"Who is your otolaryngologist?" Lydia asked.

"You mean the guy who supplies me with Viagra?" He winked at Sidney, who responded with a wicked chuckle. With Jake gone, he hated sitting at an all-female table. "Wait," he said to Howie, "I'll walk you to the lobby."

"That woman Willa," Howie said as the two old men approached the exit. "Is she available?"

"How should I know?"

"I think she's sweet on me."

"Fat chance," Sidney said.

The women lingered over their decaf coffee. "Willa," Harriet said, "is the only person around here who lets you get a word in edgewise." The others agreed that eating with a nontalker had its advantages. For lack of anything better to do, the breakfast table residents began yet another round of the Why-Are-You-Here game.

"I'm here," Harriet said, "because I couldn't find any more teenagers willing to shovel snow or cut grass. They all grew up and moved out of the neighborhood."

Looking grimmer than usual, Jake dragged himself to the table. "They canceled my VA appointment," he said, lowering his body into a chair. "When I stopped at the front desk to pick up the week's menu, the receptionist told me Yetta passed away."

"Which one?" Bertha asked. "The Yetta with the great-grandchildren triplets?"

"No, the Yiddish teacher."

His table responded with dutiful shock and respect; they recognized that death was an inevitable staple at SVM, and for some, an extra perk. Lydia wondered about the funeral.

"Tomorrow in New York," Jake said. "Can't go, nobody to drive me, and I don't take public transportation on my own anymore."

Lydia touched Jake's shoulder in sympathy. "I'm so sorry."

Jake sighed. "Yetta and I went back many years in the Bronx. She lived across the street. I remember union organizers used to hold meetings at her parents' house." He broke off and sighed. "Nu, what can I tell you?" Jake choked up. "As a kid she attended the Workman's Circle School. My family was Orthodox, but Yetta's folks wouldn't have any of that."

"Was she first generation?" Harriet asked.

"Came here as a baby like me, a greenhorn from Krakow. Her father was a big shot with the garment workers. He also wanted to make Yiddish the national language of Jews." Jake shook his head. "Yetta gone. Can't believe it."

Flo grew strangely philosophical. "Elephants and turtles have a long life too. They leave this world when they're supposed to. So when they go, everybody understands."

"Human beings aren't elephants and turtles," Lydia said.

"The way I see it," Flo said, "I used to go to the synagogue. But then I thought, why bother God with my troubles? He knows what He's doing."

"Pass the Smart Balance," Jake said.

"Yiddish is a lost cause."

Jake bristled at the comment. "You don't know anything about it, Flo. They teach it at universities these days. It's not dead yet."

"Waste of time," Flo said.

Jake put his large, sun-spotted hands up to his forehead to shade his eyes. The bright sunlight coming through the window was giving him trouble. "If Yetta were here now, she'd give you a klopp."

Always the peacemaker, Lydia intervened. "But I do want you to know, Jake, I'm distressed that she's gone. I'll miss her."

He made an effort to throw off his gloom. "And I'll miss *me* when I'm gone."

"You'll be the only one who does," Flo said.

———————

*Wednesday, October 2.* It's taking me longer than expected to get over this phantom malady. I welcome the chance to lie quietly in bed and reread passages of Dr. Holmes, who fills his pages with too many words, even though another side of him cries out for restraint. When one of his characters, the old Master, retreats from sharing certain innermost thoughts, Holmes commiserates: "That which means so much to me, the writer, might be a disappointment, or at least a puzzle, to you, the listener...The very minute a thought is threatened with publicity it seems to shrink towards mediocrity..."

During the passing week, I've engaged in numerous mediocre rehearsals of what to say to Eric when we finally meet. Words won't ripple from my mouth, I'm sure. He actually phoned from Verdant Valley the other day. Our conversation would have been funny if it weren't so sad. He spoke in a pitch lower than low, and my voice sounded as if it had been pushed through a wire strainer. Most of the time, he couldn't understand me, nor I, him. We do better face to face.

Otherwise, I've enjoyed tuning in to Classic Arts Showcase and hearing Mozart's Violin Concerto Number Four in D Major, actually three times! They repeat a lot. SVM kitchen staff members continue to bring me daily meals. A housekeeping aide comes in to do laundry and keep things tidy. Ethel visits every day and thinks I'm ready to eat downstairs with fellow boarders, but it's too soon. I'm still not Willa Warsaw, whoever that was.

Ethel keeps me up to date on any new characters at the breakfast table and Fritzi's latest outrageous gossip. I can well imagine the nasty things she has to say about me. Ethel, on the other hand, is the good angel. I remember when the first Rosh Hashanah arrived for me without Aaron, she slipped an envelope under my door. The L'Shana Tova card she made in art class was a bright yellow sunflower painted on green background, accompanied by an invitation to drop in for tea and honey cake, "sweetening the new year," she put it. Always on my side, Ethel also scribbled, "When I hear your music through the wall, I feel less alone."

Right now the classical music station is playing Bach's Air from Suite No. 3 in D Major at full blast. And these apropos comments by Holmes have resonated with me all morning long:

> ...there is a great amount of affectation in the apparent enthusiasm of many persons in music...whether it is good or bad, the work of a first-rate or a fifth-rate composer; whether there are coherent elements in it, or whether it is nothing more than 'a concourse of sweet sounds' with no organic connection...Go to the great concerts where you know that the music is good, and that you ought to like it whether you do or not.

I'll share that with Eric, who'll be amused. Together in the SVM auditorium, we sat through some glorious recitals by pianists, violinists, and operatic soloists, and I learned to hear with Eric's ears. Or tried to. I don't have the technical knowledge, the vocabulary to describe the finger work of a viola player, or the breath technique of a singer, but the color and emotion are obvious even to a know-nothing like me. Awake at night, I recreate his reaction to each performance we attended, hear his analysis, his criticism. Once he reminisced about his life on tour and described the numerous times he met his old friend, Marcel Marceau, the king of pantomime. "Several times, I sang on the same program with him," Eric said. "After the show, we would go out for a late dinner. Marcel never stopped talking."

Very early this morning, I had another anxiety dream in which the SVM bus had dropped me off at a gigantic opera hall and drove away without me. As I wandered alone through a labyrinth of orchestra seats and balconies, my handbag somehow disappeared, everything gone, money, checkbook, credit cards, my identity. Panicky, I ran from row to row but couldn't remember which row was mine and kept moaning, "I must find it. Please help me. Help me find it."

Waking up, although I felt supreme relief to be spared an entire week of difficult phone calls to American Express and several banks, the dream troubled me. Was there something else I had lost? I meant to discuss it with Ethel, but this afternoon when she dropped in to deliver a heavy bag of Gala apples, she gave me a scare.

"You need to leave this apartment and mingle with human beings again," she said, and then stopped abruptly, turning pale. "Finding it hard to breathe." She gasped so loudly it frightened me. I had never heard that dreadful wheezing sound from her before. "It's OK," she said in a faraway voice. "I'm just a little worn out."

"Get some rest."

"I'll be fine." After she left, wearily dragging the oxygen tank behind her, I felt guilty. Ethel wastes too much energy on others. Her cheeks are chalky, and she has lost at least ten pounds. She needs more loving care than someone like me can give.

# CHAPTER 5

———◆———

"Anyone going to the antisickness lecture this afternoon?" Flo the Faux Blonde asked in a bright voice. She had just seen a poster in the Gedalia Ginsfarb Fitness Garden. "It's a lecture on incontinence."

"Interesting to see who shows up for that one," Jake said.

Sidney offered a meaningful comment. "Incontinence is good for the economy. Adult diaper sales are booming." He and Jake were debating the definition of antisickness when Fritzi Schnell stopped by their table with sorrowful news. "They're dropping like flies around here," she said.

"You have the soul of a poet," Jake mumbled. He glanced around the table. "I thought Willa would be back today. And where's the one with the oxygen pipeline?"

Fritzi, in her glory, almost burst with her message. "Didn't you hear?"

"What's her name? The gal who always tries to do the right thing," Jake said. "Did she do the wrong thing for a change?"

"Ethel died yesterday." Fritzi, after making sure she had left a properly dampening effect on the table members, rushed off to spread the word to a couple of Ethel's Knitting Club friends seated across the room.

Jake's gruff voice sounded softer. "Sorry, I didn't know." There was a silence, and then Bertha wondered out loud whether Willa would show up to eat breakfast and whether her absence had anything to do with Ethel's death. "Lately, they got to be real close," she said.

Flo and Harriet apologized for making a quick getaway because they had signed up for an early bus trip to a nearby synagogue. "It's a journalist speaking at Congregation B'nai David on the situation in Israel," Flo said, happy to be leaving SVM for the morning.

"There's always a situation in Israel," Jake said.

"B'nai David serves a delicious dairy lunch," Harriet added. "Free."

"That congregation has a surplus of *tsaddikim*," Jake said, although no one seemed to be listening to him except Lydia. "A legend in the Talmud says there are thirty-six tsaddikim in every generation. They're the do-gooders who can save the rest of us from disaster."

"Does that thirty-six include women?" Lydia asked.

Jake dodged the question. "No one knows who they are, and they don't even know each other, but the continuation of the world depends on their righteousness. If you ever discover one, you have to keep it a secret."

There seemed nothing else worth talking about. They redirected their attention to breakfast. When Jake looked up from his fried eggs and challah toast, he saw Willa standing behind an empty chair on the opposite side of the breakfast table. She wore a mannish black suit with a navy turtleneck shirt, no makeup on her face, and no jewelry to relieve the black.

The table occupants looked down at their cereal bowls. "We just heard," Bertha said. "Is Ethel's funeral tomorrow?"

Willa shook her head. Her eyes looked as if she hadn't closed them since God created heaven and earth. "Cincinnati," she said. "Ethel doesn't have anyone here, just cousins in Ohio."

The table members exchanged quick glances. "Sit down and eat something," Bertha said. "Starving yourself won't bring her back."

"She deserves a memorial service," Willa said, in a louder voice that somehow carried to the next table, which wasn't laughing. "It's the right thing…" She didn't finish.

Lydia touched Jake's arm and asked him to officiate. "Any kind of Jewish service, just something dignified, out of respect," she said.

"I didn't know the woman all that well."

"Jake," Lydia said, and the tone of her voice settled the issue.

"Well, if means something to somebody."

Hugging herself, Willa the Wordless Widow swayed from side to side in a timeless way and made no sound. Before anyone could console her, she crept away from the tableau of elderly people, seated immobile, captured in time like a frieze carved in ancient marble.

———

*Wednesday, October 9.* Such a sad day. By eleven this morning, a white-headed throng had already gathered in the Sim Shalom Activities Room to remember Ethel. I had never gone to any of these memorial services before, and the number of people surprised me. Bertha, who attends even when she doesn't know the deceased, once explained her reasons for showing up at such events. "It may be someone I say hello to in the elevator or pass every day in the lobby. I don't remember names. So to make sure, I go to all of them anyway."

Friends or strangers, the old people assembled, bearing witness to the inevitable, paying forward an insurance premium to be collected later, a calculated risk. They had no idea what size crowd they themselves would draw one day. The room was so packed that two custodians had to scramble for more chairs.

Familiar faces gathered: Diana, Goddess of the Hunt, with her new asthmatic boyfriend; Flo the Faux Blonde, Harriet the Happy Housewife, Lydia the Encyclopiddia, Renee Richmond, Bertha the Bingo Baby, Fritzi the Schnellbomber, and a solemn procession of anonymous Snow Whites who clumped in with walkers or without walkers, all ladies dressed casually in pastel cardigans they had received last Mother's Day. And seated on the back row, a handful of respectful SVM staff members, not smiling for a change.

Others didn't need seats. They lingered unseen, hovering near the ceiling: Clara, who had overdosed; Yetta, bearing the decal removed from her door: Yiddish Spoken Here; Ethel herself, who did the right thing by attending her own funeral; all the elderly residents who had passed away in isolated apartments over the years; unknown phantoms; unremembered faces; deleted lives.

It was a good time to remember the honorable SVM dead, continuing to battle for attention with those who still breathed; every erased soul demanding to be recognized. In early hours, while passing through deserted corridors, I've sensed those ghosts fluttering like moths around the hall lights, a swarm of spirits who once lived here in the years even before I came, all those who talked and ate and slept here, those who dozed in the lobby or crept back and forth during sleepless nights, all those anonymous souls wrapped in pain and loneliness who never reached the morning.

Jake began Ethel's memorial service with prayers in Hebrew and in English. I stood and recited the Kaddish for Ethel because there were no family members to do it. The other residents couldn't hear me, but that was OK. You can get by saying Kaddish with nobody but God hearing you. It's the one time the residents of SVM forgive you for being inaudible. Otherwise they turn unruly if anyone dares to address an audience without a microphone.

Jake gave a loose-jointed talk on ethical behavior: the value of morality toward not only the Jewish people but all humankind. Whatever is hateful to you do not do to another person, that sort of thing. From there he waltzed into the proper ethical education of present and future generations of all Americans, Jews, and non-Jews. He emphasized logic and sensibility and mentioned Spinoza a few times. I think Oliver Wendell Holmes, with his disdain for superstition, would have liked it. Jake even launched into reasons for leaving behind an ethical will.

"A *what?*" somebody yelled from the back row.

"This was done by our ancestors," Jake said, raising his voice, but visibly peeved at the informality. "The handing down of values for our children, *Pirkei Avot*, the Ethics of the Fathers."

"What about the mothers?" asked Flo, in the middle of everything. "The mothers have always had more ethics than the fathers."

"Them too," Jake said, and continued, finally making his point. "With an ethical will, our ancestors left behind a legacy of morality. These days I think all American parents should draw up ethical wills to teach their children and grandchildren the difference between right and wrong," he said. Then he spoke gently about Ethel and called her a role model for always doing the right thing.

"That was the inheritance she left to all of us. I called her Ethel the Ethical," Jake said, winding down. "She was. And we are her children."

A voice in the audience boomed, "How can we be her children? We're the same age she was."

Jake ignored the question but remembered to say, "One thing more. I've been asked to read some original verse by Ethel's best friend. I'm not very poetic, and anyway, this one should have a female reader." He turned to Lydia. "Would you do the honors?"

"I forgot my glasses," she said.

And then there was a turn of events that surprised everyone, even me. "No," I heard myself say, "I'll do it." My mind tried to recapture some of the technique Eric had taught me during that memorable voice lesson in his room at the nursing home. Shaking my arms and hands to relax, dropping my jaw, and taking deep breaths from the diaphragm, I projected as loudly as possible. It was a poem written the bleak night before the funeral. (Included here is a copy in case anybody cares.)

### Ethel's Eulogy
by Willa Warshaw

Let us now praise lonely women
Whom life's circumstances smother,
Leaving only faded albums
Of a daughter and her mother.

Let us now mourn single women
With no children of their own,
God, their only living kinsman,
And our heritage their stone.

Let us now praise silent women
Drawing inward to themselves,
Leaving only tidy cupboards,
Hidden thoughts on hidden shelves.

My unpredictable voice came through breathier than ever, air hissing from a punctured balloon. Whether they could hear or not, the crowd listened in respectful silence, and later two members of the SVM professional staff asked for copies. That afternoon Carlos, the maintenance man, removed Ethel's Oxygen: No Smoking sign from the door. It left a ghostly outline, which will be painted over before the next resident moves in.*

(*Note: I recorded funeral details to share later with Eric at Verdant Valley. The above entry written one hour before his devastating phone call that wiped everything else out of my mind.)

———

By the next day, the breakfast-table entourage had forgotten Ethel's memorial service until Jake reminded them. "You mean to tell me nobody in that audience ever heard of Spinoza?"

"Your talk was nice," Bertha said. "A little long."

Renee Richmond sipped her tomato juice. "And too Jewish."

Jake gave her a curt nod, turned away, and said, "What happened to you, Sid? You weren't even there."

Sidney the Savvy Salesman shook his head. "When you've sat through one of those, you've sat through them all."

"So where did you go?" asked Lydia. She poured skim milk on her cereal and didn't notice that more than a few drops splashed on her new beige cardigan.

Sidney, bone white and dehydrated, spoke in a distant voice. "Don't know. Maybe I was in the Fourth Dimension."

Renee Richmond directed an aside to Bertha. "He should have stayed there."

The Ha-Ha Table, overhearing the remark, issued a few weak chuckles. With two of their principal laughers gone for good, they lacked the volume of former days.

Flo the Faux Blonde seized the helm. "Renee, you were dressed to kill when I saw you in the elevator the other night. Heavy date?"

"No, people here are always looking at you," Renee said. "From your earrings to your shoes."

Sidney came to life. "You think they're looking at your shoes? They're watching the floor to keep from falling down." He reached for the Sweet'N Low. "Enough with the girly talk. I had too much of that in my life."

Fritzi wrestled the conversation away from Sidney. "I've was just talking to Ziporah, the one sitting over there across the room next to the mirror. She keeps saying she wants to go to the moon."

Jake, who had just switched to driving a mechanized vehicle scooter, said, "I'd go too, but how would I get my new scooter up there?"

"You wouldn't need it," Sidney said. "You'd be weightless."

Jake pointed to the pancakes left untouched on Sidney's plate. "If you don't start eating more, man, you'll be weightless. *Ess, mein kind.* Eat!"

———

*Wednesday, October 10.* Dr. Holmes, what do you carry in that black bag of yours? I'd welcome a miraculous nostrum this morning, any fluted vial of liquid forgetfulness you'd offer, quinine, powdered sassafras, spirits of turpentine, or even those Purgative Pills, the kind your patients took to flush their bodies of ill humors. Eric and I need an audible (!) conversation face to face, but my head throbs and my throat burns. This horrific cold—or whatever it is—prevents me from visiting him today.

The phone call last night triggered it off. They were keeping him longer than he expected at Verdant Valley, and he didn't like it. "I want to come home," he said in a soft voice that barely carried from the phone to my ear. "I miss you."

It caught me off guard. He had never spoken those words to me before.

"Miss you too," I answered almost mechanically." Long pause. "What can I do?" I meant it more as a rhetorical question, but Eric surprised me by turning more practical than a Romantic hero should be.

"Can you get me some transportation?"

"What do you mean?"

"Could you help me escape before this Friday?"

My heart pounded in my chest. Help him leave Verdant Valley, and then what? Smuggle him back into SVM? At first, it seemed heroic, something out of a movie or opera, free spirits in rebellion and Willa to the rescue. Then it all came crashing down from sheer impossibility. Even if I wanted to, I had spent the day flat on my back, coughing, laden down with unidentified germs; how could I manage a coup of that magnitude by Friday, just two days away? And why me?

"Did I hear you right?" I spoke slowly, pausing after each word. "You want me to take you out of Verdant Valley and bring you back to SVM?"

"Yes."

My head was spinning. Obstacles paraded before my watery eyes in a grand march: the elephantine details, the challenge of renting a wheelchair for him, hiring a medical transport company, finding a dependable aide to help Eric get from Point A to Point B. On my own, even if I managed to sneak him through a rear entrance without being stopped, I'd face the agonizing solo of getting him undressed, helping him span the chasm from wheelchair to bed, navigating perilous trips from bedroom to bathroom, the onerous pulling, bending, pushing, stretching, and under it all, knowing I'm not strong enough to keep him from the floor should he fall. It would be a rerun of Aaron's final months, left forever in my bones.

Eric and I remained silent for a while. Our voices had lost their way in our throats. "Don't worry," I said before hanging up. "We'll think of something."

I'm sweating, Dr. Holmes, as I scribble away feverishly. You say that women are made to please; how long must we remain on the job? Even if I were ten years younger, kidnapping and carting Eric back to SVM is not my responsibility. Where he goes next is not up to me. We're not a couple; I'm no relative. What would Ethel say is the right thing to do here? No matter how compassionate a woman may be, she's better prepared to share the delight in a man's dream than the terror in his nightmare. And why the Friday deadline?

Scrambled thoughts. Can't call him back. No voice left. Feel rusty nails jammed into my tonsils. Tomorrow ask SVM nurse to check me for strep. Superbug, superbug, fly away home. They'll stuff me with antibiotics like a turkey. Everything exploding. Phone ringing again. Let it ring. Too damned tired to lift the receiver.

# PART FOUR

---

*Something intensely human, narrow, and definite pierces to the
seat of our sensibilities more readily than human occurrences and
catastrophes. A nail will pick a lock that defies hatchet and hammer.*

*OWH*

# CHAPTER 1

———————

"I RECALL YOUR WIFE, MAY she rest in peace," Bertha said, blotting her lipstick on the blue cloth napkin at breakfast. "You fussed with her when she wanted to get that walker."

"Fuss? I never, ever raised my voice to Ida." Sidney drained his coffee cup and motioned to the Haitian waiter to bring a refill. "She always did what she wanted."

Bertha wasn't about to let the subject go. "You told her she didn't need it, and the only reason she wanted one was that all her girlfriends had those nice walkers, the handy ones with the lids to them that you could sit on or store away odds and ends underneath the seat."

Sidney sounded reluctant, as if he would rather not discuss it but found it hard to stop. "Ida didn't need one. I spoke to that doctor who used to live here—what was his name?—Bernard something, and he explained why so many older women get hunched over. They depend too much on their walkers and don't straighten up. He said bad posture increased the hump in their backs and made their osteoporosis worse. When I tried telling that to Ida, she just laughed and had the physical therapist order one anyway."

Sidney stood up with caution and rocked back and forth on his feet to strengthen his balance. "What difference does it make?" he said. "She's gone, and now my daughters boss me around. They took over my bank account, my credit cards, my car. I used to enjoy balancing the checking account." He sighed. "The women in my family always had their hooks into me."

"Poor Sidney," Lydia said, watching as he painfully lumbered through a nest of tables and walkers on his way to the dining room door. "He seems to fret now more than usual." She turned to Jake. "There's a word you don't hear much these days—'fret.'"

"One of us is missing again this morning," Jake said. He inclined his head in the direction of Willa's empty chair.

Lydia glanced at the dining room entrance. "She must be sleeping late. Jake, notice how people today don't say 'sleeping late' anymore? They say 'sleeping in.'"

Jake made a sound that was close to a snort. "In what? Nightgowns? Pajamas?"

"No, just in."

"Maybe Willa has come down with another mysterious *krankheit*," Jake said. He half stood and eased over to the seat of his nearby scooter just as Fritzi breezed in and grabbed a chair vacated by Renee Richmond, who had left for an appointment with a new Moroccan hairdresser capable of doing wonders with hiding bald spots.

"*Krankheit?*" Fritzi said. "Who's sick now?"

"None of your f—" As an ex-newspaperman, Jake debated with himself on whether he should borrow an appropriate adjective from Renee Richmond, and for Lydia's sake, decided against it. "Beeswax," he said, and sped away to the Gedalia Ginsfarb Fitness Garden for the weekly session on maintaining balance.

In the doorway, Jake nearly collided with Harriet, who carried bad news. "The cleaning lady says Willa's in bed again. Later today I'll bring her a bagel and cream cheese." She gave him a benign smile. "It's the right thing to do."

"Good idea," he said, more enthusiastic than usual. What he learned later about Eric's second phone call to Willa would shock Jake and sadden him more than he wanted to admit.

---

*Thursday, October 10.* Eric's message this evening was even worse than his plea last night to rescue him from Verdant Valley. I had just finished a bowl of chicken matzo ball soup delivered to my apartment by a young Namibian man who works in the kitchen by day and at night studies to become a social worker.

"There's bad news and good news," Eric said.

Good news, bad news, the tired old joke. There's nothing bad about you, Eric, I thought, except that cruel illness, and it's not your fault.

"The good news is, I'm better."

"So when are you coming home?" A long silence at the other end of the line. "Eric? You still there?"

"Not really," he said. Or at least that's what I think he said.

It was time to try another approach. "Did your niece ever come from Seattle?"

"Rochelle and her husband Kevin are here now."

"That's nice."

"We—or rather—they decided it costs too much to fly cross-country anytime something goes wrong. The front desk always calls Rochelle. She's my only next of kin."

I took a deep breath. He was going to tell me something I didn't want to hear. "She's in charge. She can put me in another nursing home whenever she decides it's time." He stopped.

"You're moving to Seattle?"

"That way Rochelle is closer."

"But three thousand miles away?"

"I know." He waited for me to supply a few more words, and I couldn't. "It's not fair," he said at last.

"When will you go?" Perhaps we could meet one more time at least to say good-bye in person, anything better than this fuzzy connection. He and I can barely communicate under ordinary circumstances, and the phone makes it worse.

"We catch a plane early tomorrow. Kevin stays behind to deal with the moving."

"The dirty work."

"He's a good person. They're both good kids."

"And they've decided this is what's best for you?"

"Yes."

What could I answer? "I suppose it's the right thing to do," I said like a robot.

"I hate going. We wanted to work on your voice. I like being with you."

How it happened, I don't know, but words that came to me sounded strong and metallic, utilitarian and cold. I told him that whether we liked it or not, it was happening; we had to accept reality and keep going, no matter what.

"Sweet of you to call," I said, completely drained.

"I'll miss you," he said. "Very much."

"Miss you too. I'll send cards and letters."

"I don't want to be a burden to you."

"No burden. I want to. Good-bye, Eric." I hung up and immediately regretted it. Call him back. Beg him. Let's think this through. There must be some alternative, another route. That's what I would have said twenty years ago or ten or even five. Fight it. Argue. None of this feeble acceptance. At least burst into an all-consuming aria of operatic despair. If only I could sing.

What's the point? Reality stares us down. We've no route ahead involving the two of us together. We've only memory while it lasts, and there's no future in it. It's not as if we're a bona fide married couple, a united force pitted against—pitted against what? The power of time? The mirror says it all: two single people no longer young, survivors of a past life not spent with each other. Each of us remains alone to face in private whatever lies ahead. And no, it's not fair.

# CHAPTER 2

———◆———

THE NEXT DAY AT THEIR oatmeal orgy, Jake reminded his captive audience of the duty not only to care for the Jewish people but to demand justice for all fellow humans. "Otherwise, we have no share in the world to come."

"What do you mean by the world to come?" Bertha asked. "Where is it?"

Jake raised both arms and shouted, "Look around! It's here right now! There's nothing else." And then with his fierce, dark eyes, he dared them to contradict him.

Everyone preferred to ignore the outburst. The order of seating seemed upside down. Fritzi had an appointment with the podiatrist and was absent. Diana, Goddess of the Hunt, filled the chair vacated by Lydia, away spending a month with her Minneapolis daughter, a klutz, according to a recent evaluation from Fritzi. "She calls herself a certified public accountant, but Selma on the third floor used her for taxes and told me it was the only time she ever got audited by the IRS."

"My perfect grandson made an adorable remark yesterday," Bertha began even before she sat down and tucked her fuchsia brocade smock under her ample backside. "That boy is a genius. He said to me, 'Grandma, from the head up, you're like everybody else, but the rest of you is a mess.' Isn't that brilliant?" Spreading a paper napkin into her lap, she glanced around the table. "Whatever happened to Eric? Is he back at Verdant Valley for good?"

"Moved to a facility in Washington state," Jake said as he shoveled hash brown potatoes into his mouth.

"I never know what to say to somebody like that who's been so famous and doesn't talk much," Bertha said.

"We used to chat waiting for the physical therapist to show up," Jake said. "Eric's a gentle person, never married except to his career. He once owned a farm here when these SVM grounds were nothing but a cow pasture. The guy traveled all over the world, but when he retired, he came back to his old neighborhood. He said this whole area felt more like home to him than anywhere else."

Diana leaned in Jake's direction. "And what did you talk about in your lecture yesterday, Jake? You're so brilliant. Isn't he brilliant?" The others at the table seemed less enthusiastic.

"I called it 'Seniors Trapped by Technology: The Curse of the Twenty-First Century.' Just about everybody in the audience last night was complaining about the latest electronic tchotchkes invented by twenty-four-year-old millionaires who don't understand anything about old people."

Bertha said she didn't attend and refused to frustrate herself voluntarily. "IPads, you-Pads," she said, waving her hand as if to dismiss the whole lot. "Apps, shmapps. Dumbphones, smartphones. Who cares?"

"Lately, I've noticed some of the younger newcomers have them when they move here," Diana said. "Too complicated for me! I mean, everything is so small. Why don't the manufacturers leave enough room to spell out what the different buttons mean in letters large enough to read without your glasses? I'm talking about putting simple words like 'on' and 'off' in black letters. No more white letters on white backgrounds. And just 'on' and 'off.' Is that too much to ask, instead of confusing substitutes like 'power' and 'volume' or dumb little pictures that explain nothing? I still don't know how to turn my cell phone on and off."

"Do you realize they make devices now to trace every move an elderly person makes?" Jake said. "We'll be walking around with cameras planted in our *pupiks*."

Diana frowned. "I don't exactly know this Yiddish word."

"What are you, Presbyterian? It means navel, belly button."

"Oh. I thought it was located further down, another word for tush."

"Which is an Americanized version of tokus. And let's not get bogged down in that naked-butt business again," Jake said. "Back to the rotten facts. They're working on medicine bottles that tell your doctor when you miss taking your pills. And you'll have sensors in your knee caps to announce, 'Watch it! You're about to fall down!' Which means we'll be afraid to move."

"So nothing will be sacred?" Diane asked.

"It'll replace prayer," Jake said. "You won't have to plead with God to watch over you."

"That's terrible," Bessie said. "I wouldn't want any stranger to see me going to the bathroom, would you?"

"Look," Jake said, "we already have cars that drive themselves. Mark my words, some day everyone will make love by remote control. And when all the new information falls into the wrong hands, and it will, old people will be exploited more than they are now."

"Too depressing. What's your next lecture on?" Diana asked.

"The Boils of Job: A Metaphor for Old Age."

Diana looked confused. "Job?"

"The righteous fellow in the Bible who got thrown for a loop."

"Oh," Diana said, "*that* Job. I always thought they spelled his name wrong. It should be J-O-A-B. Otherwise—"

Jake finished it for her. "Otherwise, you think it has something to do with unemployment."

Diana batted her false eyelashes at Jake. "I forget how his story ends. Can you give me little bitsy hint?"

"Depends on which way the rabbis slice it." Jake drained his coffee cup, set it down, and prepared to leave. "Listen, I don't know what's wrong with our friend Willa. I haven't seen her in days. She's not sick enough to go to the hospital or to a nursing home, but she never comes out of that apartment. If she doesn't show up for breakfast by tomorrow, we should send out a search party for her."

———————

*Sunday, October 13.* No strep, but the sore throat remains. The nurse said I didn't need antibiotics from the drugstore. Gargling with baking soda and aspirin helps although I dislike gargling on aesthetic principles, all that officially approved regurgitation. What's next, castor oil? I can't shake this inertia, and Oliver Wendell Holmes has yanked the rug out from under me with these words: "Do you say old age is unfeeling? It has not vital energy enough to supply the waste of more exhausting emotions."

The good music station is now playing Chopin's Etude Number Three in E Major Opus 10, easy for me to identify because wasn't there once a popular song called "No Other Love" back in 1950, when songwriters set words to Tchaikovsky and Chopin?

Ethel used to tease me about my enjoyment of solitude. "Voluntary solitary confinement," she called it. These days, breakfast in the dining den is out. I need more, not less, time away from people. Regrets. I still don't have Eric's address or phone number in Seattle. What's the name of his new place? Don't remember. The front desk says nobody left them that information. Right now even his niece's first and last name escape me. No way to reach him.

Yesterday Jake phoned, of all people. He said I sounded depressed (ha!) and wondered about my research on Dr. Holmes as a possible anti-Semite. Before I could answer, "I'm too sick to be bothered," Jake grew peeved, ordering me to investigate at once and report back. "Find out," he said, "was Holmes good for the Jews? It's a possible topic for my next lecture."

His question rattles around in my vacant mind. Holmes may or may not have been good for the Jews, but he wasn't bad for them either. He couldn't have been a bigot, growing up as he did in a liberal Unitarian atmosphere, his father, a minister, at odds with conservative parishioners who accused him of heresy. Out of curiosity maybe it's worth looking up if I can stop scratching. Worrying about Eric has given me a rash; I itch all over.

Some time ago, Lydia lent me *Amiable Autocrat*, a biography by Eleanor M. Tilton. Last night when I took the volume in hand, the stiff, yellowed pages fell open as if some unseen presence knew exactly what chapter to choose, and before me lay an obscure poem in which Homes describes sitting next to unwelcome strangers while attending a theatrical performance on a hot August evening. The biographer notes, "Holmes could recognize a prejudice when he saw one." Although the verse runs on and on, couplet after wordy couplet, tomorrow I'll ask the front desk secretary to make this severely edited copy for Jake's enlightenment:

### Excerpt from "At the Pantomime"
### by OWH

My patience slightly out of joint / My temper short of boiling point / Amidst the throng the pageant crew / Were gathered Hebrews not a few / Black-bearded, swarthy,—at their side / Dark, jeweled women, orient-eyed /...Next on my left a breathing form / Wedged up against me, close and warm /...The show went on, but ill at ease / My sullen eye it could not please / In vain my conscience whispered, "Shame!" / I thought of Judas and his bride / And steeled my soul against their tribe / My neighbors stirred; I looked again / Full on the younger of the twain / A fresh young cheek whose olive hue / The mantling blood shows faintly through / Locks dark as midnight that divide / And shade the neck on either side / So looked that other child of Shem / The Maiden's Boy of Bethlehem /...And thou couldst scorn the peerless blood / That flows unmingled from the Flood / Thy scutcheon spotted with the stains / Of

Norman thieves and pirate Danes! / The New World's foundling, in thy pride / Scowl at the Hebrew at thy side / And lo! the very semblance there / The Lord of Glory deigned to wear.

That says it all, the doctor's shame at automatically rejecting Hebrews, the impure history of his own non-Jewish background in comparison, and his recognition that the Semitic folks at the theater are the relatives, the mishpachah, of Mary and her son. Of course Jake will argue the point. He'll doubt Holmes could be classified as a liberal. True, he wasn't a flaming abolitionist, gung-ho about ridding the country of slavery. I'm sure Jake will mention our biblical years as slaves in Egypt and wonder why Holmes didn't openly support freedom for all human beings. Must mull that one over and come up with some kind of dodge that doesn't take too much thinking. "No one escapes ambiguity, not even Dr. Holmes," I'll say.

That answer makes me second-guess my own passive choices. My mind doesn't stray too long away from Eric. Why did I let him go without a fight? Is he too far away for me to repair the damage? Can I think of another route open for us?

# CHAPTER 3

———◆———

THE FOLLOWING DAY, WILLA JOINED her fellow residents for a breakfast of hard-boiled eggs and corn muffins. She quietly took her seat and listened to Sidney mourning the loss of the SVM Jewish War Veterans chapter, recently disbanded.

"Only three of us left," he told the women at the table as he shoveled stewed prunes into his mouth. "Last year we had twelve guys and two army nurses. Later it came down to just the two women, Jake, and me. Then Rosalie, the one with emphysema, switched to assisted living and the other, Lenore, broke her hip, so we went out of business."

That wasn't the only sad news. Doreen, the dining room lady, dropped by to tell them she was leaving her job in a couple of weeks because her husband, an engineer, had lined up a position with the National Institute of Standards and Technology near Washington, DC. "Will you guys miss me?" Doreen asked, giving Sidney a sly wink.

"Breakfast won't be exciting without you," he said. "Can't you commute?"

Doreen shook her blond head. "It's hundreds of miles from here."

"Hire me as your chauffeur," Jake said. "I'm still driving."

Doreen skirted the comment and moved away, an indulgent smile still on her face, as Sidney told Jake that he should have given up his Buick years ago. "What do you mean?" Jake said, slightly insulted. "I can see fine in the daytime."

Flo said she had been driving since she was sixteen but had to stop. "These days," she sighed, "it's hard to depend on my children to take me places. And taxis cost a fortune."

Bertha claimed she was a late bloomer. "Papa never taught me to drive. When my husband Simon died at thirty-nine, with three young children, I learned to drive if we wanted to get anywhere."

"Your husband passed away young," Lydia said. "It must have been difficult."

Bertha recited a story they had heard a number of times before. "We had a clothing store in a poor neighborhood. They burned it during the riots after Martin Luther King was shot. But I learned how to give permanent waves and opened a beauty parlor in my basement. I managed." A smile came to Bertha's thin lips. "When I first got my license, I was afraid to drive anywhere. My father's cousin Nathan lived down the street, a very observant man, the beadle at the Orthodox synagogue. Whenever I had to take the kids somewhere, I'd ask him to go along. I thought if a religious person was in the car, I wouldn't have an accident."

"Superstitious nonsense," Jake said, his mouth full of corn flakes. He turned his attention to Willa. "So welcome back, stranger. We haven't seen you in weeks."

The women greeted her and whispered among themselves about how much she had aged during her time away. Jake seemed almost jovial. "How's it going? While in sick bay, did you read anything provocative like The Sex Change of Oliver Wendell Holmes? Maybe that's what they meant in those days by transcendentalism."

She didn't waste her breath answering him, but Jake refused to let go. "Tell me, Willa, ever find out more about Holmes? Maybe he was Jewish, and his real name was Oliver Mendel Hooha?"

Willa shrugged. She had forgotten to bring the book containing that Holmes poem and couldn't remember offhand any lines to quote from "At the Pantomime," especially in front of an audience. "I don't know," she said. She busied herself by brushing corn muffin crumbs from her lap.

Jake persisted. "It's a dilemma. Richard Wagner hated Jews, but that didn't make his music less glorious, did it? Or did it?"

Willa concentrated on swallowing the rest of a tedious corn muffin. "Perhaps."

"Could be," Jake said, "without Wagner, the Nazis might have won."

"It's sad to think of all the elderly Jewish War Veterans gone," Harriet said.

"Everybody from the Second World War got old too soon," Bertha said. "Like my husband. When he and his buddies came home from overseas, they burned their uniforms and dressed up pinstripe suits with broad padded shoulders, remember?"

Jake resumed control of the conversation. "So what happened? Overnight we became anonymous American consumers. Before we knew it, something else was happening to us. We didn't even realize it until we turned into grandfathers and great-grandfathers. Now sixty-five years later, we look around and ask, 'Where the hell is everybody?'"

Sidney nodded his bald head in agreement. "Right," he said, "where did our buddies go so fast?"

"Where did the Holocaust six million go? Every day I still raise that question for myself." Instead of drifting into another gloomy soliloquy, Jake turned back to Willa. "You didn't answer me. Your Oliver Wendell Holmes, did he look kindly on Jews? Or was he a bigot with the best of them?"

"How should I know?"

Jake refused to let the subject drop. "Has he ever written a kind word about Jews? I want you to give me a full report tomorrow."

Willa concentrated on dunking a Lipton tea bag into hot water. Coming down to breakfast had been a mistake. She should have waited longer, too much to handle. She would slip a copy of "At the Pantomime" under Jake's door and let it go at that.

——◆——

*Sunday, October 20.* Everybody hates to see longtime staff people leave. Although Fritzi criticized Doreen all the time for wearing too-tight sweaters, showing off her perfect figure, and ignoring the women residents to play up to the men, most of us admired her cheerfulness and saintly response to chronic malcontents.

"I feel deserted when a good employee leaves," Flo commented yesterday at breakfast. "You depend on someone, get close to them, consider them a dear friend, and then they're gone."

"They don't miss us as much as we miss them," Bertha said.

She's right. We can do without one more break in continuity. Too bad human nature hasn't changed much over the past hundred fifty years. In *The Poet at the Breakfast Table*, Holmes describes his Landlady's farewell words when she sadly tells the boardinghouse residents that she is closing the place down. Reminiscing, she speaks words that ring true even today:

> I've knowed what it was to have women-boarders that find fault,—there's some of 'em would quarrel with me and everybody at my table; they would quarrel with the Angel Gabriel if he lived in the house with 'em, and...tell him he was always dropping his feathers round, if they couldn't find anything else to bring up against him....and one wants this and another wants that...then a sharp word cuts...and a hard look goes right to your heart. I've seen a boarder make a face at what I set before him, when I had tried to suit him jest as well as I knew how...and I've laid awake...all night. And then when you come down the next morning all the boarders stare at you and wonder what makes you so low-spirited...Boarders sometimes expect too much...Some days the meals are better than other days; it can't be helped...And there is boarders who is always laying in wait for the days when the meals is not quite so good as they commonly be, to pick a quarrel with the one that is trying to serve...

When SVM holds their standard regulation farewell party for Doreen, I'll give her a copy of the above as a souvenir but will eliminate the conclusion of these remarks, which are cloyingly old fashioned: "And though I don't calculate there is any board-houses in heaven, I hope I shall…meet them that has set round my table one year after another, all together, where there is no fault-finding with the food and no occasion for it…"

I don't plan to meet Doreen in heaven or anywhere else.

Studying Holmes and scribbling in this journal have become uncomfortable; my eyes bother me a lot. For relief, I'm listening to more music than ever, including the Saturday afternoon opera from the Met, my favorite being *Samson et Dalila*. The Saint-Saens aria that touches me most is *"Mon coeur s'ouvre à ta voix."* It really hits home. My heart opens to a far-off voice and to the music he loves.

Although I'm a little blurry this morning, Holmes did stop me in my tracks with this observation, and I must record it: "…the musical faculty might be said to have a little brain of its own…a private language all to itself. How can one explain its significance to those whose musical faculties are in a rudimentary state of development, or who have never had them trained?…music can be translated only by music…Pure emotional movements of the spiritual nature,—that is what I ask of music." And now thanks to Eric, so do I.

Enough of all this eyestrain. Today I'll call Dr. Rosen's office to make an appointment for that cataract operation. Perhaps there's a better way for me to see Reality more clearly.

# CHAPTER 4

———•———

In addition to probiotic yogurt, the latest sensation to hit the breakfast table involved the unexpected departure of Sidney the Savvy Salesman. "He needed dialysis three times a week, and he's gone to Verdant Valley for good. He won't be coming back," Fritzi said, dropping by briefly on her way to the gynecologist. "And no breakfast for me. My cab is on the way."

After she left them, the others faced a dreaded truth. Sidney's daughters had switched him to the top floor of the long-term facility. It could happen to anyone.

"Diabetes. Sidney noshed on too many eclairs from the bakery," Flo said as she smeared a heavy layer of nonfat cream cheese on a kaiser roll. "I knew he wouldn't stay here much longer, especially after his daughters took his car away and wouldn't let him drive anymore."

"I'll miss Sidney," Bertha said. "I liked the way he pronounced 'bananas.' He called them bah-nah-nahs."

Lydia added invaluable information. "He never ate the banana at breakfast. He'd lock it inside his post office box if he had to go somewhere after breakfast, remember, Jake?"

"Right. And then he'd forget to pick up his mail for days. The mail carrier must have loved finding all those rotten black bananas."

"Excuse me, is this seat taken?" An erect, smartly dressed woman in a gray business suit pulled out the chair that had once been Sidney's. She immediately informed the group that her name was Tessie and wondered if any of them were addicted to computers the way she was. "I moved in yesterday," she added. The residents noted her perfect coiffure and heavy eye makeup, mumbled a welcome, and returned to their yogurt.

Already saddened by his loss of Sidney, Jake fell into one of his pontifical moods. "We may be the last generation that avoids the Internet. That's my next lecture. 'The Electronic Age: Is It God for the Jews?'"

Renee ignored the pun. "Now they force you to use all these gadgets that tell you things you're better off not knowing. Wasted time. I'd rather accomplish something important and get a Botox shot."

When the newcomer mentioned she had taken Internet courses at the community college, Jake said, "So let's call you Tessie the Techie."

She smiled. "I'm willing to give computer lessons if anybody wants them," she said, pouring a small box of Cheerios into her bowl. "But first, I have a question," she said, after a strained silence. "What do those letters SVM mean?"

Bertha shrugged. "Everything is initials these days. You read the newspaper and they mention something just one time and then the rest of the article they use the initials for it. Who can remember? You have to go back and start all over again. And you never can find it."

Jake spoke to Tessie as if she were a very young child. "You see, when you use initials and abbreviated words these days, few questions are ever asked. People assume you know what you're talking about. Even if you don't, you're supposed to pretend you do. It's quicker and easier. Now if someone wants to learn what the initials actually mean, I'm told your damnable Internet can supply fifty million answers, but it's simpler to accept the initials on faith and go on with one's life. Otherwise, you become bogged down."

Tessie couldn't believe no one knew what SVM stood for. "Haven't you ever looked it up on Wikipedia?"

"Ninety percent of people here avoid computers," Jake said. "An enlightened few use them to play solitaire all day."

Tessie turned to Willa. "What about you? Want to learn how to use a computer and solve the SVM mystery with me?"

Willa didn't think she liked Tessie—too slick, too sure of herself—but she might be helpful in finding Eric's Seattle address. That way he could receive messages in a stamped envelope, the normal way letters should be delivered.

"Perhaps," Willa said.

"What are you two whispering about over there?" Jake asked, more irritable than usual. "My rule at this table is we talk to the whole group so everyone can hear and join in. No private conversations."

Tessie gave him an incredulous look while Bertha changed the subject. "Know what? It's Jake's birthday today."

Jake threatened that if she or others made a fuss over it, he'd move into Verdant Valley with Sidney. "When a guy turns ninety, he's not in the mood for frivolity," Jake said, and added, "Mum's the word, or they'll send out a damned cake and a band of reluctant Ethiopian and Nigerian souls rounded up from the kitchen. I don't want to hear them sing 'Happy Birthday' any more than they feel like singing it."

"I never observe birthdays," Renee said. "I was born three months premature."

"Jake grunted. "That explains why you are the way you are." He turned his attention to Willa, who hadn't spoken much but seemed more alert than usual, as if she had important news to convey.

"You're looking a little less dragged out today," he said to her after the others left for the Gedalia Ginsfarb Fitness Garden for a health lecture on assessing acid reflux.

Willa took a deep, deep breath. "Remember a deaf couple who some-times ate with us?"

"The army colonel? Goldstock? Goldbaum?"

"Don't know. His first name was Chip."

"Passed away some weeks ago didn't he?"

Willa nodded. "His friend Gertie lives on my floor."

"That woman is hell to understand, all those slurred words."

"Saturday night she followed me down the hall and kept making sad little noises."

"Like what?"

"Whimpering. And then she cried out."

"In pain?"

Willa shook her head. "Just scared. She kept saying, 'Alone! Alone.'"

Jake suggested they move into the lobby to continue their talk. His face red from the strain of shifting his body, he mounted the shiny black scooter and twisted a silver key that revved up the motor. "We won't be disturbed in that far corner. If we're too close to the door, strangers pass by and offer their two cents' worth."

They settled into an alcove half hidden by potted Boston ferns. "It was heartbreaking," Willa said.

"Let me guess. You spent the whole evening playing social worker."

"Wrong. I suggested Gertie get help, but she couldn't hear me."

"So what did you do?"

"I didn't want to leave Gertie wandering in the hall. We went back to her apartment. That's when I tried to dial 911."

"Did you get them?"

"No, Gertie pulled my hand away. She insisted we reach her son, Philip."

Jake saw Bertha approaching and gave her an impatient wave that indicated her presence was not needed. She stiffened and hobbled away, her feelings hurt.

He turned back to Willa. "I once chatted with Philip in the elevator. He's a doctor. Lives a good two hours away from here."

Willa continued. "Gertie grabbed a scrap of paper taped to the wall next to the kitchen phone and gave me his number to call."

"How was your voice holding up?"

"Not well. I hoped no one but her son would pick up the receiver."

"And did he?"

"Thank God."

"Was he upset? I guess not so much as you."

"'My mom gets very emotional,' Philip said to me. 'It's nothing serious.'"

"What's the world coming to, Willa? Doctors today won't even make house calls for their own mothers?"

"No, he promised to come right away."

"You must have been worn out by then." She smiled; it was one of Jake's rare expressions of concern for anyone other than himself. "I gave Gertie a thumbs-up to let her know Philip was his way."

"That was it?"

"She hugged me and didn't want to let go."

"The woman exploited you."

"I took her to the lobby. She needed people around her."

Jake raised bushy gray eyebrows badly in need of a trim. "Me, I'd have told her to get lost."

Willa laid a gentle hand on his sleeve. "No, you wouldn't, Jake."

He looked directly into her eyes for the first time during their conversation and then looked away. "So you stayed up all night with her while she waited for her son."

"No, I was dog tired. No voice left. I kissed Gertie and left her with the front desk receptionist—"

"Who, I'm sure, was thrilled."

"Then, for the first time in months, I slept through the night."

Jake restarted the motor on his scooter. "Next time, try melatonin. Less wear and tear on your nervous system," he said as he zoomed away on his scooter.

---

*Monday, October 21.* Back to the sad moods. This afternoon I tuned into my satellite TV channel and discovered baritone Dietrich Fischer-Dieskau, performing "Morgen" by Richard Strauss. The anguish in the singer's voice reminded me of Eric and the physical limitations he must endure every day in a new place on the other side of the country. I doubt that he ever thinks of me.

Meanwhile, each morning Tessie the Techie claims she's overwhelmed by unpacking and waiting for technicians to hook up sundry electronic doodads. Her conversations with me are filled with mysteries like 4 K Ultra HD and OLED TV and constant references to tablets, which I visualize only as the kind of liver pills Dr. Holmes would dole out in rectangular brown bottles. As if I care, she never stops praising the wonders of her smartphone.

"I have a Yahoo e-mail account, a Gmail account, and take pictures, all on one device, everything I've always wanted to do," she said at breakfast.

"Can you fry an egg on it?" Jake asked.

As the days pass by, I'm beginning to think better of Tessie, an independent sort who never doubts herself. That attitude took her on an around-the-world voyage, the only female passenger on a freighter complete with an Albanian captain and what she called "an international crew of soreheads." All this happened the year she turned eighty, or so she says.

Over a mug of black coffee at the SVM café, Tessie revealed another secret. "I'm a late-blooming feminist," she said. "I raised three lively boys and never had time to burn bras or read *The Feminine Mystique*. Bette Friedan and her gang of women's libbers stuck me as phonies." She stopped talking to answer a brief call on her cell phone. "Just a fellow I've been seeing," she said afterward, but didn't go into details. She continued her life story. "I was a divorced single mother long before it became fashionable. It kept me too busy to join NOW or read *Ms.* magazine. After my kids were old enough, I finished college and worked with an agency that arranged adoptions of babies from overseas." Then she wanted to know about me.

"I have a voice disorder and can't talk much."

"That doesn't mean you shouldn't speak at all," she said, but seemed happy to continue the conversation on her own. "Although I agreed with the Equal Rights Amendment, it wasn't until I retired that there was a chance to catch up on all the feminist writers I missed when they were first published. Speaking of which, I attended one of Jake's talks the other day about 'The Boils of Job—Part II.' Know what? Jake is an old-time sexist. I mean, he gave Job a big build-up but didn't mention much about his wife, except that she advised him to renounce God and die already. I mean, she was the one who had to put up with him through thick and thin, wasn't she?"

"Maybe."

"I'd advise you to look it up on the Internet, but you don't do the Internet, do you?" I shook my head and wished she'd let me alone, but she didn't. "So what are you reading these days, Willa?"

"Not much. I have a cataract operation coming up next week." Tessie isn't a soul mate who would tolerate my obsession with Oliver Wendell Holmes. Her comments on Job did inspire me to find a copy of the Jewish bible in English and research his afflictions. The more I thought about his wife, the more unfair the story seemed. That night I took up a ballpoint pen and scribbled this with abandon:

### A Woman Ignored
by
Willa Warsaw

Someday I'm going to write a tale,
Biography, a probe,
Of much-maligned and put-upon
Neglected Mrs. Job.

The whole world knows her husband's plight,
His sackcloth and his boils,
Job's patience is a metaphor,
His image done in oils.

But meanwhile, who prepared his food?
Who vacuumed up the ash?
When did she get away to shop?
What did she do for cash?

They say she gave Job punk advice,
The worst that wives can levy;
(Of course, the men who wrote the script
Would make guess-who the heavy.)

And while the arguments raged on,
She let the drama play,
Then reappeared to bear some kids,
Nice going Mrs. J.!

I showed the poem to Tessie, who wants to send a copy to a friend at Planned Parenthood, which makes me think all those hours spent at the computer have addled her gray matter. But I must confess that her feminist tutorials ring true. Tessie drives me to question even the writings of Dr. Holmes. Where are the flesh-and-blood women in his work? Why isn't he more explicit? What's he hiding? In *The Poet at the Breakfast Table*, when he hints at a bona fide sexy rendezvous between a female boarder and the shy Young Astronomer, Bostonian Holmes leaves me dangling with this: "There was no place so favorable as the Common for the study of the heavens. The skies were brilliant with stars, and the air was just keen enough to remind our young friends that the cold season was at hand." (Note: the cold season? Is the weather changing or does the punster physician Holmes hint that runny noses and coughing are just around the corner?) "...her heart heaved tumultuously, her color came and went, and... she managed to avoid a scene by the exercise of all her self-control...The two lovers...at last found themselves under the Great Elm..." where the Young Astronomer invokes the Greek myth of Andromeda, the stellar constellation named for a maiden chained to a rock and rescued by Perseus who earned her love.

Concluding the scene in the most graphic paragraph of the entire book, Holmes describes the Young Astronomer's burning passion:

And then he began something about a young man chained to his rock…endless questionings that led him nowhere, and now… only one more question to ask. He loved her. Would she break his chain? He held both his hands out toward her, the palms together, as if they were fettered at the wrists. She took hold of them very gently; parted them a little; then wider—wider—and found herself all at once folded, unresisting, in her lover's arms. Then they walk home…and the autumn air seemed full of harmonies as when the morning stars sang together.

That's it, Dr. Holmes? Nothing more? Your love scene doesn't work in the twenty-first century. After babbling on, page after page, you abruptly restrain yourself from any sensual details whatsoever. Instead, you pander to all those delicate Victorian females in their overtight corsets. You realize your sweet young readers won't go for a steady diet of philosophical ideas. Bring on the love interest! Strange how you ramble on forever about the errors of the Boston Natural History Society but waste a perfect opportunity to explain the birds and bees to clueless maidens. Surely you doctors knew the score, even in Beantown.

Those same adoring young women flooded you with purple sonnets and waited breathlessly for you to finish your lectures before they bombarded you with genteel invitations to tea. In that sense, you had much in common with Eric, also a performer, an entertainer always in demand, an artist surrounded by female admirers in love with his songs and personality. I once asked him if crowds of women waited outside his stage door, and he answered, "I had my share." Perhaps even now in that Seattle nursing home he is trailed by geriatric groupies who meet him for clandestine trysts at the podiatrist's.

Oliver Wendell Holmes, you didn't write about raw sex on purpose. You were a man of your time. Why see your reputation ruined and your work banned? You played it safe, like a shrewd Yankee trader, and sold tons of books. But face it, your century has vanished just like mine. Although fans insisted your poem "Old Ironsides" saved that venerable rust bucket from the scrap heap, today a greedy billionaire would convert it into a floating casino and make a fortune.

And frankly, Dr. Holmes, sometimes you can be an annoying prig. Recall a chapter in which you introduce two significant words. You challenge a dim-witted tea party crowd to guess what those words are, and after some inept answers, you self-righteously set them straight:

> The great division between human beings is...the IFs and the AS'es...IF it were—IF it might be—IF it could be—IF it had been. One portion of mankind go through life always regretting, always whining...the other...look at the conditions in which they find themselves. They may be optimists or pessimists...but, taking things just AS the facts,...if one should count the IF's and the AS'es in the conversation of his acquaintances, he would find the more able and important persons among the AS'es...and the majority of the conspicuous failures among the IF's.

That may have inspired readers long ago, but today your words ring pompous and smug, too antiseptic, too rigidly pat. Indecision is as much a part of old age as arthritis. Old bones lose density; often we float whichever way the wind blows to avoid wasting energy. I've learned that in every stage of our lives we can wander lost in a mishmash of choices. Circumstances push us in directions we don't want to go. Able or klutzy, win some, lose some. People make life-changing choices, sensible or not, and who dares judge whether we are successes or failures? So if a woman's role is to please, does that mean she must always make concessions at the expense of never pleasing herself? Even if she's old enough to know better?

Tessie has just phoned to inform me her computer is up and running. She has already located a long-term facility for the elderly in Washington state. It's called Rhododendron Ridge for Persons of the Jewish Faith, otherwise known as RRFPOTJF.

"Fritzi thinks that's where your boyfriend moved," Tessie said.

"He wasn't my boyfriend," I snapped, upset that she had been talking with Fritzi.

But even with his address in hand, do I shower him with bouquets and cheery overpriced cards? Or wait patiently until he sinks from memory? IF it could be, what? If I take the facts AS they are, so? This *IF* and *AS* drivel of Holmes exhausts me. I keep forgetting which word means what, and it's not worth the effort to look it up each time.

# CHAPTER 5

———

NOTHING EVER REMAINS THE SAME, least of all the rent-paying population of a retirement community. At SVM a fresh batch of actors moved in, understudies waiting in the wings, silvery-skinned, white-haired thespians delivering similar interpretations of earlier scenarios. They sported identical wrinkles in old familiar places, suffered from the same ailments, and complained as much as the acts they followed. Freshly painted sets welcomed them; vacant chairs beckoned at Willa's breakfast table. Flo the Faux Blonde moved to a more expensive residence in Sarasota at the invitation of a long-lost Alpha Epsilon Phi sorority sister; Lydia the Encyclopiddia, after a bout of pneumonia, reluctantly entered Verdant Valley Assistant Living; Bertha's children switched her to a special dementia facility. Howie the Unwholesome Wholesaler departed this life in the midst of a poker game. As Jake put it, "He was losing anyway."

Much to her daughters' relief, Fritzi decided against moving in with either of them. SVM allowed her to retain her position as its foremost hit-and-run Schnellbomber. In fact, Jake renamed her The Schnellstbomber. "I nominate her for fastest on the draw," he said, "the Yenta of the Year." As for Willa, Dr. Rosen took it upon himself to slice cataracts from both her eyes and substitute the clarifying truth of artificial lenses.

Recovering, Willa spent her lonely days applying antibiotics and eye drops. Tessie the Techie had departed for an out-of-state retirement haven called Kosher Kaverns, which she described as "a wild place with Wi-Fi, hot tubs, and gefilte fish not out of a jar." Once settled, she missed what

223

she had left behind and complained about widespread inertia at her new place.

"The men here lie low," she complained to Willa. "Daytime they refuse to break away from hibernating in their apartments, except those who habitually snooze in the lobby. And all the women look like worse-for-wear Diane Keatons. Or try to."

When Tessie bought a new smartphone, she used it exclusively to pester Willa with daily calls. "How about relocating to Kosher Kaverns? Let's share an apartment," Tessie said, but Willa considered it an option second only to getting a root canal. Although she admired Tessie's gumption, she didn't want to spend the rest of her days in the company of a hyperkinetic electronics addict.

And Jake, finding it burdensome to supply pet names for the newcomers at the breakfast table, took a cue from Oliver Wendell Holmes, who, in his final book, according to Willa, identified characters by number. Impressed, Jake established his own numerical nomenclature system and informed Willa that she was Number One. He labeled himself Number Seven because, as he punned, "I'm still in my prime."

"What do those letters SVM mean?" Number Eight asked. A retired chemist, he was an asthmatic little man, who just arrived the day before and found his way to Willa's table for breakfast.

"You're a scientist?" asked an auburn-haired woman with irregular eyebrows, one always darker than the other. "My husband was a nuclear mathematician. The only thing I could read off his papers was the page number."

"Maybe SVM is listed on the periodic table of the elements," Jake said, "along with sodium, Valium, and Metamucil."

Number Eight did not accept that. "It has to mean something. Why would they call a retirement home SVM?"

"If you read the Bible—" Jake began.

Number Eight cut him off. "Not my cup of tea." He motioned to the aide serving hot drinks. "I'll have my coffee now." The Bolivian waitress filled his cup with hot water and a leaky tea bag. He frowned but remained stoic.

"I'm saying *if* you read it," Jake said, "you'll find a self-identifying Supreme Being. Who is this Being? He answers, 'I am that I am.' Well, what my point is, SVM is what SVM is."

The chemist shook his head and bit into a buttered croissant. "Nonsense."

"In this place," Jake said, "nothing makes sense and everything makes sense."

"That's an easy way out," Number Eight said.

Jake continued, undaunted. "The point is, SVM is open to interpretation. Remember the What's-In-A-Name contest, Willa? People made it mean whatever they wanted…food, home, family." He noticed confused looks on nearby faces. "So why not have SVM stand for the advice Moses gave to Joshua when they approached the Promised Land? *Chazak ve'ematz:* be strong and courageous."

Number Seven couldn't hide his impatience. "Because the Roman alphabet letters don't correspond to the Hebrew words. You're mixing apples and oranges."

"What's wrong with telling old people to be strong and courageous?"

"It has nothing to do with the letters SVM," Number Eight said, under his breath.

Jake persisted. "Why not? When you can't be strong anymore, at least you can lie to yourself that you're brave."

"No matter what your version of bravery may be?" Number Eight asked. "Or even if you're just self-aggrandizing, like some arrogant oddballs in this place?"

He glared at Jake, who answered, "Those who want to believe it won't know the difference."

"But you're just deceiving yourself," said a woman he called Number Four.

Over his cup brimming with decaf coffee, Jake gave Number Four an exasperated look and resisted an urge to raise his voice. "You are if you think you are." He took a sip. "And you aren't if you think you aren't."

Number Four thought that was wishy-washy. Others considered it profound.

"You don't pull letters out of thin air and use them to name a retirement community," Number Eight yelled. "It's no acronym. It's meaningless."

"And that bothers you?" Jake asked softly.

Willa couldn't remember when she enjoyed a breakfast conversation more. Theology versus science. It was like classic Oliver Wendell Holmes, except the vocabulary of his imaginary debaters would have been classier.

Stimulated and now able to view the world more clearly, Willa registered for an adult-education course jauntily labeled "Conquering the Web When You've Been Through the Mill but Aren't Over the Hill." And though Jake condemned "all that electronic dreck," one morning Willa took a cab to Best Buy to commit the worst of sins. She bought a laptop. The technical tyrants at the store tried to teach her how to use it, but instead of absorbing the wisdom of the experts, she worried about falling off a tall stool at the instruction counter.

After weeks of frustration, she mastered enough slight-of-hand to consult the Internet on a burning question. What did the letters SVM mean? What was their significance in the scheme of things, their orbit in the universe? She asked Wikipedia, but they didn't know either.

At least now she could receive Tessie's e-mails, mostly painful Jewish jokes Willa never bothered to read. Because Eric knew nothing about using the Internet, she bombarded him via snail mail with overpriced thinking-of-you greeting cards on which she scribbled newsworthy tidbits like, "They're painting all the laundry rooms, wish you were here." She brazenly signed everything, "Love, Willa." Eric never wrote back.

She continued to miss him and attempted an original light poem entitled "On Guard, Nelson Eddy!" boasting these immortal lines: "I don't send cards to Thomas Hampson / Old Placido doesn't rate them / They both have talent more or less / (I don't exactly hate them) / But you, my baritone divine / Can figure what my plot is, / A song of praise and school girl mush / An ode to Eric's glottis." She read it through five times and then daintily tore it into pieces one-inch square.

In the middle of the night, she thought about phoning him and whistling themes from popular operatic arias learned from Classic Arts Showcase, but she was afraid of making him feel worse. Although her voice remained as unpredictable as usual, for the first time in years, she resumed speech therapy with a woman named Mrs. Chatsworth, who promised to help her communicate more clearly with those around her. On days when even the new techniques failed her, Willa substituted a shy smile or a tiny compliment here, a brief platitude there, and dodged all lengthy verbal entanglements.

Remaining cheerful wasn't easy. Willa couldn't fight a tearful, breathless sensation that overtook her one morning at breakfast after sitting through another acrimonious debate between Jake and Number Eight over the basic meaning of SVM. She put her hand over her eyes.

"Sick again?" Jake asked.

"I'm all right. Just get me out of here."

Jake abandoned his scooter at the table, took her arm, and shuffled into the lobby, where they perched on a stiffly upholstered love seat.

"What is it?" Jake asked, genuinely worried.

"I was getting better, and now everything seems to smother me again."

"Something hurts you?"

"Nothing physical." She swallowed hard. "Two months ago a crippled man, Will Warnburg, moved into the apartment across the hall. One day the front desk delivered a letter to my box, and I opened it by mistake."

"Easy to mix them up," Jake said. "Willa Warsaw, Will Warnburg."

"The envelope even contained a large insurance check."

"All I ever get are solicitations from the Democratic National Committee."

"I slipped it under Will's door with a note apologizing for the opened mail and signed it, "Your Neighbor Across the Hall, Willa.""

"The right thing to do."

"Poor Will could hardly get around even with a walker. He took forever to shlep inch by inch down the corridor."

"Belongs in a nursing home, not here," Jake said.

"Then whenever our paths crossed, I'd say, 'Hey, Will,' and he'd answer, 'Hello, neighbor' with a big smile. I never saw anyone else talk to him."

"You're breaking my heart," Jake said drily. He hated any sentimentality unless it came from him.

Willa continued. "Three nights ago, I heard a knock at the door. Late, about nine o'clock."

"Did you call security?"

"I asked who was there, and he answered, 'Will, your neighbor.'"

"And then he invited you to his apartment to see his etchings," Jake said. "Sorry. Go on."

"He said he had a bad cold and asked if I could spare a couple of tea bags."

"You'll never get rid of him now."

"I gave him a green tea bag and hoped he'd feel better soon." Willa's eyes filled up. "He died the next day."

A silence, and then Jake tried to cheer her up. "Maybe if you'd given him two tea bags, he'd still be here."

Willa looked at him for what seemed like a long time. "You're a pitiful case," she said and walked away. In the dreariness of her apartment, she switched on the classical music station, featuring yet another baritone suffering through a mournful *lied* from *Winterreise*. She reached for a biography of Franz Schubert that Eric had once lent her. She hadn't returned it. The title in German, *Einsamkeit*, meant loneliness. Never since he left for Seattle did she miss Eric so much.

No. She missed someone else, and it wasn't Oliver Wendell Holmes. Willa ached for the man whose black-and-white photograph hung on the wall in the foyer next to her front door. "He has a kind face," Ethel once said.

———

*Monday, October 29.* I'm in shock. Just spent an eternity on two ill-fated e-mails for Tessie. The messages disappeared somewhere into the cyber catacombs or wherever missing texts go when you hit the wrong keys.

Problem is, I forget how to bring the words back, and too many thoughts evaporate without ever being retrieved. My old portable Underwood never betrayed me like this. I wanted to let Tessie know that Eric called today for the first time from Seattle. His voice sounded as if it were encased in layers of thick glass.

"Is this my beautiful lady?" he said. After days and nights of planning musical thoughts to share with him, I couldn't think of a single thing and merely wanted to know how he was and if he received the birthday card sent weeks before to mark his eighty-second birthday.

"Yes." He paused. "I must ask you something," he said in an even fainter voice, scarcely audible.

When nothing more followed, I paused, taking a mammoth breath, and then treaded water. "Today's paper features an interview with that rugged baritone, Bryn Terpel, who looks like a longshoreman. Did you see it?" Eric didn't answer right away, and when he did, it was no, he hadn't, and then more silence.

"I also read another article about a singer, forget his name, but he was in town for a concert, and they asked him which he preferred singing, opera or operetta, and he said he enjoyed operetta more because he could put more of himself into the role instead of keeping to a traditional interpretation of an operatic role. Did you ever feel like that, Eric?" By the time I finished this long speech, my own voice had disintegrated, and I wondered if it registered with him at all.

There was extended quiet on the other end of the line. Finally, he managed a complete sentence. "Yes, you can be yourself more." Another pause. "What are you doing now?" he asked.

"Hanging out with myself. What are you doing?"

"Same thing." Another long pause.

"What's new in the wild West?"

"I'm taking the bull by the horns, Willa."

I smiled but of course he couldn't see it. "Like Toreador Escamillo in 'Carmen,'" I said. He had told me he sang that role many times. "Don't ever forget. Carmen chose the baritone over the tenor."

"Will you marry me?" Eric asked.

That jolted me so much, I preferred to chatter away and not take it seriously. "Sure. Yours is my heart alone," I said, trying to remember the romantic song, courtesy of Franz Lehár and the Classic Arts Showcase, "and only you can...something, something. I forget the rest. Oh, yes. Excuse my German. *Dein bist mein gantzes Hertz*. Or words to that effect."

"Be serious. Pack a suitcase, and fly out here to Seattle. Marry me."

There it was, something neither of us had dared think about, and for once my speechlessness came in handy. It felt good not to be able to say anything.

His words grew stronger. "Sorry, can't think of anything romantic. Anyway, it wouldn't sound the way I want."

"Let me get this straight, Eric. You're asking me to marry you?"

"Yes." He was not joking. I ran for shelter. When a woman past eighty receives a marriage proposal long distance over the phone from a man of the same age, it gives her pause.

After stammering and sinking into a breathy limbo even more difficult for him to hear, I answered, "Let's talk again when we're both more in voice. I'm not even sure I heard you correctly. It may be the connection."

"You heard me quite well."

"You want me to marry you?"

"Yes."

The answer stuck in my throat. "I'll...I'll call you back. Or write you a letter. Or something. We both have to think it through." Never did I expect this. Not at this late date anyway.

Another ear-splitting silence. Before hanging up, he said, "I love you." Or at least that's what it sounded like.

"Love you too, Eric." I returned the black receiver to its plastic cradle, gently, gently as if it were Eric's hand I had been holding. My heart pounded in my chest. Reality or Romance—choose one. When it came down to it, did I really want either one of them to win? Couldn't an old woman choose a smattering of each? Or none of the above?

The decision was too important to make all by myself. At my desk *The Autocrat of the Breakfast Table* lay opened. If I read that random page, surely Oliver Wendell Holmes would point the way:

> To take up this…earthly being of ours as a sponge sucks up water,—to be steeped and soaked in its realities as a hide fills its pores lying seven years in a tan-pit,…and…at the point when the white-hot passions have cooled down…plunge our experience into the ice-cold stream of some human language or other…one might think (it) would end in a rhapsody…

Hold it. *A hide lying seven years in a tan-pit?* That completely turned me off. I skipped down to the climactic scene between two sweethearts, the teacher and the astronomer:

> I had never addressed one word of love to the Schoolmistress…It was on the Common that we were walking. One of these (branches) runs down from opposite Joy Street southward across the whole length of the Common…We called it the long path…I felt very weak indeed…as we came opposite the head of this path…At last I got out the question, __ Will you take the long path with me?

> Certainly, said the Schoolmistress, with much pleasure.—Think, I said,—before you answer; if you take the long path with me now, I shall interpret it that we are to part no more!—The Schoolmistress stepped back with a sudden movement, as if an arrow had struck her.

> One of the long granite blocks…was…close by the Gingko-tree.— Pray sit down,—I said. No, no, she answered, softly,—I will take the long path with you!

It's now almost dawn, and I haven't slept yet; there's a no-nonsense cramp attacking a muscle in my left thigh, and I can't manage the pain or anything else. Take the long path with Eric? Where does it lead? Glorious pinwheel fantasies spin out of control. My blood pressure rockets into space. When Romance and Reality collide, it's hard to know which pieces to pick up and which to sweep away.

# CHAPTER 6

———•———

HOPING HER VOICE WOULD HOLD out long enough to cover everything, Willa waited until the others had flown the breakfast table before she turned to Jake, lingering over his second cup of coffee. "Something unexpected has happened."

"What? You're speaking in that foggy whisper again."

Willa hesitated. "After a night with no sleep, it's hard to talk."

"Calm down." He leaned forward to hear better. "What's wrong?"

"Eric asked me to marry him."

Annoyed, Jake whipped off his silver-rimmed glasses. "So why bother me? I don't give advice to the lovelorn." He shifted his gaze to the scooter as if he wanted to make a quick getaway.

"Ethel's gone. I've no one."

Jake started to leave and then decided against it. "It's no great surprise, Willa. I wish someone would look at me the way you always did the minute Eric entered the room. Your face lit up like a million Hanukkah candles."

"I didn't realize it showed." She stopped and frowned. "Then Fritzi saw it too."

He answered in a subdued voice, unlike his usual growl. "I've often wondered what image of him you've built up in your mind." As he spoke, not looking at her, Jake nervously folded and unfolded an empty Splenda packet lying next to his emptied oatmeal bowl. "I mean, he's a nice guy, talented, a real mensch, but he's saddled with a condition that won't quit."

Willa took the deepest of breaths because she wanted Jake to hear every word. "He's much more. I see sensitivity and goodness. Most of all, the purity of excellence. I see Eric and hear Mozart, Verdi, Puccini."

"Know what I think? You're star-struck. You're dazzled by what you consider the glamor of his years on the stage, and you wanted to bring excitement into your life by chasing a one-time celebrity."

"Not true."

"There she is, ladies and gents, Willa the Octogenarian Groupie." He even forced a laugh out of her. "People do things in their dotage that they wouldn't dream of doing as youngsters."

"Isn't it the other way around, Jake?"

"Maybe you're just smitten with theater people."

She felt compelled to respond. "I didn't lead a sheltered life, if that's what you mean. In the ad agency, we met lots of famous actors touring in road productions. I once told Helen Hayes she had a run in her hose." Willa's voice was collapsing; she felt sorry she had confided in Jake. "Let's drop it," she said.

"Aren't you deluding yourself, trying to substitute Eric for someone else?"

"You keep coming back to that. Why would I do that?"

"How many years were you married? A half century?"

"What's that got to do with anything?"

"It's a long time to spend caring for one man, listening to his jokes, sorting his socks. His last months may have taken more out of you than you think. And then *poof*! It's over, he passes, and you ask yourself, 'Where's that person I'm supposed to look out for, the one who filled my months and years with anxiety and concern?'"

"You forgot to mention love."

Jake pretended not to hear. "Your major responsibility, where has he gone? He's out of the picture, not just away on a business trip but gone for good. So to take up the slack, you find a substitute. I don't have to be a psychologist to figure it out." Willa's eyes filled while Jake assumed a different approach. "Tell me the truth, did Eric ever discuss marriage with you before he moved away?"

She shook her head and whispered, "No."

"Maybe he's much further along now, different from the last time you saw him. Use your common sense, Willa. You're not examining this from all angles."

Although Willa wanted the conversation to end, Jake's controlling attitude annoyed her, and she fought back. "He knows what he's doing, if that's what you mean. Parkinson's affects the muscles, not the intellect."

Jake put his hand on her shoulder. "All I'm saying is you could be making a big mistake."

Willa met his slightly manic eyes and looked away. "Nothing's definite yet, Jake."

Encouraged, he landed his final blows. "And don't forget all the legal headaches of marriage at your age. The Social Security quagmire, tax problems, annuities, and doesn't his niece have power of attorney?"

"I don't know."

"Wait. I get it. For a nice Jewish girl like you, this is an act of loving-kindness, *ahavat chesed*. Right? A good deed? That's commendable, but in this case impractical. Even though the Talmud urges us to administer to the ailing, at our age we have to draw the line somewhere. Am I on the right track?"

"I feel cheated, Jake. I never knew Eric as a young man, never heard him sing, and now I'd settle for whatever is left, a kind of farewell performance."

"That's no reason to marry him. What's the big draw? Not sex, is it? Even Diana, Goddess of the Hunt, is slowing down. As she puts it, that train has left the station."

Willa refused to let him make her laugh. "My friendship with Eric is the deepest, truest kind. We were destined to meet at this time in our lives and become devoted to each other. It's beshert. Kismet."

After Jake took a long look at her, he said in a quiet way, "Wait five minutes; you'll get over it. Go back to Oliver Wendell Holmes. He requires nothing more of you than ruining your eyesight. Ever hear that saying—Holmes is where the heart is?"

Willa sighed. "You don't understand. I'm sure music has sealed Eric and me together. It's adhesive. It won't let go."

Jake wouldn't give up. "Music shouldn't control your life. You're not a musician. For you it's no more than an acquired taste, probably a recent one. Too much and it becomes an addiction."

"Our minds are still young, Jake, and music can keep them that way. The music that Eric loves is like a healing balm. Sharing it with him consoles and comforts me."

"Just because you can recognize melodies or composers?"

"More. It's the phosphorescence of music."

"The what? You lost me on that one."

"It fills me with awe and joy and makes me feel content."

Jake laughed to himself and said, "A New York corned-beef sandwich can do that for you too, but it's no reason to get emotional over it."

"Enjoying all that beauty with someone who knows so much more about it than I do, well, it's..." She stopped, exhausted.

"You're so in awe of him you've made up your mind to marry him? Awe isn't a sound basis for marriage."

"Admiration then." She examined his unhappy face closely. "I admire you too, Jake, but for different reasons."

"Look," Jake said. "I'll make a bargain with you. Stop spending time and energy trying to find out if that *schmendrick* Oliver Wendell Holmes was good for the Jews. Instead ask yourself this: is Eric good for you, and are you good for Eric? The rest is commentary."

Willa didn't want to answer. Her left arm ached. She was taking too many short breaths to project all she had to say. She felt dizzy. Not speaking, they watched a Jamaican waiter vacuum corn flakes from the floor.

"He wants us to leave," Jake said, "so he can finish cleaning up and get ready for the next meal."

With an agonized grunt, Jake shifted himself onto the motorized scooter and headed toward the French doors. Willa followed him. When they reached the lobby, he swiveled his leather seat in her direction and turned the key that switched off the scooter. "How is it that a woman like you in her eighties never managed to get a firm grip on reality?"

"I've always favored the other side of the coin."

"You know, of course, that reality wins whether you have a firm grip on it or not."

"Not always."

"So you'll join Eric in Seattle?"

"You've offered some pretty strong arguments against it."

"The suspense gives me heartburn. Are you marrying him or not?"

"I'll let you know."

Jake pounded a trembling fist into the palm of his left hand. "Rock-paper-scissors. Scissors cut paper. Paper covers rock. Rock breaks scissors."

"And a Beethoven symphony aces them all," Willa said.

Late for an appointment with his audiologist, Jake reactivated his scooter, faced straight ahead, and headed into the lobby. He tossed one final remark over his arthritic shoulder. "Three thousand miles," he said, "is one hell of a long way to travel for a free course in music appreciation."

———◆———

*Friday, November 1.* I need firmer ground than Jake. And Dr. Holmes, lately you've lost your bloom. You continue to amaze me with your insights on the elderly, but there's little help on the subject of old womanhood. You never dreamed we would stick around this long, did you? What would you prescribe for us? Your heaviest praise goes to women whose entire lives consist of pleasing their men. Or with a physician's arrogance you describe a clinical condition in which ladies (like me) go overboard on the arts: "There are certain nervous conditions peculiar to women in which the common effects of poetry and music upon their sensibilities are strangely exaggerated." (No men with similar hang-ups?)

Most of all you lose my admiration with condescending tidbits like this:

> Women find it easier than men to grow old in a becoming way. A very old lady who has kept something...of her youthful feelings, who is daintily cared for, who is grateful for the attentions bestowed upon her, and enters into the spirit of the young lives that surround her, is as precious to those who love her as a gem in an antique setting, the fashion of which has long gone by, but which leaves the color and brightness which are its inalienable qualities.

How patronizing, the Little Old Lady Syndrome, all lavender and lace, the elderly Victorian female (upper class) preserved in formaldehyde and dependent on the young for her self-esteem. My dear doctor, project yourself into the twenty-first century. What if our aging heroine is surrounded not by family but contemporaries as old or older than she is? What happens to your dainty portrait of womanhood then? Who's around to supply the self-esteem? At least you admit this: "With old men it is...different...They have no pretty little manual occupations. The old lady knits or stitches... The old man smokes his pipe, but does not know what to do with his fingers, unless he plays upon some instrument, or has a mechanical turn..." How generous of you, Dr. Holmes, to allow us our pretty little manual occupations!

Enough from the past; time for the dreaded present and my voracious computer, which taunts me with its overbite, six rows of black molars bearing alphabetic white cavities. The blinking fiend is incapable of mercy; its hellish comment, "daemon," pops up with each of my misfires. The laptop indeed laps; it laps up time, gorges itself on savory chunks of human patience. Jake is right when he warns us against allowing electronic doodads to invade minds and bodies. I should have seen it coming years ago at the advertising agency when we treated these two holy entities, time and space, as marketable trinkets. And now we sacrifice not only our identity but also the quiet core that makes us human. There's nothing in this world worth more than our own private, unadvertised selves. People like Tessie don't want to hear this.

Each of my e-mails to her requires three or four aborted tries. On rare successful occasions, she responds instantly, doling out stilted feminist responses like "You go, girl!" and other parched 1970s clichés that make her feel young, and me very old. Yesterday she suggested that I stage a clandestine tryst with Eric via Skype, as if I were some sort of adolescent Silicon Valley wizard. No, I refuse to become enslaved to every dehumanizing electronic whim that comes along.

Jake told me he was glad to see Tessie gone. He takes pride in the remarkable number of facts he carries in his head, and she considers all information as available as toilet paper. Still, Jake may be right about Eric. This obsession leads nowhere. Each day my life is like a partita, a musical variation on a free-wheeling theme. Perhaps it's best left unremembered.

# CHAPTER 7

———•———

HEART BEATING RAPIDLY, WILLA HURRIED into the Esther Essenvarg Dining Den and discovered that Jake hadn't yet arrived for breakfast. All around her, strangers occupied seats once occupied by acquaintances long gone. The former Ha-Ha Table now accommodated a circle of formidably glum individuals. Forcing a tentative smile in their direction, she couldn't manage more than a raspy, "Good morning." She would save her voice for Jake. The book review in her hand had upset her so much that she almost forgot about Eric and his marriage proposal.

Jake arrived later than usual; he had tipped over an eight-ounce glass of prune juice in his refrigerator. Willa moved into the vacant chair next to him.

"Remember Tessie the Techie?" she said.

"So far a rotten morning," Jake muttered. "Didn't have a rag to mop up the mess. It leaked all over the kitchen floor. Had to use my terry cloth bathrobe to soak it up."

Willa waved a paper under his nose. "Yesterday Tessie e-mailed this attachment."

"Don't bother me with that electronic dreck. I need a strong shot of caffeine. Over here!" He motioned to a flustered Somalian carrying a coffee pot.

"Jake, please. It took me two hours and ten minutes to download it."

Jake sipped his coffee and frowned. "Lukewarm." He set the cup down hard on a saucer. "Not that I care, but what ever happened to Tessie? Did she hit the wrong computer key and e-mail herself into the stratosphere?"

"She moved into a new condo in Pittsburgh. She has cousins there."

"Knew she wouldn't last. Not the SVM type." Jake slipped into one of his philosophical moods.

"Jake, please look at this printout."

He reached for a sliced bagel. "Social media crap. It annihilates memory. Who ever thought thinking would become a waste of time? So what will humans be like when they grow old and don't have any personal history because it's all been stolen? Meanwhile people won't know how to remember anything."

"Jake, please read this book review Tessie sent."

"That's what you're so upset about? A stupid review?"

Willa handed him a clipping, and Jake read the title in a resounding voice. *"The Crazy Autocrat in the Attic: Heartburn at Breakfast with Oliver Wendell Holmes."* He belched with feeling. "Heartburn? I'm not alone."

Willa's face darkened. "It infuriates me. My blood pressure is soaring."

"Cut back on your salt."

Willa sighed. "That's not the end of it. Yesterday I shopped at Barnes and Noble."

"You were fool enough to pay good money for that book?"

"It kept me up all night."

While Jake adjusted his glasses to read, Willa inhaled deeply. "The author is a professor at Harvard. That's the alma mater of Oliver Wendell Holmes."

Jake almost chuckled. He had never seen Willa angry like this. "So what can you do? Rent a one-horse shay, drive it to Cambridge, and give her a klopp?"

"I'll write a letter that will blast her off the map."

"Oh, a letter will really do significant damage," Jake said.

"I don't need your sarcasm." Willa's voice was nearly gone by now, her throat raw, her eyes twitching from the strain of speaking with such force.

A sour-looking newcomer with a stomach that bulged over his belt buckle like a shiitake mushroom approached the table. "Are you one of the inmates here?" he asked Willa.

Jake answered for her. "Your remark says less about us than it does about you."

"Don't get huffy with me," the man said, "I just wanted to find out if they're still open for breakfast."

Willa grabbed her belongings from under the table and stood. "Ask the servers. That's their job."

He blinked at her. "What did you say?" He turned to Jake. "I can't understand a word she said."

Willa took a substantial breath. *"That's your problem!"* she shouted so loudly that two Nigerian members of the kitchen staff emerged to see what those cranky old white folks were up to now.

"Harvard is going to hear from me!" Willa cried to the dour Ha-Ha Table as she stalked away. They glanced at the back of her head and returned to their pancakes.

———◆———

*Tuesday, November 6.* That book, *The Crazy Autocrat in the Attic*, understands neither Holmes the writer nor Holmes the physician. To call him doddering, dim, and dated all in one sentence is an affront to everyone who appreciates American literature and also those who don't.

The self-promoting author is one Kimberly Amy Donnerschlagg, PhD. Although I can't match her in graduate degrees, mine is a God-given right as an English major to put this so-called scholar in her place, even if it means neglecting Eric's proposal for just a day more. Holmes mustn't be deserted in his hour of need. This is my final draft:

Dear Dr. Donnerschlagg:

Your snide book is a devastating assault on my hero and deliverer, Oliver Wendell Holmes. If you think you are following in his witty footsteps, you are dead wrong. *The Crazy Autocrat in the Attic: Heartburn at Breakfast with Oliver Wendell Holmes* misses the mark completely. To castigate him as an opinionated male-chauvinist egomaniac is a bit harsh, although he had his moments. Granted, you did the required research but failed to reread your garbled notes. Or maybe you lost them altogether. Computers can do that to a person. That's why I prefer writing this in pen and ink, the way letters were meant to be written. (See Elizabeth Barrett Browning.)

It's only natural that Holmes describes the ideal woman as sweet-tempered, supportive of men, and eager to please. Why not? He lauds the genteel woman of his time: dainty, smart but not too smart. Female readers loved this flattering image of themselves and repaid the compliment by purchasing everything he wrote.

Of course Holmes did tag certain female writers, ones who disagreed with him, as unwomanly, but he also believed that although ladies would do better as nurses, they should be admitted to medical school to become doctors if that's what they wanted. Deep down, he didn't know why they would want to.

You lambast him unmercifully for not taking sides during the Civil War. True, he avoided politics, possibly because a few Southern rebels nested in his family tree. This may or may not have accounted for his never having marched with the abolitionists. He emphasized that slavery was sanctioned in the Bible, which most of the time he ignored or approached tongue in cheek to scandalize divinity students. (He deliberately goaded the pious to get a rise out of them. Did you miss that?)

But why do you ignore his innate tolerance? He meets anti-Semitism head on and concludes that it makes no sense for Christians to hate the tribe of which Jesus was a dues-paying member. At one point, Holmes even suggests that his exclusive Saturday Club, scientists, lawyers, and fellow writers like Emerson, Lowell, and Longfellow, entertain a famed Jewish guest, the founding father of us all. Herewith, a quote:

"I can't help wondering that the world's great men have not commonly been great scholars, nor its scholars great men. The Hebrew patriarchs had small libraries, I think, if any; yet they represent to our imaginations a very complete idea of manhood, and, I think, if we could ask in Abraham to dine with us men of letters next Saturday, we should feel honored by his company."

That's gracious of Holmes, although truth be told, never in a million years would Abraham ever want to sit down to an unkosher, boiled New England dinner with that pack of elitists. (I've heard there are still a number of them at Harvard.)

What's more, in attacking the sensitivity of Holmes, you are entirely off the mark. Here was a man devoted to his patients and his medical career. As a popular professor, his wry humor attracted a host of young medical students, who loved attending his classes at lunch time because they could goof off while he blasted primitive nineteenth century protocols. Homeopathy he especially considered the height of the ridiculous...as are your foggy assumptions.

Did you deliberately skirt over the impact of his childbed fever papers? Holmes was a physician ahead of his time. His work, *Puerperal Fever as a Private Pestilence* (note the poetic alliteration even in a scientific paper), touted the value of soap and water. Was it too much to ask that dirty doctors wash themselves and not infect the patients? Medical colleagues hooted at such revolutionary tactics and wouldn't give him the time of day. Basic rules of sanitation to protect mothers from life-threatening puerperal fever went nowhere, but once Holmes became an internationally recognized writer, a household name to readers, including the snotty British, the best physicians in Europe and America changed their minds. Celebrities carry weight even when they don't know what they're talking about. Holmes, however, knew plenty. On the other hand, much as I worship Holmes and his sense of humor, no way would I ever have wanted him to operate on me—no, not even for an ingrown toenail.

If Holmes hadn't stirred everybody up *advertising* his theories on sanitation, your own great-great-great-grandmother might not have survived by giving birth, and you, her ungrateful descendant, wouldn't even be here. Most important of all, Dr. Holmes realized that literary fame has a short shelf life. Another quote to sustain my argument:

Epilogue to the Breakfast Table Series: Autocrat—Professor—Poet.
At a Bookstore—Anno Domini 1972

A crazy bookcase, placed before
A low-priced dealer's open door;
Therein arrayed in broken rows
A ragged crew of rhymes and prose
The homeless vagrants, waifs and strays
Whose low estate this line betrays
(Set forth the lesser birds to lime)
YOUR CHOICE AMONG THESE BOOKS,
ONE DIME!

The New England prophet could foresee our own time when readers have deserted beloved hardbacks and paperbacks for online phantoms. Where are our avid book lovers of yesteryear? Is a day coming when books disappear from the face of the earth along with rain forests, extinct animals, and predictable weather?

As for you, Professor Donnerschlagg, perhaps you're too young to appreciate a writer who admits he can be long-winded and tiresome. Your immaturity is especially damaging when you take a machete to the loveliest poem he ever created, "The Chambered Nautilus." Although probably younger than you when he wrote "This is the ship of pearl that poets feign / Sails the unfettered main," his message is one that the elderly should embrace if someone would just bring it to their attention (because most of them have never heard of it and never will). Like you, I was once too young to grasp the imagery of a seashell gradually evolving, acquiring substance the same way a human soul grows. Now I get it.

Holmes, the poet, delivered that gift. The same mind that built the wonderful one-horse shay launched the ship of pearl; the same literary master who tickled us with "The Height of the Ridiculous" advised the human soul to create more stately mansions, and the same man, who swore never again to write as funny as he could, did so over and over again even unto old age.

His breakfast-table conversations were unlike any I have heard in my retirement home, where people consider it their duty to complain about the size of food portions, the lack of dependable bridge partners, and the insensitivity of neighbors with bad colds who come to breakfast only to sneeze on the hash browns. And don't blame it all on dementia. Some old people never sported much in the way of brains to begin with. In contrast, conversations among the imaginary boarders of Dr. Holmes were invigoratingly unique. I'll bet you've never heard such exquisite language among your lofty colleagues. No, not even at Harvard.

A widow, I have spent the past year cutting personal losses, which I won't go into right now. One of these, however, was the loss of a self that was. Over time I am beginning to spin a workable replacement, thanks to Oliver Wendell Holmes, who delivers a potent brand of American medicine. Bearing no expiration date, his refillable prescription extends into infinity. It is written by the wisest, most literate physician who ever graduated from Harvard Medical School. And he wasn't even an English major. You owe the doctor an apology. And if you are too stiff-necked to render it, I'll do it for you the next time I visit him.

An irate octogenarian,<br>Willa Warsaw

Having finished the letter, I slipped it under Jake's door with a note asking him for comments. He phoned, calling the text "questionably adequate unless you can muster the energy to rewrite the whole thing." He did insist that I delete the final phrase, "the next time I visit him." Jake realizes it's not meant literally but noted, "It makes you sound like a nutcase." I changed nothing.

Defending Dr. Holmes against Kimberly Amy Donnerchlagg's onslaught has cleared my mind on numerous levels. I now see Eric's marriage proposal more sharply, all the pros and cons spelled out in the boldest, most gigantic typeface available on my abominable computer. At last I know what my decision must be.

# CHAPTER 8

———◆———

AT BREAKFAST EARLY THE NEXT morning, Willa kept watch, hoping to catch sight of Jake on his erratic black scooter. Forty-five minutes late, he arrived, jerking the vehicle in choppy fits-and-starts as he crossed the room. All other tablemates had deserted the ship by this time, which suited Willa.

"Emergency appointment with my cardiologist." Jake said, panting hard as he shifted from scooter to chair. "False alarm. Gas pains. More useless pills."

Willa prepared herself for a long conversation. She inhaled from the diaphragm, paused, and exhaled slowly through her mouth. Today she didn't wish to waste any strength repeating each sentence in case Jake couldn't hear her.

He reached for the cranberry juice. "After leaving the cab," Jake said, "I stopped at the front desk to pick up my package of mail-order shirts from Haband. The receptionist asked me this to give you." He pushed a large Kraft envelope across the table.

Willa examined the return address label. "It's from someone in Washington state," she said. "Rochelle Shapfmann. I don't know anybody named—" She stopped. "Eric's niece." Willa handed it back to Jake. "Something is wrong. I'm afraid to open it. Jake, will you?"

"Open it yourself," he said. "You can't keep running away."

Willa held the thick envelope between shaky fingers and stared at it a long time.

"Look inside, for God's sake," Jake said, waited, and then gave up. "Give me that." He grabbed it from her hands and tore it open. "Just some tapes," he said as he thrust the brown envelope in her direction. "With a note. Aha! A love letter?" He handed it to her.

Willa read silently. "Eric misses his friends," she said at last. "He told Rochelle he wants me to have these tapes he made forty years ago in Milan. This one is from *Carmen* in his role as the bullfighter Escamillo singing the toreador aria. And here's another: Songs from Schubert's Wintereisse. He loved performing these romantic German songs more than anything else."

Jake brightened. "You complained you never had a chance to hear him sing. Now you don't have to move to Seattle. Play the tapes."

"There has to be more, Jake."

"What do you mean?"

"I'm going out there to be with him."

Jake shifted his gaze to a heavy, red-faced man struggling by on crutches. "So after all my advice, a still, small voice tells you to go?"

"Don't lecture me, Jake. I know all about still, small voices."

Willa paused. As she took a few deep breaths to carry her through an explanation, Jake cut her off. "No grisly details, please," he said, raising his second glass of cranberry juice. "Here's to two madcap kids tying the knot against all odds. *L'chaim!*'" He drank and then quickly emptied a miniature box of Cheerios into a bowl. "And next thing, my dear Sarah, God will tell you that you're going to have a son named Isaac and…"

"And I'll chuckle and say Eric and I are way too old."

"At least I'm flattered you came to my talk last night on Abraham, Isaac, and family. A volunteer in the activities department supplied an updated title: 'Ancient Mobility: Interactive Seniors in Genesis.'" He pointed an arthritic finger at her. "One more question. You rarely leave your apartment. You're almost agoraphobic. How do you expect to travel all the way across the country by yourself?"

Willa smiled. "Tessie the Techie has already made the arrangements for us online. She and I will fly to Seattle, where she has relatives she hasn't seen in years except on Skype. It's all settled. We'll share a hotel room."

Jake made a wry face when he heard Tessie's name. "She's matron of honor? And who's best man? Oliver Wendell Holmes?"

"Don't look at me like that, Jake. I didn't say Eric and I were going to be married."

"So Fritzi is right about you, a loose woman on the make. Not the marrying kind."

"For more than a half century, I was. That makes me respectable."

Jake leaned against the back of his chair. "Don't expect much. Eric won't be jetting off to Paris and Vienna with you. No wildly applauding audiences and champagne corks popping. At this new place, your days will be like a rerun of SVM, the same old tedium you're leaving behind."

Willa stared at him as if she had never seen him before. She put her hand on his deformed shoulder. "Jake," she said, "promise you'll continue those lectures for the residents. You need listeners, and they need you."

He lowered his shaggy head, much in need of a good haircut, and pretended to sip from an empty coffee cup. "I admire the tribe as a whole," he said. "It's just some of the individuals who get to me. Including myself."

She hadn't finished her prepared remarks. "I was just going to say..."

"Why didn't he ask you to marry him before he moved so far away?"

Willa shook her head. "I don't intend to marry Eric. Not this trip anyway."

"No? You're not getting any younger."

"Jake, you don't understand my feelings about him. There's a beautiful aria in Verdi's *Tosca*. I've watched and heard a lot of singers perform it on Classic Arts Showcase. It's called 'Nissim d'arte.'"

"You expect me to know Italian?"

"I once asked Eric what it means, and he translated it as 'I live for art.' And the positive way he spoke those four words rang true. He has lived for art all his life, even now, although he can no longer sing or teach young singers. He told me he listens to the classics all day long."

"So? What's that got to do with you?"

"Be patient with me, Jake. I'm more distant from art, further away from the brilliance of Mozart and Beethoven than he is. I can't sing or read music, but somehow now I'm part of it too because I cling to Eric."

"That's risky."

"You're thinking of him only as he is now. When we're together, I'm aware of the other Eric, the handsome young man with a magnificent jewel of a voice that wins hearts wherever he goes."

"And after the novelty wears off, then what?"

"I'll spend a few weeks with him. If he's up to it, he'll share memories about his life and his career in music. If not, we'll hold hands and listen to Gustav Mahler. But that's it."

Jake put his crooked arm around her shoulders and gave her a mini-hug. "You're a girl after my own heart," he said.

Willa laughed. "God forbid."

He withdrew his arm in pain. "Listen," he said, "when it doesn't work out and I'm still kicking, come back here. I'm no musician. I'm tone deaf, but for Willa I would even give a free concert on a Jew's harp." He coughed lightly. "When do you leave?"

"Not right away. Tessie is teaching a course in computers. She can't join me till the winter break."

"And Oliver Wendell Holmes? Calling it quits with that old mamzer?"

Willa felt lightheaded and almost giggled. "Never."

"So maybe I still have a chance too, you hussy."

She lifted her handbag from the floor. "See you at breakfast."

"Not if you see me in hell first."

Willa laughed. "That's a possibility," she said.

———◆———

*Monday, January 7, 2014.* Our Alaska Airlines plane is running behind schedule, and here I sit stranded at JFK International Airport. Tessie the Techie has gone to buy coffee. Although her computer course ended shortly after Hanukkah, I'm glad she made reservations that avoided the

Christmas rush. Tessie keeps saying to me, "Girl, I'm gonna be your chaperone." I wish she'd stop calling me girl.

Feels good to take off my shoes. It's a perfect time to fill the four blank pages remaining in my journal. This elderly brain of mine tingles with a word it's not accustomed to using: epiphany. For years the unkosher sound of it kept me away. Wasn't it a Christian holiday or a New Testament chapter? Remove the blinders, Willa! Epiphanies blast away untruths and can strike anyone, including self-absorbed old Jewish ladies like me, too vain to order an airport wheelchair.

Even when we're old, it's sometimes easier to see ourselves through the eyes of our younger selves, but I remember what Dr. Holmes wrote in his later years. He reminded the reader that the elderly don't consider themselves "the helpless, forlorn creatures which they seem to young people," and he asks if "the young folks suppose that all vanity dies out of the natures of old men and old women."

It doesn't have to happen, but some of us do turn on ourselves. By now we should know better than to sweep our own generation into one anonymous heap, everyone lumped together in the same decrepit category. These days I try harder to decipher the lines in each well-worn face that passes by and wonder what inner force drives some of us to give up and others to keep enjoying the scenery year after year. Such compassion requires patience, a commodity in short supply as we grow older.

Hurry, Tessie, with that coffee! When she returns, she'll expect to hear more details of our trip to points west, especially what will happen when we reach our destination. What's next? Not able to read music, I'll play it by ear.

They've just announced that bad weather will prevent our plane from landing for another two hours. Tessie says we may have to spend the night here. OK, I can kill eight hours just as easily as eight decades. Across from me sits an erect, white-haired woman, my age, elegant in a cream-colored suit, a gold cross displayed on her green satin blouse. For a quarter hour, she rummaged through her Coach bag and took inventory. Then she carefully draped her Burberry raincoat around her shoulders and headed for the ladies' room across the concourse. Minutes later I noticed she had left her expensive purse lying on the floor.

The dozing passengers around us, including Tessie, didn't notice, and being old fashioned, I worried more about petty theft than terrorist bombs. It wasn't very smart of me, but I transferred to her seat and waited there with our two handbags perched in my lap. She rushed back, panicky; when she saw there was nothing to fear, she calmly took the pocketbook from me. "My memory," she said, "is not what it was. When things slip my mind, I thoroughly dislike myself."

"We both have a good forgettery," I said, and together the two of us laughed like longtime friends.

I'm still convinced there's too much self-hatred among the elderly. We not only don't tolerate ourselves enough, we're quick to find fault with others like us. At SVM I never knew my fellow residents. I could see only the scanty remnants of lives. It wasn't fair to judge harshly all those contemporaries numbed by years, not fair to decide who they were from what they had become. And the darkest joke of all? They understood no more about me than I about them.

Last night I scribbled on an envelope an observation of Oliver Wendell Holmes, and now there's plenty of time to recopy it here:

> I do not know what special gifts have been granted or denied me; but this I know, that I am like so many others of my fellow-creatures, that when I smile, I feel as if they must; when I cry, I think their eyes fill; and it always seems to me that when I am most truly myself I come nearest to them and am surest of being listened to by the brothers and sisters of the larger family into which I was born so long ago.

It sounds good anyway. When we meet, I'll kiss Eric warmly, pose questions never before asked, and hold his hand as we spend the hours absorbing Handel and Schubert. We'll even try our luck with a few more voice lessons if he's still willing. Time spent together is good medicine for us both. I want him to know how much I cherish him, his vast musical knowledge and his grand resilience and courage. I want to help him recall the joy he once gave his audiences and his students. And before leaving, I'll forge some treacly verses about loving him forever, not an original idea but hard for any poet to resist.

Time doesn't expand; we must hurry. When our visit ends, Tessie and I will return to the SEA-TAC airport for a cross-country journey to Boston. In my suitcase lies a handwritten note from that Harvard professor, Amy Kimberly Donnerschlagg, who has invited me to be her personal guest at something called An Asymmetrical Symposium on the Life and Works of Oliver Wendell Holmes. I was dumbfounded to hear from her.

She wants to present what she refers to as "your amusingly touching letter" at a banquet for her colleagues at the end of their five-day conference. "It's a time for letting off steam," she writes, "and this would be an entertaining highlight, capturing the irresistible spirit of Dr. Holmes as seen by someone closer to the nineteenth century than the rest of us are."

I don't consider that an insult. Professor Donnerschlagg has a sense of humor, no surprise. How could an authentic Holmes scholar not become infected?

"You're selling out," Jake said although I saw it differently. My original letter didn't mean to be funny, and if that's her interpretation, the laugh will be on the professor. It's the best I could do at this stage of my life on that demonic computer.

Thanks, Dr. Holmes; you've been networking for me at Harvard as only a conscientious ghost can. Amy Kimberly Donnerschlagg even promised a guided tour of the Harvard Medical School, where you once served as dean. I'm game; we octogenarians have a certain cachet, don't we? Everyone will be polite, solicitous, and condescending to the old lady. They'll write her off either as a crank or an adorable eccentric. Jake feared they may peg me a crackpot, but at least I'll be pegged as something.

Most of all I'm indebted to someone else. Dear Aaron, are you reading these words over my shoulder as I write? Such an upbeat ending! I can hear you laughing. Sweetheart, the swift seasons have roared by, and no earthly power could pull them over to the side of the road for a speeding ticket. To quote my late friend, Yetta, "What was, was."

Instead, let young and old study that poetic masterpiece of Dr. Holmes, "The Chambered Nautilus." We can take instruction from his spiral creature and its web of living hope. We can learn that in painful moments a new identity always beckons to us. "This is the ship of pearl," the poet declares, and whenever a durable old mollusk washes ashore, the ocean wave roars in our ears; "Grow or diminish. You mustn't—can't—return to the past or remain unchanged."

The little doctor has offered us a powerful prescription, one I'm inclined to fill and refill. Yes, even if it's only a placebo. In his practice, he has attempted to diagnose what is real and what is fancy, or as he puts it, "the whole Order of Things, which can hardly be completely unraveled in any single lifetime."

And what if the medicine of Holmes doesn't work? What if he's an advocate of sometimes you con and sometimes you con't, a charlatan selling philosophical syrup of rhubarb, a blowhard quack? Should we sue for malpractice? We'll see.

But first Tessie the Techie and I must board our plane for Seattle.

# FRITZI'S CODA

—————

THAT WOMAN WILLA HAS CHECKED out of SVM. Nobody knows where she went, and believe me, I've tried to find out. Willa always kept to herself. Maybe she didn't want anybody to think she belonged in a place like this. Lots of people do that when they come to SVM. You would too. You wouldn't want people to think you got old, would you? She was never a grouch like Jake or desperate like Diana, who learned how to work the library computer and found a man on the Internet. He wanted to meet her face to face and said he couldn't because his sons emptied his bank account, and he was flat broke and could she send him the fare to fly here from his home in Hawaii? She was so happy to find a man who paid attention to her, she mailed him a big check to cover the plane ticket and a month's rent. It's the last she ever heard from him. That's when she stopped coloring her hair. Now she looks like the rest of us.

Willa was more quiet, if you like that type. She was better than some I could mention. She would come to breakfast, eat, and leave right away. We didn't know much about her, but maybe there wasn't that much to know. One thing's for sure: she thought the world of me. Everybody does.

—————

### The Chambered Nautilus
### by Oliver Wendell Holmes

This is the ship of pearl, which, poets feign,
 Sails the unshadowed main,__
 The venturous bark that flings
On the sweet summer wind its purpled wings
In gulfs enchanted, where the Siren sings,
 And coral reefs lie bare,
Where the cold sea-maids rise to sun their streaming hair.

Its webs of living gauze no more unfurl;
 Wrecked is the ship of pearl!
 And every chambered cell,
Where its dim dreaming life was wont to dwell,
As the frail tenant shaped his growing shell,
 Before thee lies revealed,
Its irised ceiling rent, its sunless crypt unsealed!

Year after year beheld the silent toil
 That spread his lustrous coil;
 Still, as the spiral grew,
He left the past year's dwelling for the new,
Stole with soft step its shining archway through,
 Built up its idle door,
Stretched in his last-found home, and knew the old no more.

Thanks for the heavenly message brought by thee,
 Child of the wandering sea,
 Cast from her lap, forlorn!
From thy dead lips a clearer note is born
That ever Triton blew from wreathed horn!
 While on mine ear it rings,
Through the deep caves of thought I hear a voice that sings:__

Build thee more stately mansions, O my soul,
    As the swift seasons roll!
    Leave thy low-vaulted past!
Let each new temple, nobler than the last,
Shut thee from heaven with a dome more vast
    Till thou at length art free,
Leaving thine outgrown shell by life's unresting sea!